Trent took her face between his hands and kissed her.

It wasn't much in the way of a kiss.

It reminded Jennifer of films of soldiers and sailors celebrating the end of war by grabbing the closest available female and planting one on them. More a celebration of the moment than anything to do with the individuals.

Trent lifted his mouth, still holding her face. He was so close that his grin was almost out of focus.

Then it was gone. She looked up, right into those dangerous eyes. Hot and intent.

So hot that they seared the air she drew in with a quick breath.

His gaze dropped to her mouth, and the heat she'd drawn in as oxygen became a lit fuse racing through her body.

"Jen."

And then he kissed her again.

Dear Reader,

The seed for *The Right Brother* came several years ago, standing in a long holiday checkout line at a bookstore with my brother. He announced to the woman behind us that I was an author. (Why, oh why, does he do this on the worst of hair days and when I'm wearing burly jackets and muddy snow boots?)

The woman was gracious enough not to comment on my hair or my attire. Instead, she said that she used to love to read, but she just didn't have time anymore. I noted her basket brimming with children's books. Oh, yes, she said, she wanted her children to read, but she was too busy to read herself because she was doing so many things for her kids.

Genuinely curious, I asked if she expected that her kids would stop reading when they were adults. No, of course not, she started. Then she stopped dead, staring at me. After a moment, she muttered, "Do what I say, not what I do."

As this story of Jennifer and Trent started growing into *The Right Brother,* it drew from that encounter and thoughts about parents who might sacrifice in their own lives exactly what they want their children to value.

So, in light of that introduction by my brother, it's particularly appropriate that the title is *The Right Brother.*

Oh, yes, and the woman got out of line, and when we parted she was looking at books for herself, so her kids could do what she did.

Patricia McLinn

THE RIGHT BROTHER

PATRICIA McLINN

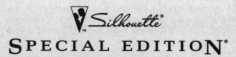

Silhouette®

SPECIAL EDITION®

Published by Silhouette Books

America's Publisher of Contemporary Romance

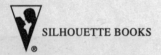 SILHOUETTE BOOKS

ISBN-13: 978-0-373-24782-0
ISBN-10:   0-373-24782-6

THE RIGHT BROTHER

Copyright © 2006 by Patricia McLaughlin

This edition published by arrangement with Harlequin Books S.A.

® and TM are trademarks of Harlequin Books S.A., used under license. Trademarks indicated with ® are registered in the United States Patent and Trademark Office, the Canadian Trade Marks Office and in other countries.

Visit Silhouette Books at www.eHarlequin.com

Printed in U.S.A.

Books by Patricia McLinn

Silhouette Special Edition

A Stranger To Love #1098
The Rancher Meets
  His Match #1164
†*Lost-and-Found Groom* #1344
†*At the Heart's Command* #1350
†*Hidden in a Heartbeat* #1355
**Almost a Bride* #1404
**Match Made in Wyoming* #1409
**My Heart Remembers* #1439
The Runaway Bride #1469
††*Wedding of the Century* #1523
††*The Unexpected*
  Wedding Guest #1541
††*Least Likely Wedding* #1679
††*Baby Blues and*
  Wedding Bells #1691
‡*What Are Friends For?* #1749
‡*The Right Brother* #1782

†A Place Called Home
**Wyoming Wildflowers
††Something Old, Something New…
‡Seasons in a Small Town

PATRICIA McLINN's

childhood summers in Illinois were long, mostly sunny
and filled with stories. She and neighborhood friends put
on plays for captive parental audiences, and once ran away
from home, heading for Hollywood to become the first
eight-year-old Oscar-winning screenwriters. (Alas, Dairy
Queen came before the train station and seriously depleted
the runaways' capital.)

Patricia made a detour of practicality into sports journalism,
working at papers in Rockford, Illinois, Charlotte,
North Carolina and Washington, D.C., before returning
to storytelling. Her books have topped bestseller lists,
gathered awards and—most important—drawn wonderful
letters from readers. She loves to hear from readers through
her Web site, www.PatriciaMcLinn.com, or at P.O. Box
7052, Arlington, VA 22207.

For Gin, greatly missed.

Chapter One

Jennifer Truesdale's cell phone rang. She stopped sweeping at warp speed and eyed the miniature tormentor sitting on the dusty counter, wondering what bad news it could bring this time.

Wasn't it enough for one afternoon that Meyer's Auto Repair had called to say the car needed new brakes and two tires? That her best friend, Darcie, had phoned and said she couldn't help clean the dealership after all, because she had to work. That the town's biggest gossip had probed for confirmation that her older brother's marriage was in trouble—as if Jennifer would know. That the middle school assistant principal had called to report Ashley had been disciplined—again—for defiantly remaining in the hall after the bell had rung—again. Thank God school was out next week.

Although, then she'd be juggling keeping track of Ashley with her job.

The phone continued to ring. The way today had been

going the caller could be her potential buyer backing out. The man's static-ridden message on the real estate office's answering machine had announced he would arrive tomorrow morning to look at the dealership. She should have known a real, live prospect was too good to be true.

Jennifer leaned the broom against the counter and opened her cell phone.

She quickly realized the official voice on the other end was not the potential buyer—so, at least for now, a buyer for this barely breathing dealership remained a possibility.

"Mrs. Stenner?" It was the woman from the state she'd talked to several times, most recently last winter.

"I've returned to my maiden name—Truesdale."

"Ah." The syllable held a wealth of understanding.

Jennifer pushed back a strand of hair that had escaped the bandanna she wore in a futile attempt to keep her hair clean. The woman told her briskly, but not unkindly, what Jennifer had already suspected—they'd had no luck tracking down Eric Stenner to collect the child support he owed.

As she listened to the detailed explanation, Jennifer looked through a clear patch of the plate glass window she was still hours away from washing. This afternoon was slipping away even faster than the sun that was about to disappear behind a sheet of gray clouds rolling in from the west and flattening the sky over Drago, Illinois.

"Thank you for your efforts, Ms. Dorran," she said.

"Oh, I'm not done trying, Ms. Truesdale. I just didn't want you counting on the money in the near future."

After they hung up, Jennifer found herself swiping at the counter with the sleeve of the old jersey she wore. From her box of cleaning supplies, she grabbed a spray bottle and cloth, going to work on that counter as if it were the enemy.

No, she definitely wouldn't count on child support. She

would count on herself. And she would make it. She had to make it. For Ashley. If she could just hang on until the real estate market picked up in Drago.

That's why the appearance of a potential buyer for the car dealership had seemed like such a miracle. Selling Stenner Autos would produce a commission that would plug that gap beautifully for her, along with saving this place from bankruptcy. But she only had seventeen hours before the potential buyer's arrival.

She wished she had more time. More time and more money.

Heck, as long as she was wishing for time and money, she might as well throw in wisdom. And with a soon-to-be-teenage daughter, patience. Yes, she most definitely needed patience.

But right now she didn't have time to worry about patience.

Especially when she also had to fix dinner, try to impress on Ashley the necessity of following the rules, tear her away from endless debating about what to wear tomorrow, get her to do her homework and go to bed. Maybe, if Darcie's shift had ended by then, she'd keep on eye on Ashley while Jennifer returned here to clean. Ashley would be incensed, proclaiming that at nearly thirteen she didn't need a babysitter. But she'd go to sleep, and someone she knew would be there, in case she woke up. And it would make Jennifer feel better.

Jennifer gave the now-shining counter a pat before resuming sweeping debris into a dustpan that she then dumped into a nearly filled trash bag.

Seventeen hours to wipe out more than a year of being abandoned and who knew how many months of neglect before that.

Abandoned. Neglect.

The words' echo rapped against the inside of Jennifer's ribs.

The dealership. She meant the dealership.

That's what she needed to be thinking about. Selling it would tide them over until the technology company Zeke-Tech moved to town, bringing employees who would need places to live. Then her efforts as a real estate agent would really take off.

But first, she had to sell Stenner Autos, which had stood empty since her ex-husband ran it nearly into bankruptcy.

With that commission in the bank she wouldn't have to work so much, and she'd have more time to spend with Ashley. Maybe more patience, too. Wisdom? Well, you didn't get everything you wished for. Or that you needed.

Jennifer dropped the full trash bag with others piled near the front door and snagged a fresh one, heading around the high counter and into the general manager's office, the last place to sweep. Then she would wash the windows and desks. Floors, too. Water stains marked the ceiling, but fixing that was beyond even wishing for. There was only so much she could do in seventeen hours.

She swept quickly in the near dark. She'd have to bring lightbulbs after dinner.

Jennifer heard the soft whoosh of the main door that she hadn't bothered to lock behind her when she'd hurried in with the cleaning supplies. Her heartbeat stumbled.

Not from fear—Drago wasn't that kind of town—but from a premonition.

It couldn't be the buyer. It couldn't. The phone message had definitely said tomorrow morning at ten.

It had seemed a miracle that between the old machine's pops, distortion and sound-blurs slices of clarity made "Stenner Autos" and "ten tomorrow morning" recognizable. She'd also pieced together a phrase about "interested" and something about coming into town. As for his name or a phone number to call him back to fill in the gaps, forget it.

But she hadn't minded. She'd been more than happy with the miracle of "Stenner Autos" and "ten tomorrow morning."

She eased to the office's open door and peered around its

edge. Against the front window's lighter background of gray she saw the outline of a man standing a yard inside the door, feet slightly spread, hands on lean hips, head tipped back as he scanned the ceiling. She couldn't see his face, but she was certain he was frowning. He *would* look at the ceiling first. Damn.

She didn't recognize the outline as anyone she knew. So who—?

The potential buyer. A day early.

A stream of words she never used—because sure as heck if she did, Ashley would hear and feel free to use them—rocketed through her head.

Okay, okay. If it was the client, she couldn't do anything about his being here. And she couldn't do anything about his seeing the place looking like this. But she could try to slip out without his seeing *her* looking like this. Tomorrow, in her navy-blue suit, he would see only a calm, confident professional whose words would carry enough weight to talk away any objection, including water stains on the ceiling.

She would edge out the door, staying low to take advantage of shadows from the counter, and slip down the hall to the back door. It might be tricky using the key without making noise, but—

The dust of empty spaces, old paper and who knew what else, all stirred by her broom, wrenched a sneeze from her. Then another and a third.

So much for remaining unnoticed. Still, she automatically dodged behind the office door.

The sneezes came so hard and fast that for a moment she could only lean on the broom and gasp.

Footsteps headed across the showroom toward her.

"Who's there?"

Damn. She straightened away from the broom.

"Hello?" the voice repeated. It sounded vaguely familiar. So maybe it wasn't the client. Maybe it was a friend or neighbor who'd stopped by. Not from any interest in buying Stenner Autos—nobody in Drago could afford it—but maybe to help.

"Who's back there?" It sounded more like a command than a question.

He shifted and she could see the way he moved. No, he wasn't anyone from Drago. She was sure.

Escape was hopeless. She stepped forward to the office doorway reluctantly, but determined to not be apologetic or wimpy. He was the one who had no right to be here.

"Who are you?" she demanded. The sneezes—and the irritation—lowered her voice and added a rasp.

He stopped beside the counter and peered at her.

"Sorry, I didn't mean to startle you." His tone held less command, more gentleness now. But broad shoulders, several inches of height above hers and dark coloring still made him a commanding figure. "I was driving by and stopped to look inside. The door was open."

"The door might not have been locked, but it wasn't open."

Her sharpness stemmed partly from the fact that he'd startled her, partly from the knowledge that she'd been wrong. It *was* someone she knew.

In fact, she realized with a sickening spasm in her stomach, it was both the client *and* someone from Drago. Originally from Drago, anyway.

"Sorry again." He drawled out the words, his face shifting into a grin. Most women probably found that expression charming. "Though, you should have the alarm switched on, being here alone."

She could hardly imagine a man she would find less charming at this moment than this particular one.

Her ex-husband's younger brother, Trent Stenner.

She hadn't seen him in years. When she'd still been going to

Stenner family gatherings with Eric, Trent had been noticeably absent. But she couldn't mistake the broad cheekbones divided by a strong nose with a distinctive thin scar angled across it.

"I'm Trent Stenner," he said. "I called the real estate office about seeing the dealership."

He hadn't recognized her.

She could hardly blame him, but still…

He'd grown more solid and more confident in the years since they'd seen each other. She'd grown…well, she'd like to think wiser, but the downside of *wiser* was that it went with *older*.

"Tomorrow." Her voice started in the sneeze-induced lower register, and she made sure it remained there. Just in case. "You're supposed to be here tomorrow. You came early to catch—" She swallowed the word *me*. Maybe, just maybe, she could still present herself as a real estate professional tomorrow, if she got out of today without his recognizing her. "The agent."

His dark eyebrows popped up. But she was done with placating Stenner men. Heck, this one had never even pretended he liked her.

"No," he said evenly. "I just got to town and it was spur-of-the-moment to stop by here. Like I said, I was driving by."

He gestured toward the window, which showed a shining car parked next to her aged compact.

"Why did you come to town a day early?"

"Just the way my schedule worked." That didn't sound like the truth. By comparison, his statement about spur-of-the-moment did ring true.

So what could have brought him to Drago a day early? In fact, why was he here at all? It wasn't as if he'd shown any interest in visiting his hometown for years.

And why on earth would he suddenly get it into his head to look into buying the dealership?

Eric had spent time at Stenner Autos, letting customers shake hands with the owner's star quarterback son. Trent had stayed far away. Once he was in college, he'd rarely even returned to town.

"Looks like you've been doing hand-to-hand combat with the dirt." Trent brushed his finger over the trailing cuff of her long-sleeved jersey, snapping her attention back to the immediate situation.

Could he possibly recognize it as one of his brother's? It had been years, but it did have Eric's old high school football number on it. Wouldn't that be perfect—he hadn't recognized his brother's old wife, but did recognize his brother's old shirt? She had to get him out of here fast.

"I have to get back to work. Come back tomorrow."

"They left you to clean this whole place by yourself?"

"It's my job."

"Big job for one person."

She grunted and turned away, wielding the broom.

He didn't budge. "Will you get in trouble with the boss because I saw the place like this?"

"No. Now, please go."

The door whooshed again.

As Jennifer turned to identify her new interruption, a familiar voice came.

"Hey, Jennifer. I saw a strange car out front—"

Darcie Barrett walked in, appearing as casual as someone could appear in the uniform of the Drago Police Department, wearing a gun, handcuffs, indestructible flashlight and other accoutrements dangling from her black leather belt. Knowing Jennifer was alone at the dealership, Darcie's cop instincts must have gone on alert at seeing the unfamiliar car out front.

Jennifer started toward Darcie, but before she could catch

her friend's attention in order to signal her, to warn her, to shut her up, Trent turned too, effectively blocking Jennifer.

"Darcie Barrett," he said, extending a hand and a smile. "Trent Stenner. You probably don't remember me. I was a few years behind you in school."

"Trent. *Stenner?*"

Jennifer tried again to catch Darcie's gaze, but her friend was fully occupied with staring at Trent, just short of slack-jawed. "I remember you, I just never expected you to be here and—oh, my God, you're the person who called Jennifer about the dealership listing?"

"Jennifer?" he repeated, sounding puzzled. Then he looked over his shoulder toward her and repeated with no puzzlement, but a lot of other emotions she couldn't sort out, "Jennifer. Jennifer Stenner."

She pulled the bandanna off her hair, refusing to run her hands through it or otherwise try to arrange it. But she stood straight, head up, jaw level with the floor, the way she'd been trained.

"Yes, Jennifer," she said. "Jennifer Truesdale."

Trent's lips moved in silence. Possibly with a curse. He dipped his head infinitesimally in acknowledgment.

Jennifer looked him directly in the eyes—eyes she couldn't see because he'd turned toward her, leaving his head backlit by the window and his face in shadow.

Darcie looked from one to the other of them.

"I…I think I hear my radio. In the car." Darcie's words were a blatant lie. She had a radio on her shoulder that wasn't making a peep. She eased a couple steps toward the door. "I'll just…"

Neither Jennifer nor Trent said a word as Darcie slid out the door and got in her car. Jennifer's peripheral vision told her Darcie left the car door open and kept her gaze on the showroom. She'd bailed on being a participant in the upcoming discussion, but she was there as backup.

Jennifer took a step to the left. Trent shifted, too, to remain face-to-face. Now the window revealed half of his face and the shadow masked the other half—as her face would be half in shadow, half in light to him.

She saw an extremely masculine face. No prettiness in it as there could be with handsome men, but rather strong, broad lines. His dark hair was cut short, emphasizing his distinct hairline and the shape of his head.

Trent broke the silence. "Why did you let me— Why didn't you tell me who you were?"

"That would have been rather awkward, don't you think?"

"Any less than this?" His words were dry.

"No. Perhaps not."

"You… You were hired to clean the dealership?"

"I have the listing. Cleaning is a bonus."

His mouth twitched, as if it had started a grin, then abruptly stopped.

"The listing? *You're* the agent? How the hell did you get the listing?"

His tone held no anger. Solely astonishment.

Which she could understand. The divorce had not been amicable. If the decision had been left to Eric or his parents she would never have had anything more to do with anything carrying the Stenner name, including Ashley. But those decisions hadn't been up to the Stenners.

"Judge Hector Dixon assigned the listing to me," she added, certain he would recognize the name.

Judge Dixon had done a great deal more than that.

After Eric left town so abruptly, just as divorce proceedings were revealing what a shambles he'd made of their finances, the judge had helped the employees try to keep the place running during a search for a buyer. When that had failed, the judge had negotiated with the creditors and the manufacturers to keep Stenner Autos from going directly into bankruptcy.

"Still, tight-knit little Drago, huh?" This time Trent's tone held an edge. "All the connections clicking right along to keep the haves having."

In a way he was right. It had been the judge's way of helping her out. But she could tell by his tone that it didn't sit well with him.

She was not going to let that cost her a potential buyer. Right here, before she even had a chance. She had too much riding on this.

"Connections don't change that this dealership offers a good business opportunity to the right owner. You know Zeke Zee-kowsky is bringing part of his high-tech operation to Drago, don't you? There'll be new residents as well as more people coming through, so there'll be a bigger pool of customers for the dealership, along with possibilities for related business."

"I don't—"

"A smart businessperson looks beyond personal concerns in making a decision."

"Whoa—I'm not anywhere near making a decision. You'll have to wait, learn to be patient, like everybody else."

His emphasis gave the words significance, even if she hadn't already interpreted it from his look. She'd gotten that look a lot. The look that said people thought she was accustomed to getting what she wanted when she wanted it. The look that said they thought life had been easy—too easy—for her.

"You should be ready to make a decision. This is a great opportunity. Combining Drago's new prosperity with a name that has meant a lot in this community for a long time is a smart business move."

"I'm only here to check things out," he said firmly.

Check things out. That could be as little as the cursory view he'd already had.

"Thoroughly checking out the dealership and this wonderful business opportunity will start with returning tomorrow at your scheduled time," she said, as if nothing else were possible. "Then looking around town, talking to other Drago businesspeople and studying the projections I've put together." Updating those projections had prevented her from starting the cleaning earlier.

She felt her breath back up behind her closed-off throat as he looked slowly around the empty, dim dealership, then back at her.

"All right."

He headed out, and she let a breath out in small, inaudible drafts.

"Ten tomorrow," she said, holding the door open for him.

Darcie got out of her patrol car, studying them as she approached.

"Ten," he confirmed. "But don't bother cleaning anymore. I've already seen it this way, so it would be a waste of energy."

He and Darcie exchanged nods in passing. She came to stand beside Jennifer in the doorway. When Trent raised his hand in farewell as he backed out, Jennifer consciously eased one hand's grip on the door to return the gesture.

"Whew, he grew up nice, didn't he?" Darcie said.

Jennifer emitted a noncommittal grunt.

"Is he still playing pro football?" Darcie pursued.

Jennifer controlled the urge to wince. A beat later she realized she didn't need to—didn't need to control the urge, didn't even need to wince.

Because Eric wasn't around to rant about how his talentless brother had the career Eric should have had, only Eric wouldn't have been living like some damned monk. And the way he played—Christ, he never got his name in the paper. Lunch-pail player, John Madden called him on *Monday Night Football*. F—ing boring, was what Eric called him.

Eric would have had a spectacular career. Eric would have been a star. Eric would have been living the high life. If only he'd had some luck. If only things hadn't gone against him. If only she hadn't dragged him down.

"Retired after last season," Jennifer said.

Trent's car rolled out of sight. She and Darcie stepped inside.

"Oh, yeah. I remember. It was all over the *Drago Intelligencer*. Well, if that's retired, sign me up for the old folks' home, especially with Zeke back in Virginia for three weeks." Darcie grinned at Jennifer. She didn't return the grin. "Oh, come on. Trent's a babe. But he doesn't seem to think that gives him carte blanche to roll over people."

"I wouldn't care if he was Genghis Khan. All I care about is if Trent's truly interested in buying Stenner Autos. Or if he's yanking my chain for some unknown reason."

"Why would he do that? I only saw him for a few seconds, but he didn't seem— Hey, what are you doing? He said not to bother cleaning anymore. Besides, you've said all along that a smart businessperson would look past a little dust and dirt to see this as a great opportunity."

"I'm not relying on him meaning what he said *or* being a smart businessperson."

Trent Stenner anticipated.

Even more than his honed reflexes, the ability to anticipate had given Trent a career in football. And anticipation had allowed him to put his solid but unspectacular income to work with investments that now amounted to a sizable nest egg.

He studied—game films, prospectuses—and then he used that knowledge. It had been his way since he was a kid, right up until thirty-six hours ago.

But in the past thirty-six hours, he'd forgotten all about studying, which had resulted in failing to anticipate finding Jennifer Truesdale Stenner acting as a skivvy at Stenner Autos.

His first reaction to the woman he'd startled had been empathy. Sorry he'd given her cause for worry by walking in on her as she worked alone in the dealership, and impressed by the way she gave no quarter verbally.

In the oversize and dirty shirt and with that faded scarf covering Jennifer's trademark blond hair at the same time it dropped shadows under her eyes, the woman had looked delicate. Almost fragile.

Glowing and confident. That's how he remembered Jennifer. Always on Eric's arm. Always smiling. The golden couple—literally, with their nearly identical fair hair.

Quite a contrast.

But he still should have recognized her. Because he should have anticipated how things worked in Drago. The Dixons, Truesdales and Stenners had been doing each other favors for generations. Although, from what their parents had said, Judge Dixon hadn't done Eric any favors in arrangements with the creditors. Trent hadn't been interested in details of Eric's problems, but it had been hard to miss their outrage during his dutiful phone conversations.

A phone call had started all this, too. A phone call from his father.

As a rule, his mother made the calls, then pulled his father into the conversation. The only other time he'd heard from Franklin Stenner had been the day Ella had had her heart attack. So Trent had been surprised—and worried—to hear his father's voice when he answered the phone.

This time, though, his father had asked him to come out to Florida to their retirement home, a shock of another kind.

"I have something to discuss with you," his father had said. And would say no more.

Now, thirty-six hours and thousands of miles later, Trent felt the muscles in his forehead contract into a frown as he turned his rental car onto the Interstate ramp thirteen miles outside of Drago. It was only a few miles down the Interstate to reach Pepton, where he'd find the closest motel.

Unlucky thirteen, his father had said of those miles. If the Interstate had passed as close to Drago as it did to Pepton, Drago's businesses would have benefited. That was Franklin Stenner's eternal regret.

Exiting at Pepton, Trent decided Drago hadn't lost much by not acquiring shoe-box motels, chain restaurants and all-night gas stations. From what he'd seen, Drago remained as it had been when he was kid. Wide streets flanked by mature trees so regularly spaced they looked like sentinels. Neat yards around solid houses. Pepton used to look like that.

He checked into one of the box motels, mentally retracing the steps that had brought him here.

He'd made the red-eye out of San Diego last night for Florida. This morning—God was it only this morning?—over one of Mom's lavish breakfasts, complete with homemade coffee cake, his father had told him what he wanted.

"The dealership should be in Stenner hands," his father had said. "You're a Stenner. You should feel this as strongly as any of us. I'd go back and run it again myself, except…"

He'd looked out the glass doors to where Ella Stenner had been weeding tubs of blue flowers after Franklin dismissed her, saying, "We're going to talk business."

"Mom doesn't want to go back," Trent had surmised.

"The doctor says she can't take living in the Illinois

weather anymore. Never bothered her before, but that's what this fancy specialist says."

Trent wondered if Franklin would have listened if the doctor hadn't been a fancy specialist—and no doubt expensive.

"Eric—" That was the only word Trent got out.

"Last thing in the world I want is for Eric to go back to Drago. He did his damnedest. No one can fault the boy. It was that harpy Jennifer Truesdale. Saw her chance to make the big time, got her hooks in him in high school and never would let go. Demanding this, demanding that. Drove the boy right into debt.

"He's much better off since he divorced her. It's a damned shame courts automatically give children to the mother, but that's the only downside. Now he's making a new start, and without that albatross of a woman, he'll get the success he's always been meant to have."

Before Trent could form a response, his father had knocked all thoughts of Eric from his mind.

"But that leaves the dealership that's carried the Stenner name proudly since your great-grandfather started it sitting closed and for sale to satisfy those damned jackals of creditors. For sale to anybody who comes along! You're going to change that, Trent. You buy our dealership, so we can make it something proud again. That's what you're going to do."

Beneath his shock, part of Trent had recognized that these words were the closest Franklin Stenner had ever come to asking his younger son to do something for him. It sure as hell was the closest he'd come to indicating he thought his younger son could accomplish anything.

But Trent wasn't anybody's fool. Even his father's.

He looked around now at the cookie-cutter motel room as he stowed the last few clothes he'd brought in the closet, and his mouth twisted. Well, not a complete fool, anyway.

He'd made his father no promises, despite the older man's

sales pressure, which only would have gotten worse. That's why Trent opted to fly to Chicago and drive to Drago right away, rather than stay overnight as his mother had wanted. Trent left their house in Florida barely three hours after arriving, promising only to check out the dealership.

The same promise he'd made to Jennifer Stenn—no, Truesdale, she'd made a point of that—less than an hour ago.

A Jennifer Truesdale he hadn't recognized. Not from his memories and certainly not from his parents' descriptions. What he'd been told and what he'd seen didn't add up.

Trent pocketed the motel key card and the rental car keys again.

In order to anticipate, he had to study. In order to study, he needed the right information.

He closed the flimsy door and headed for a return trip to Drago.

Might as well get started with uncovering the right information.

Chapter Two

Trent had been gone from Drago a long time—long enough to rate as an outsider, if he hadn't always been one.

He supposed an insider would accept it as business as usual that word of his return got around so fast—as evidenced by the arrival hard on his heels of half a dozen people at the surprisingly full café.

But even he was not entirely surprised when Darcie Barrett strolled in, giving him a narrow-eyed nod. He doubted he'd been here five minutes before someone called her.

Darcie sat at the counter while he finished his dinner of fried chicken—real fried chicken, with the skin on and more than a passing acquaintance with oil—green beans, tomato slices and early season corn so fresh he barely stopped himself from moaning with pleasure at each bite.

No one would have heard, because two of his high school football teammates, among the first to arrive after him, sat opposite, talking and laughing over old plays, old jokes and old triumphs.

He remembered the good. He also remembered the bad of those years. But then most of the bad had been in private, away from the public eye.

With his dinner plate empty and first Fred, then Bobby saying it was time to head home to their families for their own dinners, Darcie moved in.

"You want some pie?" she asked, sliding into the bench opposite him as Loris cleared his plate.

"You angling for my tip, Darcie?" demanded Loris. "I was about to ask the boy."

Darcie's gaze traced his neck and shoulders, both showing the result of long, hard years of training. "Boy?"

"He's a boy to me. I remember him comin' in here in diapers." Now that was one effective way to prick a man's ego. "Yup, him as dark as Eric was fair. Just goes to show, doesn't it? Peach or apple pie, Trent?" she demanded before he could consider what it might be going to show.

"Peach. Do you have any—?"

"Cinnamon ice cream. Yes I do. It's gotten to be a favorite around here, and I tell everyone you're the reason it's on the menu."

She bustled off to another table.

"That's true, peach pie and cinnamon ice cream's a specialty because of Trent Stenner—that's what she tells everyone," Darcie said. "So I've got to believe she was telling the truth about the diapers, too. I wonder if ESPN would be interested in a we-knew-him-when piece that included that tidbit."

His mouth quirked. "I wasn't exactly a darling of ESPN when I was playing. If you'd offered them a we-knew-him-when piece then, they would have said, 'Who?' And now I'm not even playing. So you'll have to content yourself with trying to embarrass me to the home crowd."

"And don't think I won't," she said cheerfully. Then her tone changed. "What are you going to be doing now that you've retired?"

He smiled at Loris, who delivered his pie, turned it so the point faced him, then dug in and enjoyed the first sweet, spicy, warm, cold pleasure.

"Now, why did that sound like an official question?"

"Not official. Professional, maybe, but not official. And it's natural to have some professional curiosity, because it sounds like you've been practicing to go into my line of work. I heard you started off asking questions the minute you walked in the door."

He kept eating his pie.

"Plan on becoming a detective, Trent?"

"Strictly amateur."

She sat back in the booth, contemplating him. She made no effort to hide that she was trying to decide about him. When she started talking again, he had no idea what decision she'd made.

"The only reason she won't hear that you've been asking questions about her finances is that nobody would want to make her feel bad that her ex-brother-in-law was nosing around her business."

Okay. They were going to be honest. Even if they didn't mention Jennifer Truesdale by name. A wise precaution since Loris's Café clearly still ranked as Gossip Central.

"You don't think her having the listing on Stenner Autos makes it Stenner business, too?"

That would make her the only one benefiting from the dealership at this point.

And wouldn't his father love to hear that.

"No, I don't," she snapped.

She went on almost immediately, talking all about how Drago was a strange mix of everybody knowing everybody else's business and respect for people's privacy. A flow of words meant to cover that initial, blunt response.

He only half listened. The three words—*No, I don't*—had coalesced fragments he'd been picking up into a whole he didn't like.

He swallowed the last bite of peach pie. It didn't taste quite as sweet as its predecessors.

"Remember Zeke Zeekowsky?" Only when Darcie asked that abrupt question did he realize they'd fallen into a silence.

He knew it was a different question from whether he recognized the name. Most people who kept up with technology at all would know the name. But *remember* keyed the question to here in Drago.

"I remember him. And I hear you're to be congratulated. Wedding's soon, isn't it?"

Her smile nearly blinded him. "Not soon enough—and thanks."

In the interests of cutting to the chase, since she must have asked the question with an eye to heading somewhere, he added, "I also heard Zeke's starting a computer lab in town, and signed a license for a hot new program with a Drago kid and he's moving a division of Zeke-Tech here."

"Yes, he is. But moving a division of a company isn't easy. It's going to take a while. It's going to take a while to get to the point where Drago feels real benefits. It's started—a trickle here or there, spurts when the media descends—but the steady, reliable flow, that won't come for a while yet."

"I can see that," he said slowly.

What he didn't see was what it had to do with his brother's ex and his questions.

"The café here has more business with all the Zeke-Tech folks coming through town. And a few people are starting to rent rooms and such to the Zeke-Techers planning the move. But the big influx of folks, the ones who'll stay here permanently, put their kids in school, and—" she looked into his eyes "—buy houses, they won't come for another year or so."

And Jennifer sold homes, so her hopes for good times were another year off.

But that didn't necessarily mean she was going through bad times now.

"Are you saying—?"

Darcie held up her hand. "I'm just catching you up on the big news in Drago. That's all any of us have to tell you."

Some might have taken that last part as almost a threat. But having failed to get much concrete information about Jennifer's finances out of anyone he'd talked to, he chose to accept it as a statement of fact.

On the other hand, words didn't necessarily tell the tale. The quality of discomfort with the topic, the furrows in foreheads when he broached his parents' contention that Jennifer had come out of the divorce in the lap of luxury, the downturned mouths whenever Eric's name came up—that all came together to form a message.

But whether that message was the truth or not depended a whole lot on the messenger. The town would be hearing only Jennifer's side of the story, and one side of a story was never enough.

He took a final swig of water, wiped his mouth with the paper napkin and put it down beside his empty pie plate, then slid out of the booth.

Darcie mirrored him, standing face-to-face with him.

"I'm just telling you— My God. You used to be a runt. Did you grow or something?"

He couldn't help but grin at her, though it twisted a bit at the ends. "Since my freshman year in high school? Yeah, I grew. Or something."

"Oh, dear. Your father's at the town council meeting about the streetlights, Trent. I'm sure he wanted to talk to you about the dealership."

"No problem," Trent said, as if he hadn't remembered his father's plan to take on the town council. "I haven't seen the dealership yet anyway." Not officially. "What do you know about Eric and Jennifer's divorce?"

The hum of silence came through his cell phone.

"Mom?"

"I don't know what to say, dear. Why would you ask?"

"What sort of settlement was there?"

"Oh, I have no idea about that."

Trent rubbed his neck, then down his shoulder. "Do you know if Eric's been to see Ashley since the divorce? Word is that he's got visitation, but doesn't use it."

Another silence confirmed the truth of that tidbit from Loris.

"The children are always hurt most by a divorce," his mother finally said. "There is no arguing with that. Poor Ashley. It breaks my heart."

"You don't think Jennifer's a good mother?"

This time the hesitation was briefer. "I have never seen any sign that Jennifer wasn't doing her very best for her daughter."

Trent turned those words over. They could be high praise. Or damning with faint praise, depending on what Jennifer's "best" was.

"Okay, Mom." He wasn't getting anywhere, and he was making her uncomfortable. "If you need to get in touch with me, leave a message on my machine at home and I'll call back."

No way was he letting his father know where he was staying

or giving him the cell phone number. His life wouldn't be his own, not with Franklin's beloved Stenner Autos at stake.

"Trent."

He waited. Then nudged, "Yeah, Mom?"

"Don't get caught up with trying to understand what went wrong. It can paralyze you. And when the paralysis finally wears off, it can be too late. I don't mean too late to fix what went wrong, because some things can't be fixed, but too late to change. To make a change. To go on."

Was she talking about the dealership? His relationship or lack thereof with his father? Eric and Jennifer's divorce?

The last option went to the head of the line when she spoke again.

"No one truly knows what goes on inside a marriage. Sometimes," Ella Stenner added softly, "not even the two people who are married."

Trent couldn't pretend he wasn't surprised.

An apartment over a store.

That was where the phone book listing for J. A. Truesdale led him. Though when he'd tried calling, the phone had been disconnected.

Three businesses occupied the building's first floor. A Warinke Hardware Store on the corner, Hair Today in the middle and on this end Bulton's Antiques, with a sign that read Gifts, Jewelry, Crafts. Trade, Barter, Buy, Sell. That pretty much covered it, Trent thought.

Having examined the three store windows, he had nothing left to look at except a door tucked in next to Bulton's Antiques. Its adornment consisted of the address in those stick-on angled rectangles with reflective numbers, a doorbell buzzer, a mail slot and a peephole.

Definitely not what he'd expected.

He rang the bell.

Nothing.

Rang again.

Still no response.

He hadn't achieved what he'd achieved by giving up easily. He tried the door. And damned if the knob didn't turn under his hand.

The door opened to a miniature landing with a steep stairway straight ahead. He had to take a few steps up before he could pull the exterior door closed behind him. At the top of the stairs an equally miniature landing presented a single door at a sharp right angle. It was painted a glossy, fresh green. Wooden letters painted with flowers and strung together by rope to spell out "Welcome" hung from a spindly knocker.

Not trusting that piece of hardware, he knocked loudly with his knuckles. He tried to imagine Eric living here. Not a chance.

He knocked again.

So Jennifer must have moved here with Ashley after the split. But what about his father's declarations about Jennifer getting all the money?

This doorknob didn't turn when Trent tried it. Locked.

As he turned to start down, the exterior door abruptly swung open.

A girl—a young teenager, Trent guessed—started up at a good clip. Halfway, her head snapped up and she stopped dead, staring at him, with one foot on the next step and the other trailing behind.

He saw Jennifer in the girl. The coloring, sure. That blond hair that was so much more than yellow, because it had depths and shadings like finely polished wood. Only wood that swayed and swung. Also the hint of slender curves to come.

"Who are you?" she asked, her voice rising.

Her attitude appeared undecided, open to a number of

options, including flight. But some reluctance seemed to offset the urge to run.

"That depends on whether you're who I think you are," he said.

She jammed her fists on not-yet-there hips. "What's that supposed to mean?"

And now he saw his brother in her. In the cast of the jutted chin. In the sureness of the stance. In the curl of the lip.

Damn.

Before Trent could explore what had pushed that word to the upper level of his mind—or perhaps so he didn't have to explore it—he decided he needed to deal with the girl in front of him.

"It means that if you are Ashley Stenner, I'm your uncle. Trent Stenner."

For a moment, her eyes widened and her face softened. She looked almost as she had the last time he'd seen her, a chubby-cheeked toddler in coveralls that bulged out in back with diapers that also provided padding when her adventures in walking ended in an abrupt seat on the floor. Each time, she'd hauled herself upright, using whatever prop was handy. Then she'd stand clear, wide-eyed and pleased with herself when she found her balance, and head off, fast and unsteady.

"I know who you are." She made it an accusation. Any resemblance to the remembered child disappeared.

He ignored her declaration. "How long have you lived here, Ashley?"

"Awhile."

"Did your father live here with you?"

"What do you care?"

"Does your father ever visit?"

"None of your business!"

"Are you and your mom getting help—financial help—from your father?"

Her eyes narrowed to daggers, red pulsed in her cheeks. "I know about you," she said. "You used to be a football player. But you quit. Dad told me about you."

"Did he?"

"Yes. I know how mean you were to him. And Grams and Gramps."

"Really. When did he tell you all this?"

She flinched. But she didn't bend. "Lots of times."

"I only retired after last season. January. Have you heard from him since then?"

"None of your business."

And that was a no.

"When I left your grandparents' house this morning," he said slowly, watching it sink in that he was calling her bluff on including *Grams and Gramps* in her list of people he'd wronged, "they said to tell you they send their love."

She didn't back down. Not one iota. Instead, she launched a full-fledged bad-attitude sneer.

But it didn't last, as she did another of those lightning changes, startled like a deer and scooted up the remaining stairs. She elbowed him out of her way on the landing, and he stepped down to protect his balance.

The exterior door opened again and he saw Jennifer coming in, head lowered, a plastic grocery bag dragging down one arm.

In the half second it took him to absorb that sight, Ashley had the green door unlocked and open. But instead of slamming it on him, she spun around, holding its edge, looking as if she'd been standing in the doorway all the time.

Jennifer had trudged up one step when he spoke.

"Hello, Jennifer."

Dismay swept over her initial surprise. Then she saw Ashley in the doorway beyond him, and her pace picked up.

"Ashley, you shouldn't have buzzed him in." She stopped

on the stair below him. She would have to be even more single-minded than her daughter to get past, considering there would be two adult bodies involved. "You know the rules about strangers."

"He says he's my uncle," the girl said belligerently. She cut him a look, as if daring him to tell her mother she hadn't buzzed him in, because she hadn't been here and the door had been unlocked.

"You didn't know…" Jennifer's husky voice trailed off, and he saw her decide not to conduct this argument in front of him. "Why are you here?"

"I came to see you."

The parade of reactions to that statement was about as subtle as a brass band and a troop of men on little cycles wearing fezzes, although less suited to a festive occasion. She didn't want to see him. Maybe because she wore the same ratty clothes as before, and was even dirtier. Not a chance in hell she'd listened to him about not cleaning more.

She particularly didn't want to see him *here,* he realized when she darted a look toward the cramped living area he could see past Ashley.

Then he noticed another layer of *didn't want*: she didn't want him to have met Ashley, judging by the protective frown tucked between her brows.

Then, atop those layers, another appeared. Speculation, along with a dash of hope and a heaping helping of determination.

"You came to get the projections so you can study them overnight."

"Yeah," he lied, because what did it hurt?

His peripheral vision caught Ashley rolling her eyes.

She could tell Jennifer that he'd been asking questions that had nothing to do with business projections or the dealership. But he could tell Jennifer that Ashley's pose at the door was a lie, that she'd arrived not long ago herself and that the outside door had been unlocked. That equalized the balance of power and kept them both silent.

"I could meet you at the café in half an hour," Jennifer offered.

"I've eaten."

"For dessert and coffee then."

"Had dessert. Don't want any more coffee."

This time Ashley made no pretense of hiding the eye rolling. "Well, we haven't eaten, and I'm starved. So go away—"

"Ashley."

"Well, geez," the girl said, then subsided into mumbles under her mother's stern look. The only word he caught was *dense*.

"I'll come in while you get the projections," he said. Seeing the inside might not be confirmation of what he'd been hearing, but it added to the evidence. "Then leave you in peace to have your dinner."

Jennifer caught the left corner of her bottom lip between her teeth. "The projections require some explanation. Come in, and if it won't delay you too much, I'll start dinner then go over the projections with you."

"Okay."

"Great." Ashley's sarcasm was about as subtle as her eye rolling. "I'll be in my room if dinner's ready before midnight." She stalked away.

Jennifer pressed herself against the far wall to minimize contact. He accommodated her by also turning his back to the wall, to leave the most room possible for her to pass. But he'd been right about the effect of two adult bodies in this narrow space. There was no way not to touch.

Her shoulder brushed his arm. The sleeve bottom of her big shirt feathered across him—hip, crotch, hip—and he felt the instinctive stirring.

The top of her lowered head was under his nose. The blond

hair might be matted but it smelled sweet. Her knee bumped his leg as she climbed the stairs sideways.

Her gaze flashed to him. "Sorry."

"No problem."

Once clear of him, she shot past. At the landing she drew an audible breath, then gestured for him to enter.

A door slammed down the hallway. Jennifer seated him on the couch, excused herself, then went down the hall. He heard her open a door, speak quiet but concentrated words, close that door and open another.

He took the opportunity to look around. The couch's leather was good quality, but showed wear. Side chairs flanked a table under windows that had to overlook a parking lot by his reckoning. A wall unit held books, a modest TV and an even more modest audio unit. An aged air conditioner clogging one window wasn't turned on, even though the room was just this side of uncomfortable. A dining counter separated the living room from a kitchen that would have felt at home in a camper.

He looked down the hall and saw it made a sharp turn to the right. What were the chances he could poke around down there?

A door opening somewhere around that bend gave him his answer. He was seated again when Jennifer appeared. She had fluffed her hair, washed her face and changed into clean slacks and a shirt.

"If you'd like to look these over while I start dinner…" She handed him a binder he nearly dropped because he hadn't expected its weight.

"Would you like something to drink?" she added.

"Thanks, yes." A drink could provide a prop now, a reason to linger later. He followed her to the kitchen, taking a seat on one of two stools at the dining bar, which was empty except for a glass jar holding a yellow rose not quite opened. Not a store-bought rose, he thought, judging by the holes in two of the leaves framing the bud. She turned, a frown between her brows again.

The stool creaked as he shifted on its hard seat.

"You'll be more comfortable on the couch."

"I'm comfortable here." He could observe her. "Don't you eat here?"

"We have a little balcony. We eat there in the summer."

How little was little? He'd seen no sign of a balcony.

She poured lemonade over ice and placed the glass before him, her gaze going from the folder to him and back. Dutifully, he opened it.

"The blue tab is the historical section." She took a container from the freezer and put it in the microwave. "That incorporates figures from when your grandfather and father ran the dealership."

"No red tab? Isn't that the color you'd need for when Eric ran it?"

"The figures from that period are also under the historic section," she said with little inflection, pulling things from the refrigerator.

She'd taken out a blotchy green-and-brown item wrapped in plastic with a red sticker saying, Reduced For Quick Sale.

"The yellow tab is for current demographics. Market penetration dropped a lot, so improving it would go a long way to turning around the dealership. But even without that, it can be a success as you'll see by the information behind the green tab."

"Green for money?"

She shot a look over her shoulder. The woman could pack a lot into a look. A slice of annoyance that he'd called her on it, some surprise he'd figured it out, even amusement. "Black might have worked," she said, "with the connotation of being in the black. But green is more cheerful."

"Good choice. Because black-and-blue makes me think of pain."

Only after he said it did he remember that blue was associated with the dealership's past—and the family members who'd run it. So she could interpret him as meaning money and family.

"Professional hazard," he clarified. "You know—bruises."

But she'd already shot another of those looks at him, and this one seemed to hold understanding and sympathy, at the same time it informed him confidences would not be welcomed.

Oh, hell, maybe he was making up these emotions he was ascribing to her. He didn't know the woman, that was for sure. Hadn't known the girl, either. What little thought he'd given to her then had been that what you saw was what you got, and what you saw was vacant prettiness.

Now that she'd peeled off outer layers, he could see the blotchy item was a head of lettuce. Only it looked the way the plants Liz had insisted on buying for his place had looked when he'd returned from training camp after they broke up last year. Jennifer put the sorry, limp lump in a large bowl, ran water into it, added ice cubes, then put it back in the fridge.

He flipped to the green tab. "So green's for the future now that Zeke Zeekowsky's bringing part of his company here."

"That's right. The population is going to expand. People will not only be looking to buy cars, but service also could provide steady income. Now we have to go to Pepton. See the map with projected density of population and present repair shops?"

"Uh-huh," he said.

But he wasn't looking at maps or population density. She bent to get a pan from a drawer below the oven and Trent leaned forward to watch the way the fabric tightened over her rear end.

Not that that meant anything, he reminded himself as he straightened. She was a woman—an attractive woman—and he was a man. A man whose last serious relationship had ended a year ago and who wasn't inclined to one-night stands.

The contents of the container from the microwave went into the pan on a burner. Precooked ground beef, he thought. She added a jar of salsa and stirred slowly, blending the salsa's red around and through the darker meat. The motion was deliberate. Almost sensuous. She turned down the heat and with quick, deft movements, she shredded cheddar cheese.

She took individual bowls from the cabinet. Then she retrieved the large bowl from the refrigerator. She took out the lettuce, reduced in size but miraculously restored. She drained it, dried it, then cut that up, too, putting the shreds in each bowl.

"Questions?"

About a million. He had no idea why, of them all, "What are you cooking?" came out of his mouth.

"A version of taco salad. Quick, simple and covers most food groups."

"It smells great."

"I'd invite you to stay—"

Damned if his mouth didn't water, even after that café dinner.

"—but you said you already ate."

"Why aren't you and Ashley living in the house Eric built?"

One quick, surprised look was all he got before she faced away from him. "That has no bearing on the sale of the dealership."

Not bad. Didn't give an inch, but didn't punch a potential buyer in the nose. "I can ask around town. Most might not tell me. But even those who think they're not telling anything will give away a bit here and there."

She chopped at a pair of tomatoes with verve. He didn't care to guess whose face she imagined as she whacked away.

"It serves no good purpose for you or anyone to know all

about my marriage ending. It ended. That's all you need to know."

"I didn't ask all about your marriage ending. C'mon, Jennifer. I heard you got the house in the settlement. When you sold it, the prof—"

She made a derisive sound, then came to a full stop.

"Do you want me putting pieces together or do you want to tell me your version?" he asked evenly.

"It's not your business."

"I'm making it my business. Let's say I want to know whom I'm dealing with. I can check public records. But—" he dropped one hand on the open page "—that'll waste time I otherwise could spend studying this."

Her next words came reluctantly. "Eric had taken out a second mortgage plus other loans on the house. With income from the dealership falling... In the end, the sale barely covered the loans."

"That's when he left?"

He saw her recognize that she might as well tell him; otherwise someone in town would. "He'd already left."

It was that harpy, Jennifer.... Demanding this, demanding that. Drove the boy right into debt from the start.

He hadn't believed or disbelieved his father when Franklin said that. He hadn't cared whether it was true. He barely knew this woman. The child was a blood relation, sure, but he hadn't felt obligation to blood relations for a long time. Why concern himself with this mother and daughter now?

He swore mentally. Emphatically and repetitively.

Because he could ask himself logical questions from now until Super Bowl Sunday and it wouldn't change that he did feel an obligation.

"Now," Jennifer was saying, "if you have no questions about the projections..." *Please get the hell out of my house.*

No, she didn't say that. But then again, this wasn't anything like the house his parents had waxed eloquent about Eric building with all possible gadgets and indulgences, fit for a prince and his princess.

"No, no more questions now," he said. "I'll study the projections tonight, and see you in the morning."

Trent read every bit of information she'd given him, then he researched on the Internet and sent an e-mail to Linc, who handled his investments, asking for more information before he went to bed.

He examined the ceiling in a lot more detail than it deserved before he willed himself to sleep.

First thing this morning, he called Jerry Brookenheimer, who'd been his football coach at Drago High and still held that position, even though he was past official retirement age, "Because no one else wants the job," as Coach had said.

After setting a time to meet for lunch, Trent had come out and asked Coach what he'd tiptoed around with everyone else. "Is Eric providing for his daughter, is he helping out his ex-wife at all?"

Coach hadn't known details—apparently Jennifer had been so closemouthed that the town's gossip factory hadn't had much to work with—but he confirmed a few things Trent had surmised.

Trent had breakfast at the café, without asking any questions.

Then he drove by the house Jennifer had sold, contemplating the aggressive angles and outsize proportions. Ugly as sin, to his mind, but still considerably more comfortable than that apartment.

He found the cornfields where Zeke-Tech would be built. Then drove to the riverside bluff that gave a view of Drago's layout. Stenner Autos was a block to the west of dead center.

He went by the high school, memories surging. But what he remembered as open fields between it and the middle school now held sport fields and parking lots for a unified complex.

He arrived at Stenner Autos ten minutes early. Jennifer was there. He saw the same ramshackle car by trees that separated visitors' parking from the car wash next door that his father had added. He drove past.

Maybe it was a sense of fair play. After all, he'd already caught her at a disadvantage. Twice. Once at the dealership, again at her apartment.

He wound through downtown, daylight revealing some boarded-up windows, out-of-business posters and a general air of disrepair.

Then—to his own surprise—he ducked off Main Street long enough to go past his old family home. It sat back from the street, adding to its prominence. It was dark brick, with a peaked roof over the front door. The trim had been painted dark brown when he was growing up. Now it was a rich cream, with the door a deep blue. Sure made it more cheerful looking.

He slowed the car to a crawl. Two bicycles leaned against the front steps, as if their users had hopped off and rushed into the house. The garage door was open, a volleyball net stood in the backyard and sometime in the past decade and a half the flower beds had gone from precise right angles to flowing curves.

He returned to the dealership at the top of the hour.

Jennifer emerged from the general manager's office. He wondered if she'd done it deliberately, to replace yesterday's impression.

"Good morning. I have a lot to show you. Shall we get started?"

He nodded. Before yesterday, if he'd given any thought to seeing her again, this was the Jennifer Truesdale he might have expected to encounter.

She wore a dark blue suit, a pale blue blouse and low-heeled shoes that just missed being boringly conservative because the sides swooped down. She had her light hair pulled back at either side of her face, then flowing down her back. Hammered gold earrings and a watch were her only jewelry. Less flashy than he might have expected, but in the ballpark.

And yet, different. Different from what he remembered. Different from what he would have expected if he'd ever considered what to expect.

Something had changed in her face, he decided an hour later as she concluded a tour of the fenced compound nearly empty of cars. She was less a pretty girl and more a striking woman. But that wasn't quite it, either.

Maybe some of it had to do with her being tired. Even more tired than when he'd left her at her apartment.

Considering how much better the showroom looked this morning than it had yesterday afternoon, he'd bet she hadn't just ignored his telling her to quit cleaning before dinner, but had also come back after dinner.

"…and you'll have no trouble hiring people," she said, continuing to extol the virtues of Stenner Autos. Her voice wasn't pitched as low as yesterday, but still had that husky quality to it. "There's an eager employee pool in Drago, including several with excellent experience here at the dealership. I have compiled their names and positions."

He noticed she was talking as if he'd agreed to the deal, but he didn't object. A little trick like that wasn't going to sway him.

They'd already toured the showroom, the offices, the reception area, the break room, the service bays, the storage facilities, even a shed with the snow-removal equipment. Not a lot seemed to have changed.

"What's in that building?"

She'd clearly been prepared to skip the World War II vintage metal building at the back corner. That was one reason he'd asked. Another was he wanted to see Stenner Autos as people had come to know it recently, and that meant examining an area that her cleanup frenzy had not reached.

"Inventory. Parts."

"We saw the parts storage room by the service bays."

"This provides long-term storage."

"Let's see." He kept the words mild, but cocked one eyebrow and looked right at her, making his challenge clear.

To her credit, she didn't try to wriggle out of it, or to explain. She turned on a sensible heel and marched up the decaying wooden ramp that led to double doors, pushing aside accumulated dead leaves with one toe.

"I can…" he volunteered, extending his hand for the keys.

"I'll do it." She fiddled with keys until one fit the padlock that gripped the ends of a dirt-coated chain threaded through the door handles.

She pulled the heavy chain free, but before she reached for the handle, he stepped in. No telling what could come flying out of a building locked tight so long. Kind of like his return to Drago.

He yanked the door open, sucking out a wave of air stale with time, dust and uselessness. He blinked against that hot draft and against the gloom inside that gave nothing away. Behind him, Jennifer sneezed. Once delicately, then a second time, wholeheartedly.

For some reason that made him smile.

He cleaved a spiderweb with his hand and stepped inside, beating back the anonymity of darkness. From floor to ceiling, rows of tall metal shelving rose, divided by narrow aisles. He edged down the middle aisle, where daylight cautiously slanted in. Each shelf held ranks of boxes faded to muddles of colors and indistinguishable writing. He swiped his thumb at what appeared to be a label.

"Power cylinder for the power steering of a 1963 Ford Falcon."

"What's a power cylinder?" Jennifer asked.

"Hell if I know. I'm reading the label. Better question might be—What's a Ford Falcon?" He peered at rows of boxes stretching into dense shadow. "This place must be filled with parts from my father's time, maybe before."

He swore under his breath. He knew the man never let go of ideas and beliefs, but he hadn't known it extended to parts for long-dead cars.

"There's a flashlight in the office. I can—"

His hand shot out and hooked around her elbow. "Don't bother."

"But to see what's in here—"

"You said it before, it's parts inventory."

"But that's all I knew. I asked a former employee. But I didn't have a chance to get to this." Sure as hell she'd have tried to clean it single-handedly if she had, he thought. "We'll need a flashlight to see wha—"

"I don't want to see any more."

He was aware of her gaze. He didn't meet it, instead using his hold on her to guide her out. Stepping over the threshold, her arm came out of his loose hand, severing the connection.

He pulled the chains into place and held them while she threaded the padlock through and clicked it. He swiped his hands against each other to dislodge dust and dirt. She did the same, and he had a fleeting wish he was one of those men who carried a handkerchief so he could offer it to her.

They crossed the back lot's broken surface, passed through the sparse ranks of remaining cars. When they neared the main building, she clicked back into real estate–salesperson mode, listing each supposed highlight.

"And as you've seen," she said, wrapping up her spiel from the side doorway, "you could have a ready-to-operate service area—"

"Without the newest equipment."

"And a salesroom ready to go, as well as—"

"Run-down."

"A secured lot in place."

"Without inventory to secure."

Annoyance flashed across her eyes, stark and unmistakable. She had it controlled almost as fast as it had arrived. "I've shown you the pertinent areas. Is there anything I've missed that you would be interested in seeing?"

The whisper of a devil's voice he didn't know he had in him mentioned a thing or two it would be interested in seeing. He pushed it back down where it belonged, under whatever covered the floor of his subconscious.

"I'm sending these projections to several other investors," she said. "You shouldn't wait until this develops into a bidding war."

He snorted.

"Other investors will look at it strictly for its business potential," she added coolly, "without personal associations clouding their assessment."

"Then why not give these other investors first crack? Wouldn't it be easier to sell to them than to somebody who spent half his life trying to get away from Stenner Autos and the rest thanking the fates he'd succeeded?"

"It only seems fair to give a Stenner first crack at it. You have a name that has meant a lot in this community for a long time. It would be a real asset to you in running this business."

"If the name's such a business asset, why didn't you keep it?"

She gave him a level, would-be-cool-eyed stare. But underneath, he saw emotions churning, including pain. He felt like an ass for stirring that.

"All right, all right. None of my business. I get it. I overstepped. Sorry." But he wasn't a patsy, either. "But come on—other potential buyers?"

He let her see he didn't for a second believe in these other potential buyers. She looked back, defiant.

He almost smiled. "You're good, Jennifer. You're really good."

"Thank you."

"Uh-huh. My family ties both explain my reluctance to buy this white elephant, *and* excuse you from producing rival buyers. That's what I call making the most of what little you have to work with."

"Quit worrying if I'm trying to play you, Trent," she said. "Pretend the name Stenner isn't attached and look at the numbers. It's a good opportunity. A great opportunity. Perhaps I'm foolish in giving you first crack, but you'd be more than foolish to turn it down because of the name."

"What if I say yes?"

"Uh, we'll write up the offer," she said tentatively, as if she'd so focused on getting him to say yes that she hadn't considered what came next. "Judge Dixon has to approve, but I'm sure that won't be a problem."

He was sure it wouldn't be a problem, either. Not if she smiled at the old judge the way she was smiling at him.

"We can go to the office and write up the offer now," she proposed.

"Not now. I'm meeting Coach Brookenheimer for lunch."

She deflated instantly.

"I'll meet you at your office after lunch," he heard himself saying.

"Okay." But he saw that she didn't believe it.

"I'm not making any other promises, but I will be there."

He held her gaze. Even when he saw she wanted to look away. Even when he saw he was making her uncomfortable.

"Okay," she said again, and this time she did believe him.

Why he'd needed her to acknowledge his promise, he had no idea. And now that she had, he couldn't wait to leave.

"Don't expect me before two or three. Coach and I have a lot of catching up to do. But this afternoon, at your office we'll talk more."

"Okay. Have a nice lunch."

He had the main door open when her voice came. "One thing, Trent."

He looked over his shoulder. She hadn't moved. "Yeah?"

"You shouldn't thank the fates for getting away from Stenner Auto."

Ah, here it came. The sentimental pitch that this was as good as a family heirloom. Or he should feel Drago's version of noblesse oblige to keep Stenner Auto going so citizens had a place to buy cars and get them fixed.

"Yeah? Why not?"

"Because the fates didn't get you away. You did that. You worked hard to get away from Stenner Autos and you succeeded."

Chapter Three

Why on earth had she opened her big mouth?

Did she *want* to scare him off from buying the place?

No, absolutely not. Even if he did make her uncomfortable, with that direct, penetrating stare, accompanied by a faint air of disapproval.

She just hated hearing him pass off his success as fate. God knows his brother and father were willing to do that. It seemed wrong that Trent did, too.

...somebody who spent half his life trying to get away from Stenner Autos and the rest of it thanking the fates he's succeeded.

There'd been something in the way he'd said it, something in the way he'd narrowed his eyes until only slits of the pale color showed between the thick, dark lines of his upper and lower lashes, that had made her feel she understood. That she knew his feelings.

She'd thought when she and Eric went to college in Iowa that it meant they would start a new life, away from Drago. The school had been selected based on the best football program to showcase Eric. There'd been no question that Jennifer would follow wherever he chose to go.

She hadn't minded. She hadn't considered studying anything in particular, just wanted to get a degree.

She'd figured she'd adapt, and she had. She did okay in her classes, better, actually, than in high school. She'd made friends, especially at the beginning. She would have enjoyed staying on campus, but nearly every weekend Eric hadn't had a game or practice he'd wanted to return to Drago. "To see what the hicks are doing," he used to say. So she'd come with him. The friends she'd made on campus found other people to do things with who wouldn't be gone most weekends.

Trent had returned to Drago considerably less often. She thought back, trying to remember. He'd graduated from high school when she and Eric got married. The next summer, she knew he was back, because that was right after Eric's injury. At least one Christmas after that, too, she thought. When Ashley was about two.

That must be the last time she'd seen him.

Pretty.

The word went so far back in her memory that Jennifer thought it had always been there. It was something people said of her. Something nice. Not like Mark calling her Jenny-Poo-With-Poo-In-Her-Pants.

Pretty was good. That much she knew.

Then she'd learned its power.

What a pretty girl!

Her father had been holding her hand, trying to find a seat with a good view for one of Mark's Little League games. He hadn't been happy about having to take her, but Mom had a doctor's appointment. He walked a lot faster than she did, and he tugged her hand when she got behind.

"Already started," he'd muttered, blocked by other people climbing the bleachers.

Then a lady in the front row smiled at Jennifer, and said loudly, "What a pretty girl!"

Daddy had looked around. First at the woman, then at her.

For a second she'd been almost afraid, because Daddy's eyes had that blank look, as though he didn't even see her.

But then he did, and slowly, a smile arrived. "Yes, she is. She's a very pretty girl."

"Are you nuts?" Linc demanded.

Trent sat on the concrete steps that led to old shop fronts on Main Street. It looked like one—Zeekowsky Shoe Repair, if his memory was right—was being renovated. But the workers were either off today or taking a lunch break elsewhere.

From here he could see the café and spot Coach's arrival. In the meantime he'd have privacy for this phone conversation.

"You *are* nuts," Linc amended before Trent could respond.

Trent grinned. Imagining his friend and business manager's face, incredulity adding a ruddier tinge to his coffee-colored skin. They'd met eight years ago at the wedding of Trent's teammate to Linc's sister, started talking investments and hit it off.

There wasn't anyone Trent trusted more. There wasn't anyone who knew the ins and outs of his finances better. There wasn't anyone whose chain was easier to jerk: just edge an inch toward being a fool with money.

"You're always the one saying don't invest money you can't afford to lose," he said.

He could hear Linc's keyboard going, and knew his friend

was already researching car dealerships in general and Stenner Autos in particular.

"That's a hell of a lot different from investing money you expect to lose."

"I didn't say I expect to lose it. I asked how long it would take me to recover financially if I lost all the money it'll cost to buy Stenner Autos."

Linc snorted. "From what you said, you *should* be expecting to lose it. Small town, selling a couple kinds of cars instead of specializing—I didn't think manufacturers even let dealers do that. Thought you couldn't sell competing new cars."

"Stenner Autos is grandfathered in. Started doing it so far back they didn't have rules like that. But if the dealership officially goes bankrupt, it loses that exemption, and that's one of its most valuable assets."

"Hmph. This place has assets? Besides, if it's in the hands of a judge, how can you pull it back from the brink? Why would he let you try?"

"You don't know Drago. The Dixons and the Stenners go way back."

"Still doesn't make this a good investment. Why couldn't you start a Lexus dealership? Or Mercedes-Benz."

Trent laughed. "In Drago? Linc, we need to pry you away from that California wasteland and get you out here into the heart of the country. Status isn't a cash crop the way it is in L.A."

Linc grunted. "You said it's been losing money forever."

"Not forever. It used to support the Stenners very well."

"Times change."

"Yeah, they do." Sometimes. And sometimes, even when times changed, people didn't. "But change can be good. Turns out Zeke-Tech's bringing a division of his company here."

He'd seen signs of decline in town, but also a subtle kind

of perking up. Like the drooping flowers in a concrete planter by the café that Loris was tending with a watering can. It must have been an optical illusion, because he imagined he could see the purple flowers reviving from here.

"That's *your* town?" Trent could practically see Linc sitting up, intent with interest. "I heard about that move. Hmm, maybe this could work."

"Yeah? Well, don't count on it," Trent said, switching roles. "It will take a year, probably more, for enough folks to move here to really make a difference. And they'll come with cars. So it could take even more years before they need a new one. So your concern's well-founded."

"Yeah? When you start admitting I'm right, I know you're in sorry shape. This isn't all about the money, you know. You sure you want to climb back into that pit?"

"No. But…" He gazed down the street.

"But what?"

"As far as I can tell, my brother left his wife—ex-wife—and daughter without any financial support."

Linc growled. He was not a fan of men who didn't take care of their families. But he didn't give up the fight. "And this is your problem how?"

"Because I'm here," Trent answered honestly. "I can't say I ever would have thought to wonder how Jennifer and Ashley were provided for if I hadn't stumbled onto the knowledge. But I can't unstumble now."

"All right, all right. But how would your sinking money into Stenner Autos help your niece and her mama?"

"Jennifer is handling the listing. She'd get the commission."

"So you're going to buy this damn dealership so your niece's mama gets a commission, Mr. Bleeding Heart? You sure that's all it is? We both know you buying that place would make your daddy as happy as that man can get. You sure it's not something to do with your daddy and that brother of yours? Which makes no sense. On the other hand, for your mama—"

"Linc."

That stopped the flow of words. But after a moment broken only by the continued tap of computer keys, Linc exhaled loudly. "Well, it wouldn't be pretty if it goes belly-up, but you could recover. Eventually. Might have to come work for me."

Trent groaned. It was the direst of dire threats. "I'd rather flip burgers or join the French Foreign Legion."

"You don't get the luxury of choice when you spend your money on other luxuries. Like the luxury of playing Sir Galahad."

"This has nothing to do with—"

"Save it. With the commission going to your sister-in-law—"

"Ex-sister-in-law."

Linc made an explosive sound that combined a laugh, a groan and a healthy dose of *I told you so*. "Tell you what, Mr. Stenner. I've got some ideas we can talk about in a minute—unless you want to stay there and run it yourself."

"No way. I'll put money into it, but I'm not staying here."

"Okay then, I'll keep researching this business venture of yours. But I can tell you right now what the bottom line is."

He made Trent ask. "What's the bottom line, Linc?"

"If you want to have any luxuries besides choice, you'd better make sure that dealership becomes a success."

"I hope you had a pleasant lunch with Coach Brookenheimer," Jennifer said, professionally cordial, when Trent walked into the shoe box she called an office at Roscoe Real Estate at two forty-five.

"Very nice. Thanks. I'm making an offer on Stenner Autos."

Her mouth opened. Those parades of reactions streamed

across her eyes again. Hope, fear, relief, more fear, uncertainty, triumph quickly reined in and another dose of fear—this one clearly centered around whether she'd heard him correctly. Or whether he was kidding.

"No," he said. "I'm not kidding. Nuts, maybe, but not kidding. I'm putting in an offer on Stenner Autos."

"What—" She ran her tongue over her bottom lip. "What's your offer?"

"The asking price."

"But—" She stopped that sentence by clamping down on her bottom lip, clearly deciding that encouraging a buyer who was willing to pay full price to negotiate was not a wise move.

"So, what's next?" Trent asked.

"We… We talk to the judge."

White-haired Hector Dixon looked across his impressive desk at them.

First at Jennifer, then longer at him. It made Trent feel as if he'd overlooked something. Something more than that he'd gone crazy.

"These terms satisfy the conditions set with the creditors. Are you satisfied with the monetary amount of this offer, Jennifer?"

"I am, Judge."

"Have you received any further word from that woman—what was her name? Duran? Doring? The one who—"

"Your Honor, that's a separate matter from this," Jennifer said quickly.

He leaned back in his chair and steepled his fingers. "That's your opinion is it?"

"Yes."

The older man continued looking at her from under his lids for a moment, then turned that look on Trent.

What was going on? He hadn't had much time to do

detailed research, but he was confident Linc had given him the pertinent information in their second phone call after lunch. He knew about the deal brokered by the judge with the creditors—an unorthodox effort to avoid bankruptcy because that would end Stenner Autos' deals with the auto manufacturers and most of its value would go down the drain, gaining the creditors nothing.

He didn't recall anything about a woman named Duran or Doring. So, what was this about?

"Here's what we're going to do," Hector Dixon said, then abruptly straightened. "I'm confident the creditors will go along. Trent's going to buy Stenner Autos, and you'll get your commission—" Beside him, Trent thought he heard an exhalation of pent-up breath from Jennifer. "That'll all be straightforward as long as you and Trent agree to two conditions."

"What?" Jennifer looked puzzled.

"It's Stenner Autos, and Ashley's a Stenner. So the first condition is you have an agreement drawn up, Trent, to assign a portion of the dealership to a trust for Ashley, to be administered by Jennifer."

"What portion?" Trent asked.

"Ten percent," Judge Dixon said.

"Twenty," Jennifer countered immediately.

"Fifteen," the judge said in an *and that's final* voice.

Trent bit back a dry smile. Interesting to have terms of his acquisition negotiated without any input himself. Linc would go nuts.

The smile became harder to repress.

But a fund for Ashley was a good idea. Having it come from the Stenners made it more right.

"Twenty-five percent of the fund goes to a college account," he said.

Judge Dixon and Jennifer both turned to him, as if they'd

forgotten he was there. In the judge's face he saw approval, in Jennifer's surprise.

"Done," the judge said.

But Trent hadn't forgotten how Dixon had introduced this topic. There was another shoe to drop. And no matter how much fun it was to ruffle Linc's feathers, he wasn't going to buy Stenner Autos at any cost.

"What's the second condition?"

The judge met his gaze, and Trent let him see that he had limits. He definitely had limits.

And then the old man went and pushed those limits.

"You agree to hire Jennifer here, for one year as a manager, and you, Jennifer, agree to take the job."

"What?" Trent demanded, the implications of hiring her as a manager playing out in his head.

Linc had said large dealerships had a general manger, an operations manager, a sales manager, in addition to the head of the service department. Stenner Autos couldn't support anywhere near that staff, but would still need those duties fulfilled.

So they'd worked out a plan on the fly to hire the best general manager they could find, so Trent could dump the whole mess in his lap. It was already going to be tight to pull together the money fast to get a general manager with as broad a background as they needed.

Could they add another salary and afford to stick with that scenario?

Even with Jennifer picking up some managerial duties, the general manager would need to fill a lot of roles, which translated into being able to command a high salary.

So the answer was no. If Trent had to pay Jennifer a salary for a year, he couldn't afford the kind of general manager that would allow him to be an absentee owner.

He'd have to stick around and act as his own general manager. It was the only way they could swing it financially.

Stick around… *God*. The last thing on earth he'd ever wanted to do—run Stenner Autos.

But unless he backed out now, he'd have no choice. He needed to make sure things went well and the place made money. Both so Jennifer and Ashley would be provided for and to protect his investment. And then there was the fact that if Stenner Autos went under while he owned it he'd never hear the last of it. Not from his father. Not from Linc. Maybe not even from his own conscience.

He glanced at Jennifer. She seemed as stunned as he was.

"But—but I have a job," she said.

"I've talked to Roscoe. There's not enough real estate business to support a flea, much less a grown woman with a growing girl. You need something steady, reliable. After a year, if you want to go back to selling houses, Roscoe will take you back, and by that time there might be buyers, with these Zeke-Tech people coming in."

"She doesn't know any more about running a car dealership than I do," Trent objected.

And that brought the whole thing home. He'd have to immerse himself in the topic that had been second only to Eric's accomplishments at every dinner table conversation of his childhood.

"She's got a good head on her shoulders. She'll learn," the judge said, unconcerned. "Just like you will. So. It's settled. I'll have a side letter drawn up, and if you'd like to look it over…"

"Damn right I would. Sorry, Your Honor," Trent quickly added at the scowl from under bushy salt-and-pepper eyebrows. "I'd like some time to call my financial adviser in California."

Judge Dixon looked at the clock, then the open leather-bound calendar on his desk. "Twenty minutes. Then we'll meet here to sign the papers."

Twenty minutes.

She had the judge's office to herself for that time. It was cool and shaded. Serene in a utilitarian, masculine way. The leather chair she sat in was comfortable and pleasant.

Jennifer felt as if she were sitting on ground glass.

Trent had left looking like thunder to talk to his financial adviser.

She wished she had someone to consult, just in case Trent didn't tell Judge Dixon where to put his conditions.

Not a lawyer. She didn't need a lawyer for what concerned her. Not an accountant, either.

Judge Dixon was already doing more than she could have imagined to see that she and Ashley had the security Jennifer had been striving for since Eric left. Even before he left. When she started recognizing the mistakes Eric was making with the dealership, with their finances, with their futures. She'd tried a couple times to broach the subjects. And hadn't that gone great?

The first time, he'd laughed. Not pleasantly. "Like you know anything about business. Like you have a brain in that blond head?"

She sometimes wished she'd pointed out that he was blond, too, as was their daughter.

The second time she'd brought it up, he'd screamed at her before she'd even finished. That's when she knew their financial situation was really bad.

She'd already been saving money in an account Eric didn't know about. For Ashley's college, she'd told herself. Sometimes she wondered if at some level she'd recognized what would happen. After that screaming episode, she'd escalated her savings. But it had been hard, with Eric spending money faster than it came in.

Those savings and the one credit card she'd opened in her name alone had kept her and Ashley from living on the street until she got the job with Roscoe. Although the job with Roscoe hadn't kept them far off the street.

But maybe Trent was wrong when he'd said she didn't know any more about running a car dealership than he did. Which would mean she was wrong, too, because she'd silently agreed with him when he'd said it.

She did know a little about what *not* to do after watching the business fading under Eric. And she knew about customers who desperately needed transportation, had little money, and were afraid of being taken advantage of. Yes, she knew something about that.

None of that was the problem she wished she had someone to call to consult with about.

The problem was Trent Stenner.

And, truth be told, she did have someone she could call— Darcie. Except she knew what Darcie would say— "Problem? Working with a good-looking, intelligent and generally considerate man? That's no problem."

But it was.

First, because she wasn't entirely sure Trent was…what? Honest? On the level? Trustworthy?

There was something else going on in this situation that she didn't understand. After all his efforts to stay away—from Drago, from the dealership, from his family ties—he came back now? Why?

Was it to show up Eric? To prove he could succeed at running the dealership where his brother had failed, just as he'd succeeded at building a career in football when his older brother hadn't?

To win over his father? If so it would be the first time in her knowledge that he'd made that effort. As long as she'd known the family, Trent's coping method had been distance—and lots of it.

Not knowing made her edgy, uncertain. It was like walking on ice in early spring, not sure where or when or if it was going to crack open and plunge you into freezing water, but knowing each step had the potential.

She'd say no, she thought on a quick wave of panic. She'd say she hadn't realized until now that she didn't want to leave real estate, and she would tough out the next year of no commissions. Somehow.

Except Ashley would have to tough it out, too.

Oh, God. She couldn't say no.

She couldn't deny Ashley all that a steady, reliable income would bring. Plus, she'd be involved, making sure the dealership became a success, securing Ashley's future.

She had to say yes.

And she had to pray Trent did, too.

Somewhere, Jennifer thought she could hear Darcie Barrett cackling with glee. But she shivered at the thought of ice cracking under her feet.

"Okay to both your conditions," Trent said as soon as they'd all sat.

It might have sounded curt, but he was not in the best of moods.

"Fine," Judge Dixon said with a broad smile. "We can sign the preliminary agreement right now. I'll have my clerk—"

"Wait a minute," Trent objected. "Jennifer hasn't given her decision."

The judge looked taken aback, but whether at his own oversight or because he hadn't considered that she had a say, Trent couldn't tell.

"Before I give you an answer—" Jennifer cleared her throat, but when she spoke again, her voice was still that husky timbre that felt like someone was touching him "—I have a question for Trent."

She waited, as if not sure how he would respond to that declaration.

What else could he say but, "What's your question?"

"You…you're buying the dealership?"

He raised one eyebrow. "I thought we'd covered that."

"I mean, I wondered if you're acting on behalf of your father. If he was buying the rest of it back."

"No." He would have liked to have left it at that. She clearly wouldn't. And he supposed he owed her a little more under the circumstances. "My father won't be involved in this transaction. It's my money."

The judge got into the act then. "Franklin does retain a minority interest, however, the same as he's had since retiring. Will your father be involved in the dealership operations?"

God, no. He stifled that response. "No, he won't."

He saw another question burning in Jennifer's eyes, while her mouth remained tightly closed. Judge Dixon clearly saw it, too.

"Do you have another concern, Jennifer?" the judge asked.

"How'd you get the money, Trent?" The words shot out of her, as if she couldn't hold them in. "I mean people say you're doing okay, but this much? You didn't get signing bonuses or the big—"

She stopped like someone had hit her Off button. Or as if she'd remembered where she'd heard those assessments of his contracts.

"No, I never got big signing bonuses or eye-popping contracts," he said without emotion. It was simply a fact. "But you know what they say—it's not what you get, it's what you do with it."

Her eyes were wide. And so blue.

A memory hit him. Of looking into her eyes in just about this way the first time she'd come to the house. Sitting across the table from her. He'd said something about one of his classes—a rare foray into dinnertime conversation for him—and she'd looked at him. Probably the first time she had. And he'd seen how blue her eyes were and how beautiful and how empty.

At least that's what he'd thought. That's when he'd dismissed her.

Or maybe he'd dismissed her when she'd walked in with Eric.

Her blue eyes certainly weren't empty now. Intelligence and drive filled them. And uncertainty. But that was about him.

"I'm not going to give you a blow-by-blow account of my finances."

She started to protest. "I'm not asking—"

"But I can assure you it's my money, not my father's."

She looked at him for a long moment. Finally, she nodded.

"Okay." She gripped the chair arms, as if preparing for blastoff. "Then I accept Judge Dixon's conditions. I'll work at the dealership for a year."

Chapter Four

"So, now what do we do?"

Trent stood in the middle of the empty showroom and by his expression he felt a foreboding nearly as deep as Jennifer's while she'd signed the papers at Judge Dixon's chambers.

They'd driven here in separate cars, each of them, she supposed needing those minutes alone to get their bearings. Too bad they weren't in Chicago, where the traffic would have provided plenty of time to get used to the idea of what they'd agreed to do. In Drago, the trip had amounted to eight minutes, including time for her to make phone calls.

"Hire employees. Get more inventory. Get cars," she started.

He put his head back, looking at the ceiling instead of her. The position emphasized how his hairline curved crisply back at his temples, came to mirrored peaks below the temples before curving again to meet his sideburns, which in turn faded to a stubble down his firm jaw. The effect of that hairline was to call attention to his eyes, where dark brows and dark lashes provided a stark contrast to eyes more gray than blue.

"I talked to my guy in California about finding a good general manager, but—"

"I'm general manager," she said with a firmness born of desperation. An outsider wouldn't care the way she would. An outsider wouldn't fight as hard to make this place earn money to go into Ashley's fund.

Still angled, his head came around toward her.

"Whoa. Judge Dixon said you'd be a manager, he didn't say general manager. If we want this to succeed—"

"We can't afford to pay the salary a good general manager gets." Eric had acted as general manger, but he hadn't been a good one.

"I know. That's why I'll be acting as general manager myself," Trent said with a hint of wryness.

She eyed him. She wanted to argue. Oh, did she want to argue. What had drawn her to real estate was the idea that her financial well-being was in her own hands. How could she sit back and let him—another Stenner male—control her financial future?

On the other hand, arguing for arguing's sake made no sense. And she saw that nothing she could say would change his mind. Not yet, anyway.

"You're the owner," she said mildly, then watched his reaction.

God, owner of Stenner Autos.

The thought flashed across his face like a neon sign, even though he tried to mask the dismay. Whether it had been his own work or the fates, he certainly had spent a good chunk of his life getting away from this, and now here he was. Back. What the hell was he doing here?

And then, just as fast, his expression covered all the turmoil.

But she thought she could hear the faint *click* of a crack in the ice she was standing on.

"Yes, I am the owner." He tipped his head back again. "You're wrong about that first step, though."

"Paint the ceiling," she guessed.

"Fix the roof," he amended. "So it stops leaking. And then paint the ceiling. Then I'm going to have to hire people."

Her turn to correct him. "*We're* going to hire people." Having given in on the general manger point it was even more essential that she stake her claim to authority. That didn't mean it was easy. "I know the people to hire. You don't. I researched all that getting the dealership ready for sale."

He looked at her from under lowered eyelids. "Okay. We're going to have to hire people. How do you propose we go about that?"

Since she'd worked hard on her research, she felt only a shiver of nerves under the confidence. Faked confidence, sure, but she'd learned during her blighted real estate career that well-executed fake confidence could be as good as the real thing.

"I have a list of possible candidates for the most important jobs." She put a copy on the counter. He reached for it, but if she'd wanted him to have it she would have given it to him. She pulled it out of reach. If he started reading, he'd stop listening—another lesson from real estate. "I made some calls. I've got five people coming in tomorrow."

"Tomorrow? Good lord, you don't waste any time."

"There isn't any to waste. We should open at the end of July, so we're up and running when new models come in. We have a lot to do, and we can't wait."

"That part is going to have to wait," he said flatly. "I'm leaving in the morning. I wasn't planning to stay for more than a day or two. Now…well, I've got to get home, make arrangements, get more clothes."

"Then we'll start this evening," she said with a calm she didn't feel. This wasn't all that much different from selling a house. Once you had a prospect on the line, you didn't want to let them get away, let them think too much, let them change their minds.

And since she'd sold exactly one house—a whopper of a sale, true, but the seller had been her best friend's mother and the buyer had been her best friend's soon-to-be husband, so it didn't exactly qualify as a compelling feat of salesmanship—she knew about letting buyers get away.

Would Trent change his mind? Renege on the deal?

"I'll call right now to switch the appointments," she added.

"Nobody'll want to change their plans and come in this evening."

"Are you kidding? Around here, folks would walk on nails for a good job."

Already thirsty and knowing he had an evening of talking ahead of him when the interviews started, Trent strode across the main drive to get a soft drink from the machine nestled under the trees that divided customer parking from the car wash next door.

You had to give Drago its due. He couldn't imagine many places where a vending machine left outdoors and basically unattended would remain standing, much less operating and—judging from the *clunk-clunk-clunk* resonance of his deposit—with its change intact.

His father had added the car wash to Stenner Autos to ensure every car that left the dealership was clean. It also drew business off the street.

Apparently it had kept operating even when Stenner Autos didn't. Either that, or this soft drink was going to be a year or two old.

He took a tentative swig. Nope, not a day over six months.

Peripheral vision had saved his neck more than once on the football field, now, with his head back to drink, it caught someone approaching.

Ashley.

She appeared headed for the machine, too, probably for the same purpose. She hadn't spotted him.

After lining up the interviews for this evening faster than he could have believed, Jennifer had suggested they meet back here at five-thirty to prepare. "That will give us time to get dinner beforehand," she'd added.

He'd opened his mouth to say he didn't eat dinner that early, especially since his stomach was still on West Coast time, two hours later.

He hadn't said the words.

She had Ashley's schedule to work around. Was school still going? Those sorts of family considerations weren't part of his experience. So, he would follow her lead for now.

He went to the motel, packed so he could get an early start tomorrow and called for a plane reservation. He decided to call his parents later. After he knew more about how this was going to work.

He stopped at the café to buy a sandwich for later and returned to Stenner Autos with the sun blaring full in the main showroom window. Inside, he'd found Jennifer moving tables and chairs around, while Ashley slouched against a wall with a headset's earplugs firmly in place, eyes shut and one heel tapping time against the wall.

"Stop that."

He'd said it without any heat, but loud enough to reach through the electronic noise the girl was listening to. Her eyes popped open. But it was her mother who jolted as if she'd had a live wire applied to her skin.

Trent kept his main focus on the girl. "Your mother just washed the walls. You're putting marks on it."

She looked at him blankly.

"Here." He grabbed a towel Jennifer had been using to dust surfaces that looked clean to him, and tossed it at the girl. "Clean those heel marks."

Ashley's eyes narrowed. He could practically see the smart-ass words bubbling up. Then she flicked a look at Jennifer and back to him.

Uh-huh. She was wondering if he'd snitch to her mother that she'd been out when he'd arrived at the apartment last night.

Let her wonder.

Another lesson learned from football. Whenever possible, you didn't commit irrevocably to a play until you knew which way the ball was going.

"Now," he continued, hefting the table Jennifer had been rearranging by shoving one side, then the other in a laborious zigzag, "where do you want this?"

Jennifer gaped at him for another beat before she went into action, directing him where to put that table, plus two others and about a dozen chairs. All the while Ashley, cleaning the scuffs on the wall with ill grace, had watched him as if he was the snake about to swallow her mongoose.

When Jennifer said there was nothing more for him to do, he'd come out for the soft drink. And maybe a little to get away from his niece.

So, of course, here she was, one hand digging in a pocket for change.

"Oh." She stopped, startled. Then immediately shifted to sullen. "It's you."

"Yup. It is." He took a swallow. "Your mom need any more help?"

"I wiped all those dumb chairs. What more do you want?"

The kid sure did lead with anger.

"To know if your mom needs my help."

"She said everything's done but putting forms on a bunch of clipboards, and she wanted to do that herself," she added hurriedly.

"Good enough. What do you want?" He gestured toward the machine.

She teetered for maybe half a second. Then she slid her hand out of her pocket, letting coins clunk back to its depths. "Root beer."

He put in coins, pressed the button, retrieved the can and handed it to her. She mumbled a syllable that might have been thanks.

In silence, they each took a swallow. He almost felt sorry for her then. She was younger than the kids he'd worked with at the high school he and a couple teammates had adopted, but he recognized the signs. She wanted to leave, but she didn't want to retreat.

She took a second, long swallow. A nearly stifled belch followed.

He smiled. Just a little, but she saw it. In an instant she was an outraged diva, reining in her justifiable wrath with the greatest of self-control in order to deliver a stunning put-down.

"My dad," she declaimed, "was the best quarterback this town ever saw."

Trent thought about that. In his memory he saw Eric, only a sophomore but already the varsity starter, dropping back for a pass during a high school game, looking over the field before him, the play developing the way it was supposed to, his confidence complete.

"I suppose that's true."

"And you—you weren't much of a player at all."

That same memory continued in Trent's head. Sitting in the

stands, his middle school game, played on a mudflat far from the glory of the varsity field, now long over. In that moment, Trent had seen the potential for the deep defender to intercept the pass Eric was about to throw.

He'd sat forward, watching the play, while also playing it in his head, with him as that defender. *Ignore the receiver's fake, take two quick steps to cut inside, and have a clear shot at the pass.* He didn't need the dazzling skills Eric possessed, he didn't need the impressive size some linemen possessed. He needed quick feet, the ability to see possibilities ahead and the faith that he could turn those possibilities to his advantage.

The defender on the field didn't make that play. Eric's pass reached the receiver and became a touchdown. But from that point on, Trent had honed his quick feet, his ability to see ahead and his faith in his abilities.

"Not then, I wasn't much of a player," he agreed with his niece. "But I worked and I got better."

The girl flushed. Blotches marbled her skin. She was too young not to want the fairy tale of her handsome prince of a father, and too old not to recognize some of the truth about him. He felt sorry for her.

"He hurt his knee," she said defensively.

Someone more accustomed to dissembling would have recognized that by giving her father an excuse, she'd highlighted his failure. By saying the words, she'd acknowledged that, unlike what Trent had just said about himself, Eric hadn't worked hard and he hadn't gotten better.

"He did hurt his knee." He eyed her. He could let it go. But he wasn't sure that was for the best. "You know how many NFL quarterbacks have played after that same injury? How many college players? They had to do a lot of rehabilitation, but they played."

"I'm not going to discuss this with you," she said haughtily. As if he'd started this pissing match.

"Fine. I've got something else to discuss." He gave her no chance to respond. "You don't leave that apartment without your mother's permission again."

"You can't tell me what to do."

"I can tell you what I'm going to do, though. If I find out you've gone out like that again, I will make sure your mother knows." He tipped his head. "Or I might decide to deal with you myself."

Her eyes flared wide, but only for a second, then the diva returned. She stalked off.

"We're ready for—Ashley?" Jennifer had come out the door and started toward them. Now that her daughter was making a beeline for the street, she changed her path like the arrow on a magnet swinging around to follow true north and went after the girl. "Where are you going?"

The girl stopped with an air of martyrdom during a brief exchange that Trent heard only part of. It included surly snippets about *Done everything you asked, just want to go home and watch a movie* and *It's broad daylight* from Ashley and *Are you sure you're feeling okay?* and *Be careful,* then, finally, *Call me when you get there* from Jennifer.

Then his niece walked away, while Jennifer looked after her.

Her shoulders lifted, then dropped in what looked to be a sigh that started from the depths of her toes, before she turned and zeroed in on him. Frowning, of course.

"What was that about?" she demanded when she got close enough.

"Family bonding. Ready to start these interviews?"

She looked at him, uncertain. "Ashley didn't look happy with you."

He nodded, unperturbed. "Exactly. Just the way I'm bonded with all of my family."

* * *

"Agreed?" Trent asked.

Jennifer was thoroughly unsettled—not by the interviews, which had gone remarkably well—but by Trent Stenner.

That episode with Ashley in the parking lot had started her feeling of being unsettled. Could he really be that blasé about his niece's apparent hostility? And what about equating it with his other family relationships?

Her concern wasn't based on any maternal ideal that an uncle should be crazy about Ashley. It was based on practicality. If Trent felt that way about family, she came back to her original question: why was he here?

And most important, what impact might his motivations have on the dealership's future?

She couldn't complain about his behavior tonight. He'd been pleasant and professional and relaxed. With both the interviewees and with her.

The problem with that was she kept forgetting he was Trent Stenner. Trent *Stenner*.

In the minutes she'd allowed between interviews, she'd found herself relaxing into an honest, open discussion with him of the candidates' merits.

And then she'd catch a glint, a light in his eyes…. Sometimes she thought it was a look of interest, though not quite the I'm-a-man-interested-in-you-as-a-woman look. Sometimes it was a look like someone trying to work out a scam. But as the scammer or the scammee?

If he was trying to scam her that would be awful, but the result could be just as bad if he thought she was trying to scam him.

And then it would hit her again. Trent. *Stenner.* He was Trent Stenner! What was she doing being relaxed and honest and open with him?

It was like slipping into a pleasant dream, then slapping

your own face to bring yourself back to reality. Not a great way to spend an evening.

"So, we're agreed?" His repeated question pulled her attention to the present.

They'd locked up and turned everything off except safety lights guarding the back lot. Now they stood under the trees, Trent with one foot on her car's bumper, her leaning against the closed driver's door. She would have dust on her slacks. But she was too tired to stand straight.

The past thirty hours had held more than a week should.

"Agreed?" she asked.

He gave her a searching look from under those dark brows. In this more-shadows-than-light, he looked more dangerous than ever. Dark and powerful and contained. The containment seemed most menacing of all.

"About hiring Jorge to head service."

"Oh, yes, absolutely."

Jorge O'Farrell was young, sharp and hungry. He'd had his own garage in Chicago that had burned down under mysterious circumstances. Some folks in town whispered about the mob. Whatever the cause, he'd returned to Drago and moved in with his parents. He'd smiled when he'd said that was great motivation to work hard so he could afford his own place, but his dark eyes had remained intense.

"As long as his references check out," Jennifer added. "I'll start on that tomorrow."

"Good. I like Carol and Herman for sales. And you can't argue with Hank's experience. I know," he added before she could do more than open her mouth. "As long as their references check out, but since Hank worked here for four years, his shouldn't be any problem. Okay, then, since I'm going to be general manager—"

That sounded decidedly grim. Decidedly, to stem any arguments from her, she thought. And grim, because he dreaded holding the position.

"—that brings us to sales manager. There's Chelchem."

Bert Chelchem, Eric's sales manager, was the top candidate on paper.

She sighed. "He has experience and certainly knows the dealership. And with neither of us experienced in running a car dealership…"

"I don't like him, either," Trent said.

"Either? I never said I didn't like him."

"You didn't have to."

"I never meant to—"

"Don't worry. He didn't have a clue. And that pretty much wraps up the file on Bert. What about Mr. Warner?"

Jennifer almost smiled. Elliott Warner had been sales manager under Franklin, so Mr. Warner is what Trent grew up calling him.

"You heard him—he won't work any more than part-time," she objected.

"Part-time's okay. You can fill in the rest."

"Me? Sales manager?"

"Hey, you're the one who wanted to be general manager."

"General's easier to do than sales manager. You have to really know about selling and all that."

He chuckled. "Then you should agree that you're a better choice for the job than I would be."

"But you—you played football."

"Yeah. And that would mean what?"

"People like to buy cars from celebrities."

This time he laughed. "Honey, I'm no celebrity. Not even here in Drago. Just a working stiff on the football field who showed up every day. But I am the guy who's putting in the big bucks for this operation, so I say I'm General Manager,

Mr. Warner's part-time Sales Manager and you're part-time Sales Manager and, uh, part-time Assistant General Manager. Yeah, that's good. That way you're officially over Mr. Warner, so there's no question you have authority to make decisions."

And no question that she reported to Trent, as the General Manager. But the fact that she'd be reporting to him as his assistant wasn't the reason for her reluctance. What did she know about selling cars? Nothing about cars, and judging from her performance in real estate, not much about selling.

"Trent, I don't think—"

"I do. It's settled."

"But—"

A light swept over them, and they both jerked around, as if they'd been caught doing something they shouldn't have.

"Everything okay?" came Darcie's voice, only a second before she became visible beyond the light.

"Just fine," Jennifer said when Trent didn't answer immediately. "We started interviews tonight. We're just recapping."

Jennifer suddenly became aware of the thrum of Darcie's police car in the background, along with chatter over the police radio. She'd been so intent on her discussion with Trent she hadn't heard them.

"I heard about the interview session. How'd it go?"

"Good." Jennifer gave Trent a quick look, uncertain. Then she leveled her chin and repeated, firmly, "Good."

"Great. And I hope you know you got a fantastic deal, Trent," Darcie said. "Congratulations."

"For getting all this?" he asked dryly, with a sweep to the dealership's lumpy shadows behind them.

"Sure. But more for getting Jennifer's help as part of the deal. You'll be thanking your lucky stars. I guarantee it. She's—" She interrupted herself to listen to the radio. "Gotta go."

Her teeth flashed white in a grin as she backed out, waving through the open window.

Trent turned to Jennifer. "Sounds like you and Darcie are good friends."

"Yes, we are."

His dark brows drew down. "Were you before?"

"In high school? No. We got to know each other five or six years ago."

She and Darcie happened to sit next to each other at the annual Lilac Festival dinner-dance that spring. Eric had been at the head table.

"Mingling with the peons, huh?" Darcie's question had had an edge.

Later, Darcie had come around a corner to find Eric berating his wife. *What was she doing mixing with the ordinary people—* he probably would have said peons if he'd known the word— *when she was a Stenner? How dare she make a spectacle of herself because she was in another one of her stupid moods?*

Darcie retreated, as people always did. But Jennifer had caught a flash in her expression that went beyond the embarrassment most people showed. A flash that somehow transformed into words in Jennifer's head.

You don't deserve to be treated this way.

The words had circled in her head. Intriguing, a little frightening.

Later, Eric left with a group, stranding Jennifer. Darcie had offered her a ride home. They hadn't become friends that night, but Jennifer thought it might have been the start.

She blinked, abruptly aware of silence in the here and now. Trent was watching her.

"Darcie marrying Zeke is kind of a surprise, isn't it?" he asked. "Kind of strange, a tech genius and a small-town cop. Even if they did know each other as kids."

"A surprise to them, maybe, not to anyone else." She smiled. "Actually, Darcie would tell you it's wonderful *and* strange. Separate, they're fantastic, and they're even better when they're together. Wait until Zeke comes back. You'll see."

"Okay. I'll wait. Zeke's gone a lot even though they just got engaged?"

"It takes a lot to prepare to move part of a company halfway across the country. Darcie understands. Besides, she's not exactly a clinging vine."

But he still looked skeptical, and it irked her. How could he doubt Zeke and Darcie when he hadn't even seen them together?

"How're they going to keep the wedding private?" he asked. "Won't the media be crawling all over town? In a town this size it won't be hard to track them down. Or maybe they want to be tracked down—you know, that saying about any publicity is good publicity."

"No, they don't want it. But Drago rallies around its own. Sure reporters ask nosy questions and dig for information, but everyone gives them blank stares if they don't want to answer." It struck her that apparently people hadn't done that when Trent had asked about her. She hurried on before he could point that out. "In the meantime the journalists eat at the café, buy gas and—"

"Too bad they won't buy cars here," he muttered.

"But the Zeke-Techers will. Well, you have an early flight, right?" she added briskly, not liking the trend of his thoughts. "So, I'd better let you go."

"Yeah. When I have an idea of when I'll be back, I'll let you know."

Were those his doubts or hers that made his vagueness sound so ominous. "How long do you think that might be? There's so much to do."

"Minimum of a week."

"A week?" Dismay dripped from her words.

"I'll have to drive back from California so I have my car here. And that's after everything else I'll have to pull together there."

"What kind of car?"

He hiked up one eyebrow. This time she had no trouble reading his reaction. He wondered if her question represented the appearance of the material girl he so clearly had expected.

She drew in a breath. So what if he misjudged her? A lot of people did. Sometimes it worked to her advantage. And, besides, she couldn't control what he thought of her.

"BMW," he said.

She immediately shook her head.

"What do you mean, no?"

"You can't drive a BMW around here."

"The hell I can't."

"You'll need to drive a dealer car. Just like your father did. As a rolling advertisement for Stenner Autos."

"Damn. Okay, you've got a point."

She started to turn away, ending the discussion now that she'd won.

"But—" His emphatic syllable brought her head back around to face him. "If I have to drive a dealer car instead of my own, then so do you."

"Mine's the same make as half the new inventory we'll be getting."

"Not exactly a rolling advertisement for Stenner Autos, though, is it? I've heard that car when you finally get it started."

She hated that he was right. She hated that her car was only one manifestation of her earlier messed-up priorities, which had put getting a degree and preparing for a career low on her list.

"Okay." She said in a low voice. "I'll use a subcompact."

"Luxury SUV."

"Compact."

"Station wagon."

"Sedan."

"With all the extras."

"Trent—"

"Extra safety features."

She sighed. "Okay."

Pretty as a picture.

Jennifer had watched the float carrying the Lilac Queen and her Court go by. Everyone smiled and clapped, and people dashed into the street to snap pictures of them, while the girls on the float smiled and waved, and smiled and waved.

She'd turned and told Mom she wanted to be on that float someday. Her mother had entered Jennifer in her first pageant that year.

"Did I hear right? You're giving up the Beamer?"

Linc had been leaning back in the easy chair, legs stretched out, hands behind his head, watching Trent pack. Now he sat straight, gaping.

"Yeah. Ike's going to keep it in his garage," Trent said. "Take it out for a workout now and then."

"I just bet he is. Have you seen that man drive?"

"Don't remind me. But he's keeping it for free, and I don't have time to find anywhere else. Besides, he knows I'd kill him if anything happens to it."

"And you're satisfied about this place?" Linc circled his head to indicate the town house. He'd brought papers that needed signing, saving Trent the drive to his office, but he'd flatly refused to help pack.

Trent was packing personal items that would go in storage. Surprising how few things he had once he eliminated clothes and other necessities he'd take to Drago and the household stuff he'd leave for the renters.

"He seems like a good guy." He'd been lucky. A player just traded to the team from Boston needed a furnished place he and his wife could rent. "It's a hell of a lot better than renting to a group of rookies who're barely housebroken. Besides, you looked over that lease agreement. So I expect it's airtight."

"It'll do." High praise from Linc. "But leaving here, your friends, your car, your home—even if it isn't exactly the Taj Mahal. I never have understood why you wouldn't get a real house. That's weird enough, but leaving like this—I never expected this of you. And for what?"

"Go ahead, rub it in—remind me I swore up and down when you brought that Lexus dealership offer to me that I wouldn't have anything to do with selling cars. Ever."

"Oh, that part doesn't surprise me. I could have talked you into it if I'd really thought it was the right thing. I meant that you'd have anything to do with Stenner Autos. That's what surprised me—not the cars, the family part."

Trent shrugged.

It didn't dislodge Linc's penetrating gaze. "You're a weird breed, Stenner. It's not that you don't like families and all that goes with them. You do. Because you sure spend enough time with mine."

"They're good people."

"Yeah, they are. But sometimes it's like you…I don't know, like you drink in my family like a man dying of thirst."

"Are you saying I'm like a family—what? A family vampire?"

"Vampire? Hmm." Linc finally shook his head with regret. "No, not a vampire. More like a parasite."

"Gee, thanks, Linc." The fact that Trent laughed—and meant it—showed how comfortable he was with the Johnsons.

It was also rather nice knowing that if he ever told Mama Johnson that Linc had described him as a parasite on the family, she'd have her son's hide.

"Okay, okay, maybe one of those parasites that sort of helps the host. But also is having a fine time hanging on. Unless you're a masochist." He seemed to consider that. "Nah, you're no masochist. So you really enjoy it. But you get enough of whatever you need by hanging around with the Johnsons instead of with your own family."

"My own?" Trent snorted. Linc was among the few people in the world who knew the story of the Stenners from Trent's viewpoint. "Right."

"Okay, so you don't want to get cozy with Ma and Pa Stenner—although it does seem that one word from your father and—"

"Linc."

"Fine, fine. I won't say it, even though it is the truth. I'll just get to my point and say that you don't want to get cozy with your parents or your dear old brother—I understand that. But why not start your own family?"

"Yeah, I can just see that. I'm sure I've learned great skills in being a father. Or a husband."

"Plenty enough people who don't find what they want in the family they were born into build a good family themselves."

"Not me. It's the last thing I want."

Linc stared at him for another long moment. Then he shook his head. "Well, whether you want to or not, you're going to be dealing with family of sorts, since you'll be working with your sister-in-law—"

"Ex."

"So you keep saying," Linc said, as if scoring a point. "But there's nothing ex about your niece. She's family. You can't deny that. And you're not only going to be with her mama, you're going to be working basically for that sweet little girl."

Not so little in her own eyes, Trent thought. And definitely not so sweet.

But he didn't say it. Linc would pick up the concern sliding like fog into Trent's bones, which would only extend this lecture on family.

"It's real interesting to see this Sir Galahad role," his friend continued, "from a man who's never liked being wanted or needed too much."

Wanted? All that was wanted was his money.

Needed? There clearly were things Jennifer and Ashley needed. Like lettuce that didn't need resuscitating. Like a better place to live. Like a reliable car.

When he'd made use of Jennifer's declaration about not driving his BMW in Drago to get her out of that wreck she drove, she'd blushed.

Not a cute, aw-shucks kind of blush. But the kind that looked as if it hurt. As if both the thought that had caused it and the actual flow of blood under the skin caused pain.

At that moment, he'd experienced the same weird, mixed feeling as when a Steelers running back had broken a bone in his arm from falling awkwardly after Trent's tackle. It was a clean hit, he hadn't meant to hurt the guy, he'd do it again because tackling the guy was what needed doing, and it wasn't even his tackle that had hurt him. Still, you hated to see a guy hurt.

"I'm needed to run a car dealership, Linc. That's all."

Chapter Five

"Nice ride."

Jennifer looked up from the list she was writing—already four legal-pad pages long—and found Darcie grinning at her from outside the car that had arrived today. Apparently Trent had arranged it from California.

She ignored a twinge of embarrassment over her previous "ride," and grinned back. "It's a dealer's car. Both Trent and I will be driving them."

"What do you hear from Trent? He's been gone, what? Five days?"

"Oh, he's so busy taking care of things there, it could be weeks."

"Don't worry. He's coming back. Otherwise, he wouldn't—"

"I'm not worried," she rushed to lie. "I know he's coming back."

"Yeah? Well, good. So, what are you doing here?"

"Writing to-do, to-figure-out and to-research lists that go on for miles."

"I can see that. But I meant here. In the library parking lot."

"Oh, waiting for Ashley. I checked a few things out." She gestured to the pile of women-in-business books on the backseat. "But she was still looking, so I came out here to work on my lists."

"Still looking, huh? With school nearly out, it can't be homework, and I thought she'd already read every word there was on horses, so…"

Jennifer sighed. "Fashion and beauty magazines."

Darcie bit back a laugh. "Oh, Lord. Is she still on that kick?"

Ashley had been junior princess in the spring's Lilac Festival court and had developed a massive case of hero worship for one princess. That hero worship had evaporated when the princess's feet of clay tripped her up. But Ashley had continued poring over every magazine and book she could get her hands on. Since their stringent budget hadn't run to buying copies, Ashley had haunted the library, reading the new issues on the spot, and checking out older copies.

"Not only is she still on that kick, but she's taken down the horse and puppy pictures and put posters of boys on her bedroom walls. She tells me they're singers and actors. But, I swear, Darcie, I've never seen a single one of them in my life. She told me their names, and I still have no idea who these people are."

Darcie laughed. "We're getting old, Jennifer. That's all there is to it. I hate to tell you—it's part of the process."

"I know."

"But?" Darcie prompted. "I see you chewing on your lip, so I know you're worrying about more than posters on her walls."

"It's just… This is such a tough age. And important. She

needs to take school seriously. Her grades now set the foundation for high school, and then college…. And I'm afraid with being a manager at the dealership, I won't be around as much."

"The reason you could be around before was Roscoe had no business. Just about any other job would mean you'd be around less. Just level with her. Quit trying so hard."

"I have to try hard. I have to show her how a woman can be a success. That's one reason I couldn't pass on this opportunity at the dealership…. It's not that I don't want her to be interested in beauty and fashion and even boys—eventually—but I don't want her to get obsessed. I don't want her to measure herself by her popularity. I don't want her to get her priorities so screwed up that she messes things up for herself. Important things like college. Like life." She produced a sorry-sounding laugh. "In other words, I don't want her to follow in my footsteps."

"First, that wouldn't be so awful, you know. Second, she has you for a mother, so she's way ahead of where you were. Third, you don't have to win her approval, you know. You just— Oh, hi, Ash. Wow. That's quite an armful. Here, let me come around and get the door for you."

In minutes, a foot-high stack of magazines was added to the collection of books in the backseat, Darcie had bid them both goodbye, added, "Call me if you want to talk," to Jennifer, along with a significant look toward Ashley, and they started the crosstown drive to the apartment.

"Ashley, I want to talk to you more about this new job I have."

"I know all about it. You're going to work with *him*." She made the pronoun venomous.

"You hardly know Trent—your uncle."

"I know about him. I've heard," she said darkly.

Jennifer wondered if she'd infected her daughter with her own doubts about Trent and why he was doing what he was doing. "You shouldn't just believe what you hear about people. You have to make up your own mind."

Her daughter shot her a look, but with pedestrians crossing in front of the car, Jennifer couldn't take her eyes off the road to interpret what it meant.

Unsure of her own thoughts on the topic of Trent, she shifted to the practical. "This job is going to mean changes for us."

"What kind of changes?" After that suspicious-sounding question, Ashley abruptly sat up, her face transformed in one of her lightning changes of mood. "Are we moving?"

"No. Maybe eventually, but right now I can't afford it."

"When you can afford it, will we go home?"

"Home?" Oh. Jennifer's heart constricted. Of course. The house Ashley knew as home. "No. No, we won't be going back. Even if I could afford a house, someone else lives there now, Ashley. It's their home."

"Then who cares about these stupid changes?"

She ignored her daughter's sulkiness. "I'm going to be working more. And I won't be able to adjust my schedule as much as I could when I was working with Roscoe. We'll have to be even better about planning ahead with things like parties and rides. You might have to ride your bike places more often."

Ashley rolled her eyes. Jennifer allowed herself a moment's nostalgia for when Ashley had so desperately wanted her first two-wheeler.

"I might also need you to be at the dealership with me sometimes. If there's no one to look after you or—"

"I'm not a baby. I don't need a babysitter."

"You're not a baby," she agreed. "But there are going to be times I don't want you alone at the apartment, and you'll have to live with that."

Ashley *humphed* and sank in her seat.

"This job is a great opportunity," Jennifer said, taking a

new tack. "Not many women are managers at car dealerships, and I'm going to have the chance to show it can be done."

And the chance to make her daughter proud of her.

Please, God, please let that be true.

"A job like this can give us the financial resources to do things—important things," she hurried on before Ashley could present her priority list for allocating their funds. "Like send you to a good college."

"What if I don't wanna go to college?"

Jennifer gripped the wheel hard enough to press her nails into her palms. "You are going to college, Ashley. And you are going to get a degree."

"Hey, Trent."

His first suitcase hadn't even cleared the trunk of the rental car he'd picked up at O'Hare when a voice came from behind him. He completed the motion of setting the suitcase on the motel's cracked concrete parking lot.

"I didn't expect a greeting party, Darcie."

"No party. Just me."

"I'm touched that you would come fifteen miles out of your jurisdiction just to welcome me back," he said dryly.

"Eleven miles—we cover part of the county—but who's counting? It's come to my attention that a number of inquiries are being made, and when I started tracing them, oddly, they all seemed to start in California."

Linc. He was not going to apologize for his friend acting on his belief that the best defense against any decision turning bad was gathering every iota of information possible, because Trent shared that belief.

"I'd be a fool not to gather information with all the money I'm investing in the dealership."

"If the inquiries were limited to the dealership, I wouldn't be here. But digging for information on Jennifer, her background, her finances, the divorce?" On that last word, her level tone shifted to accusatory. "Nosing around town was bad enough, but this goes way beyond that."

Along with studying and anticipating, Trent had one more attribute that had brought him a hell of a lot further than anyone had predicted: he adjusted. Even to surprises.

"Judge Dixon made her part of the deal, so that's reasonable, too."

But not something he'd known Linc was doing. When he got Linc on the phone, he would decide how much of that information to wring out of him, and whether his friend had crossed the line.

Darcie stepped closer, her eyes nearly level with his. "Here's what you need to know. The Stenners haven't done Jennifer any favors. Ever. After a long time of being blind, people in town are starting to wake up to that fact. They don't want her to feel bad or have her pride bruised. Pride's what she's got left. Along with a good brain, a big heart and a daughter she adores. You do anything to hurt her or take advantage of her in any way, and you'll have more than your conscience to answer to. Are we clear?"

"You're entirely clear."

"Good. In that case—" and damned if she didn't give him a genuine smile "—you are welcomed back. See you 'round."

He watched her car turn and head out before he hauled out the next suitcase.

Great.

Darcie Barrett apparently thought he'd returned to Drago with the sole intention of picking up where Eric had left off in making life miserable for Jennifer and Ashley.

His parents thought he was here to rescue the Stenner heritage.

Linc thought he was here from bleeding-heart syndrome. Jennifer? She seemed torn between Darcie's and his parents' views.

And him? Having rented out his town house, disposed of his belongings and made arrangements for his car, he was a man cut loose. A man who didn't know what the hell he was doing here. Right back where he'd started life and had sworn to escape forever.

Jennifer knew she was talking too fast. She couldn't stop herself. Everything that had happened at the dealership, everything she'd done, practically everything she'd thought pertaining to the business tumbled out.

Not because Trent had caught her off-guard when he'd pushed open the showroom's now-dazzling glass doors half an hour ago. Because this time he hadn't—even though he *had* arrived a day earlier than he'd told her to expect him in his one phone call since he'd left for California. This early arriving appeared to be a habit with him.

Still, the place looked great and she was prepared.

Trent Stenner had swooped into Drago and turned her life upside down. He'd raised her expectations and hopes. But until he'd walked back in the door and her heartbeat had multiplied as if it was on fast-forward, she had not let herself truly believe he would return. Oh, she certainly hadn't allowed anyone to see her doubts. She'd veneered every conversation, every encounter, every answer with impregnable and absolute confidence. And there'd been lots of conversations, encounters and questions.

But, by herself at night, watching shadow patterns created by light seeping unevenly through her worn curtains, she had worried.

"…and I've lined up want ads to go in the *Drago Intelli-*

gencer, plus three other area newspapers, but I didn't want to submit them in case you…uh, until you could look them over."

"We've hired people by using your grapevine. Why put in want ads?"

"To let more people know Stenner Autos is back in business without spending a lot of money. Want ads are much cheaper than display ads, so they make sense until we have more inventory. Plus, people around here read want ads religiously, so they'll get in the habit of thinking about this as a possible place to buy their cars."

"Better be more than a *possible* place," he muttered. "Even though nobody around here has money for a new car. Even a used car."

He hadn't been grim before.

Oh, God. What if he'd come back solely to tell her to her face that he'd changed his mind?

Panic later, she bargained with herself. *Right now, you have to think.*

What if Trent did regret his decision? If he backed out, he knew he'd lose a lot of money. On the other hand, if he'd given up the dealership as a lost cause already, he might try to cut his losses and just leave.

No, that was one worst-case scenario she couldn't let herself imagine. She'd sold her car, she'd quit her job at Roscoe Realty. And she'd promised Ashley things would be better.

Trent Stenner might be able to afford to give up, but she couldn't.

So, she couldn't let him give up. She'd just have to manufacture enough fake confidence to carry both of them.

"People still need their cars fixed," she said, so firmly that the statement sounded totally confident, even to herself. "Even more so if they're not replacing them with newer models."

"You said something about that before. But Jorge can't get the service section going until we have mechanics."

"Technicians. They call them technicians. Or techs."

He grimaced, but didn't argue. "Okay, until we have techs hired, we can't even start to let people know we're in business to fix their cars."

"Then I'll place those additional want ads right now."

She immediately turned without looking at him, and headed for the room she'd taken as her office. She heard skepticism in his grunt behind her, although she chose to focus on the fact that he hadn't stopped her.

As a sign of faith went it was tiny, but she'd take it.

"I don't want to hear any more." Trent's voice sounded angry.

Standing in the empty service bay where she'd come to look for Jorge, Jennifer could hear him, but couldn't see him.

"Yeah, I listened before, but I know what I need to know. No more, Linc."

Ah, he was on the phone. Somewhere. He was silent for quite a while, but she'd narrowed the possibilities down, and crossed to the door outside.

"All right…Yeah, yeah, I promise." Trent raised his head as she came around the corner, his gaze so intent it almost knocked her back. Sitting on a metal bench behind the building, he was hunched over, and when he spoke again into the phone, he still sounded angry. "I told you I would. I'll call you later. Bye."

He clicked off the phone and folded it shut with a snap.

"Were you looking for me?" he asked.

"No. I heard your voice, and just wondered…"

"Linc," he said, looking away. "Listen, I've got to run an errand, might be a while. Do you need me for anything this afternoon?"

"No. I…is everything okay, Trent?" she asked tentatively.

"Fine. See you later." He got up and strode past her, then stopped. His face carrying an ominous frown and his tone still angry, he added, "You look very pretty today."

Pretty is as pretty does.

She'd been in middle school before she'd realized people used that phrase to mean you had to be nice in order to be truly pretty.

Her mother always said it meant you had to work hard to be pretty. You had to eat right and walk right and talk right. You had to try on clothes for hours. You had to give up diving for dance lessons, because dance could be used for talent competition.

But it was worth it. Because when you'd come home with a trophy, Daddy smiled and said, "Way to go, Pretty Girl!" and put the trophy on your shelf amid all the shelves of Mark's trophies.

"You didn't turn the alarm back on when you came in this morning," Trent said from outside the open door of Jennifer's office.

Office? More like a locker, with just space for a normal-size person to edge between the desk and the cabinets and the bookcases lining walls uninterrupted by any windows.

Although it sure smelled better than a locker. He sniffed. Some sort of flower-something. Light. Clean.

When he'd returned from home—California, he corrected himself—four days ago, he'd discovered she'd ensconced him in the big office with the window to the showroom. The one where his father had once sat. The one where Eric had once sat. The one where he felt like a monkey in the zoo.

He'd protested, but she'd been implacable. Just kept saying

he was the general manager, and that was the general manager's office.

"You came in not long after me," she said.

"You couldn't know I was going to. Set the damn alarm when there's nobody else here." He didn't give her a chance to argue more, adding, "What time's the first interview?"

"One-thirty."

She'd been right about the want ads. Not only had applicants come in at a good clip, but people—non-job applicants—stopped by and called. Many said how glad they were to have the dealership getting back on its feet. More were curious. All were treated like honored guests by Jennifer.

Which wouldn't be so bad, except she invariably ushered them on to him, either by bringing them into his office or by transferring the call to his line, clearly expecting him to win them over with a course of schmooze.

"Okay. I'll be back by then. I'm going to lunch with Coach."

Her left eyebrow twitched.

"I've gotta eat."

"Of course you do. And I'm sure you'll be back in plenty of time to go over exactly what we're looking for with Jorge and me."

"All right, all right. I'll be back by one."

"That will be perfect."

She smiled, and he felt as if he'd salvaged himself from that eyebrow twitch. He didn't like how good that made him feel.

Then she did him a big favor.

She got that look women sometimes got. That "ahhh, now I understand" expression. As if they'd just opened the top of your head and peered down to your toes. And she said, "You're quite close with Coach Brookenheimer, aren't you?"

He expelled a breath through his nose, as if he was really irked. But he wasn't sure it counted as really irked when you were partially glad to be irked because it meant you weren't feeling so all-fired pleased to have salvaged yourself from an eyebrow twitch.

"He's not a second father or a father figure. Just a good man I've known a long time, who taught me a hell of a lot of football and a little about life." He'd had that friendship pop-psyched before by women.

"I'm sorry." She dropped her head, apparently staring at the keyboard. "I didn't mean to offend you. It's none of my business."

"For crying out loud." And it was a damned miracle that was the phrase that came out of his mouth. "You didn't offend me. And you don't have to go getting all meek and subservient because—"

That popped her head back up. And had her eyes burning. "I am not meek or subservient. I—"

"Good," he half roared.

She snapped her mouth shut. He actually heard it.

"Good," he repeated in a more temperate tone. "Because I'm not paying you for obedience. Or agreeing with me. Are we clear?"

"Yes."

"Okay. Then I'm going to lunch."

"Before you go," she said in a tone of laserlike precision, "do you have a moment to look over these figures before I e-mail them to Linc?"

He still wasn't quite clear how that connection had become so strong so fast. Linc, as his best friend and a financial whiz, had come up his first day back when he'd been probing to see if Darcie had told Jennifer about the inquiries.

He'd known Darcie hadn't when Jennifer asked if he thought Linc might be willing to answer a few questions. He'd said sure, because he figured Linc owed it to her as compensation for the nosy questions he'd been asking about her, even if Jennifer didn't know it. So, he'd called Linc, then handed the phone over.

That night, Linc had called him at the motel.

The man was smitten. There was no other word for it. Smitten. With Jennifer's good sense, willingness to learn and quick grasp of financial concepts. Cautious, but smitten all the same.

Which made Trent all the more annoyed for reasons he couldn't articulate.

"This is the breakdown of average profitability and expense percentages for auto repair operations that I was telling you about. And here I've estimated ours. Payroll and utilities and office expenses. I do think we can do better than the average on expenses for legal fees and advertising, though, don't you?"

Trent bent to look over her shoulder at the figures she indicated.

His gaze didn't reach the computer screen.

Pushing herself to one side of her chair seat to give him a clear view of the screen had shifted the fabric of her top. On the shoulder so close to him that all he'd have to do was bend his waist and his mouth could touch it, the result was that a short section of her bra strap was visible.

A couple of inches of white material arcing up, then down in concert with the slope of her shoulder. Nothing extraordinary.

And he was getting hard.

He shifted back, hoping to ease his libido and its consequences.

That put him in line to see down the otherwise demure V-neck of her top. He could see the rising curve of her breast where it disappeared under the white caress of her bra.

That was plenty.

Good lord, what was his problem?

A bra strap and a glimpse of a covered breast. As if he

hadn't seen women showing more than that most days on the street. Not to mention some outfits teams dressed—or barely dressed—their dance teams in. It was some big fashion trend to have bra straps out in the open.

So why was the area between his legs so eager to report for duty?

He had a bad feeling it wasn't because of a view of a few inches of material and a few more inches of skin. But because it was *Jennifer's* bra strap, *Jennifer's* skin.

This was trouble. Definitely trouble.

She had never appealed to him when she'd been the town's acclaimed beauty. Why would she now?

"Trent?"

"Uh, yeah. Yeah, I'm sure you're right."

"Good. I wanted your take on that before sending the figures to Linc."

"I don't know how much longer he'll do this."

"You don't want to impose on your friendship," she said with understanding.

A crack of genuine laughter coming from his own mouth surprised him. But it felt good.

"I'd impose on our friendship for all I was worth if I thought it would get me anywhere, but Linc won't stand for it. It's part of what I like about him. He knows his own value."

"Ah."

There must have been a million meanings behind that syllable. He didn't have a clue what even the first dozen were. He considered himself damned lucky to have recognized that any existed.

"Yeah. Well, you better add to that list of yours that we're going to need someone to do the books." He rubbed the back of his neck, then down across his shoulder in an all-too-familiar gesture. A shoulder, the doctor had once told him—

with ghoulish interest to Trent's mind—was the best candidate to develop arthritis in a joint he'd ever seen. "And while
you're at it, put on that magic list of yours some way to get
money coming in sooner rather than later."

"I've been thinking about that."

Trent twisted around to look at her so fast that the muscles
around his shoulder fisted tight.

"What's wrong?"

How the hell had she known something was wrong? He
hadn't grimaced. He'd learned real early not to give coaches
or trainers any excuse to hold him out of a game. Without the
physical skills of some players, he'd figured out fast that what
he could bring besides smarts and determination was reliabil-
ity. Showing up and playing. No matter what.

"Nothing. Any conclusions from that thinking you've
been doing?"

She was biting her bottom lip the way she did.

"Yes."

"Well, let's hear it."

Chapter Six

He'd felt pain—real pain—when he'd turned. He'd covered it fast. So fast that Jennifer suspected Trent had a great deal of practice at covering it up.

If he'd had to retire because of injuries, his financial situation might not be as good as people said. On the other hand, maybe he'd had the injury for a long time and covering it up had become second nature to him.

She suspected he'd had a great deal of practice covering up other kinds of old injuries.

Memory flashed vivid in her mind. A Sunday dinner at the Stenner house when she was Eric's new girlfriend. She had not yet realized that this meal had followed a common pattern—Franklin and Eric talking, everyone else silent. Trent had looked at her for a moment with total lack of interest.

She'd seen Trent watching his father and Eric with a cool indifference that caught at her, making her want to break into the conversation, to widen the circle to include everyone at the table, even herself.

Of course she hadn't.

But remembering that moment, it did feel as if it united them in a strange way. They might not be in the same boat, but they seemed to be in the same fleet.

"Parts," she blurted.

"Sorry?" He tipped his head, obvious confusion easing the pain-pinched tightness around his mouth.

"I've been thinking about parts."

"Buying them?"

She shook her head. "I mean, yeah, we'll need some, of course. But I was thinking…remember all the old inventory in that building?"

"Yeah. I wouldn't be surprised if my father cornered the market on some old part, just because someone else wanted it. It's too bad the building's metal or we could burn the place down with all that junk in it."

"No! It's not junk—that's what I'm saying. There's a demand for old parts."

"Around here? C'mon, Jennifer. You're dreaming."

"I'm not talking about a demand in Drago. We can sell them anywhere. The Internet," she added, unable to contain a surge of triumph.

"The Internet?"

"Right. We create a Web site for our inventory, and become a source for old parts. You should see the prices these things are going for."

"You've checked this out already?"

That level voice cooled her enthusiasm. Had she over-explained? Maybe she shouldn't have told him yet. Maybe she needed to do more research first.

"Yes," she said. Then she waited.

He ducked his head in a "Well?" gesture. "So, you're thinking eBay? Something like that?"

She eased out a breath.

"Maybe a few items, to start, as a way to get the name out. But we'll have more control with our own site. We can link from car enthusiast sites."

"Car enthusiast sites, huh?" He sounded as if such a concept were far-fetched. "How expensive would this Web site be?"

"It doesn't have to be fancy. These folks aren't wowed by graphics. But they get downright poetic about a 1960's carburetor."

"Huh." He looked from her to the computer. "You think it'll work?"

"Yes." She allowed none of the doubts burbling inside to seep into the word.

"One condition— I don't have to have anything to do with it. Selling cars is bad enough."

"Deal," she said immediately, relieved he hadn't quashed the idea.

"Okay, then." He grinned. "Turning lemons into lemonade—great idea, Jen." The grin slipped. "Sorry. Jennifer."

"You've been working hard these past two weeks on that research."

Jennifer's head snapped up from the computer screen. Her neck muscles screeched a double protest—at being in one position too long, then at being moved so abruptly.

Trent had been distant since giving the go-ahead to sell the parts. But she'd heard from Loris, Mildred Magnus and two other acquaintances that Trent had had a private meeting with Judge Dixon. Not only hadn't Trent said a word about it to her, she didn't feel she could ask him.

Her mind said she could—they were business associates,

after all. But each time she tried to broach the topic, her stomach threatened to lurch into her throat. She knew the reaction was a residue of her years with Eric, but knowing hadn't defeated that throat-clogging response. It made her downright cranky.

"Did you think I wouldn't? And it's not just the research." With the grand reopening at the end of July, she had a daunting to-do list. "Do you know what I've been doing this morning? Straightening out tax filing requirements, going over employees' W-4 forms, negotiating for benefits—"

"Hey. Don't shoot. I'm unarmed. I've been working hard, too. Roofers come tomorrow, and the painters next week." He dropped into the chair, seeming to rest on the middle of his spine, legs extended, arms dangling. "We deserve a break. At least I do. Since I'm not allowed to make any reference to how hard you're working, I can only vouch for myself."

"Very funny."

"How about some lunch? Not at your desk, either. A real lunch. Where someone else makes it and serves it. And something other than that rabbit food you eat. You know, something real, like a hamburger, potato salad, watermelon, peach pie and cinnamon ice cream."

"Good grief. That's not lunch, that's a Fourth of July cook-out."

He groaned. "I can't wait for lunch until the Fourth of July."

But Jennifer's mind had left lunch and Trent. "Did I tell you Zeke's company is sponsoring fireworks this year for the Fourth?"

He grunted.

"Drago hasn't had fireworks for several years because of the expense. So it will be a big deal. More people coming— both because they've missed the fireworks and because they'll be curious what kind of job Zeke-Tech does."

"Uh-huh. This is fascinating. What does it have to do with lunch?"

"We'll hold a Fourth of July cookout."

He looked at her as if expecting more.

And there was more. Her mind was already zipping through details. She pulled a fresh notepad from the papers on her desk and started writing.

"We'll have to order the meat. Premade hamburger patties would be easier, but that might be too expensive. I'll price it both ways. Hot dogs for kids. Buns. Ketchup and mustard. Something else. What else did you say? Oh, right. Sorry, Trent. No potato salad. Potato salad can go bad in hot weather because of the mayo, and we'll need the cold storage to keep the meat. But we'll have chips and sodas. And watermelon."

"Uh, Jennifer?"

"Hmm?" She was writing notes.

"You keep saying *we*."

"Of course." Loris might help her with sources for food.

"Well, my motel room doesn't have any place for a cookout and I've seen your place and, no offense, but where would you put people?"

Motel room? Her place? He thought—?

She burst out laughing. A sound so unexpected that it surprised her. It seemed to catch Trent by surprise, too, judging by his intent expression.

"Not my apartment, and not your room. Here, at Stenner Autos."

His expression lost some of its intensity. "Here? You want to feed the whole town here on the Fourth of July?"

"I seriously doubt it will be the whole town. People go away and others have their own cookouts. But it should be a good crowd. We've talked about the grand reopening, and how hard it can be to entice people when they know we want them to buy a car or get service or do something else that costs them money. This way, we get them to come to get something for free."

"Free for them. How much for us?"

"How much can it cost?"

"That's what I asked."

"Okay, okay. I'll price it out. But think about it. You can't beat the PR of feeding people for free. And it'll imprint in their minds that Stenner Autos is back. Think of the goodwill. We'll have grills, get employees to cook and serve. That'll give everyone a chance to mingle with our employees in a relaxed atmosphere."

"I have one condition, Jen."

He'd been calling her that more often lately. "What's that?"

"We talk about this over lunch."

"In a lot of ways he's easy to work with. He certainly isn't a micromanager. In fact, sometimes I wish he'd get more involved."

"That's what's worrying you?" Darcie asked, sipping her wine on the apartment balcony that held two chairs, a tiny table and Jennifer's solitary rosebush in a wooden planter. "You want Trent more involved in running the place? Sounds like he'd just get in the way of you being the big boss."

With Ashley at a movie with friends, Jennifer had invited Darcie over for wine. Darcie had returned from four days in Virginia with Zeke, and Jennifer could tell she was a little down about being separated from him again.

Plus, Jennifer figured she owed her friend a case of wine, along with several months' worth of meals. Somehow, in her toughest financial times, Darcie had always managed to pay. Now, after banking her first paychecks, Jennifer had decided she could splurge. But not over ten dollars.

Jennifer made a face at her. "Okay, maybe I have discovered a streak of megalomania. But Trent's keeping things from me. Not that I think I have a right to know things about him—I mean his personal life or his relationship with his family or anything like that. But if it has to do with the business…"

"Let me fix you up with Zeke's friend Quince," Darcie said.

Jennifer put down her wineglass on the table and stared at the other woman.

"Are you nuts?" she demanded. "What does that have to do with Trent—with the business?"

"No, I'm not nuts. But I think Stenner Autos is making you a bit crazy. You're nuts if you pass up a chance with a guy like Peter Quincy. You met him, right? The day of the news conference about Zeke-Tech coming."

Just the mention of that day and Darcie glowed, because that was also the day Zeke had returned to Drago and asked Darcie to marry him.

"Uh-huh. And he's nice. But I don't want you to fix me up with him."

"He's good-looking, charming, smart, rich and Zeke swears Quince doesn't date much, so there's no string of broken hearts."

"Still no."

"Give me one good reason. If it's Tre—"

"Because it wouldn't last."

Darcie sat back, clearly surprised, but also alert, determined. Uh-oh, she'd switched to investigative mode. "Why won't it last? Whoa. You can't believe just because Eric is an idiot—"

"It's not just Eric. It's every man. Like Zeke."

"Zeke?"

Jennifer nodded. "Like you said back in the spring, he'd had this image of me in high school. And when he first came back to town, when he looked at me, I saw some interest."

Darcie's expression did the strangest thing. As if memories

wanted to make her face stiffen, but newer knowledge wouldn't let the muscles fall into old habits.

"Darcie, don't even pretend you're worried about Zeke. You know how long that interest in me lasted? A minute. Until the very next time he looked at you. He looked back at me, and he *thought* he was interested, but it was gone." She snapped her fingers. "Gone."

"Jennifer—"

"No, no, I'm not trying to make you feel sorry for me, Darcie. Especially not about Zeke. Because with him, for the first time, a guy kept looking at me after that sex-interest light went out. And it's amazing to have Zeke as a friend. As for other guys—" she shrugged "—that's the way it is."

Darcie's eyes grew soft and her smile turned misty. "It only takes one."

Something stopped Jennifer's breath high in her chest. Something so eye-tearing and mouth-curling happy for her friend. And yet so achingly wistful for herself.

"It only takes one," Darcie said again, putting her hand over Jennifer's. "And then it makes no difference if it's never lasted before."

She didn't argue. Not because she believed it would be that way for her, but because she knew Darcie wanted it for her, and that touched her.

"What are you two doing out here in the dark?"

Ashley's voice startled Jennifer. She blinked back moisture in her eyes and saw Darcie was doing the same.

"Discussing your uncle buying the dealership, and your mom's new job," Darcie supplied.

"What about it?"

At Ashley's abrupt suspicion, Darcie gave a silent whistle.

"Just talking," Jennifer said mildly, and Ashley relaxed.

"That's all you two ever do," she said. "Talk and talk and talk."

"Hey," Darcie protested. "You and your friends are no slouches in the talking department."

"But you two talk about *nothing*. We're talking about—" Was that the squeal of brakes Jennifer heard as her daughter halted? "Stuff."

Her maternal antennae quivered, but Jennifer changed the subject. "How was the movie, Ashley?"

A quick smile raised her lips before she clamped them down. "Okay."

"Did you and Courtney run into anyone you know?"

"Oh, you know, the regular people. Mandy and Becky were there," she said, naming two princesses from the Lilac Festival's court. "They said hi to you. And Warren—he actually deigned to come to a movie."

Warren Wellton was a bit of a sore point with Ashley. He'd been slavishly devoted to her for years. When Zeke came to town Warren had made an ill-fated attempt at fame by trying to steal from one of the nation's best technological minds. Darcie had caught him, then paired him and Zeke on computer-related community service.

Zeke had recognized Warren's true aptitude for technology. Not only that, he'd had his company license a program Warren had created, helping the Wellton family's finances considerably.

The upshot was that Warren had suddenly become important, busy and much more sure of himself. He was no longer Ashley's faithful retainer whom she had taken for granted for years.

Her daughter professed herself relieved to not have him *following me around like a puppy dog,* but Jennifer knew she missed Warren.

"Plus Jonas—you know, the guy you hired at the dealership. And Sarah's brother, Barry." She yawned hugely. "I'm going to bed now. Mom, I'll do the grocery shopping for you tomorrow. I can use the cart."

Jennifer's brows hiked up, but she said only, "That would be great, sweetheart. Sleep well."

Ashley kissed first Darcie, then her mother on the cheek and wished them good-night before leaving.

Jennifer and Darcie stared at each other in the dim light.

"Let's recap," Darcie said. "Glowing smile, the movie was just *okay,* complete list of who was there, the sudden desire to go to bed early, and butter-wouldn't-melt-in-her-mouth goodness. Clearly meant to reassure and/or distract the maternal watchdog."

Jennifer groaned.

"And the verdict is?"

"A boy," they said in unison.

"Her first crush. Probably the star of the movie." Darcie shook her head in wonderment. "All I can say is, count yourself lucky she's still just a kid. A few more years and this'll really be a problem."

"Gee, thanks."

Trent had put off making this phone call as long as he could.

"I'm not going to make it for the Fourth, Linc. You know I'd make it if I could. I love the Fourth with you guys."

"Yeah, and us guys," Linc said with only a shadow of his usual teasing for that Midwestern term, "are going to have the best one yet. Everybody's coming. Tracy and Ben are flying in from Chicago—and don't think it's gone unnoticed that you haven't contacted them since you've been in Illinois. We've got a great beach house rented and Mama's already baking."

Trent groaned.

Apparently feeling Trent had been sufficiently chastised—and he did hate to miss a Fourth with the group of friends who had coalesced around the Johnsons like iron filings around a magnet—Linc asked, "So what are you going to do for the Fourth out there in the vast wasteland of cornfields?"

"Feed the town."

"Is that some metaphor for living in the breadbasket?"

"No. That's the literal truth. Feed the town. A free cookout for all of Drago to advertise Stenner Autos' grand reopening."

After a silence, Linc asked, "How much is it going to cost you?"

"The whole day."

"Dollars, Stenner. How many dollars?"

"I have no idea. Jennifer's handling all that."

"Well, you'd better find out, fella, because that's your money."

"Are you saying we can't afford it?" he asked, torn between hope that he could fly west for the holiday weekend after all, and a sinking at the pit of his stomach at the prospect of informing Jennifer.

"How can I know if you can afford it when you don't know how much it is?" Linc asked. "Actually, it sounds like a really good idea. Make sure you have new cars around. Nothing too pushy, just models folks can see while they're there. Casual. You know, it really is a good idea. I'm surprised you came up with it."

"Not me. Jennifer. I'll pass on your thoughts about the cars."

"So what are you going to do at this thing?"

"Supervise."

"Thank God. Just tell that Jennifer of yours not to let you near a grill."

Jennifer pushed back from her computer screen and stretched her tight back.

Amazing that the phone had been silent long enough for her back to tighten up. She linked her hands overhead and bent to the right.

She was almost afraid to let the thought form, but maybe, just maybe, she was getting the gist of these tax requirements, so her order of IRS bulletins and informational booklets would be pared from her initial, panicked send-me-everything-you've-got to a mere four dozen or so.

But her to-do list for the Fourth of July and the reopening at the end of the month stretched for miles. In the meantime, day-to-day financial issues and duties accumulated faster than she could sort them. Layer upon layer of paper formed on her desk, each layer weighing down and compacting the previous layers, the way geological ages compacted dirt. She expelled a deep breath as she bent to the left.

Coffee. She needed coffee. No, better make that a soft drink. As long as they didn't have customers—or income— yet, she'd told Trent to keep the thermostat set high to save on air-conditioning.

Coming out of her windowless office she blinked at the bright—and hot—midafternoon sunlight streaming through the showroom windows. Despite the financial issues piling up, they were making good progress in other areas. They'd hired more people, including a pair of high school boys to clean the back building and compile a list of the old parts that were there.

She'd talked to Warren Wellton about a Web site. She'd had to bite her lip to keep from smiling when he informed her that he was far too busy himself, but he had a protégé who could do the Web site and, as a personal favor, he would oversee the work. A thirteen-year-old entrepreneur with a twelve-year-old protégé.

If she'd had just one thought in her head about business at that age, how much different her life, Ashley's life, might be now.

But she'd make it up to her daughter. She had to.

She had her hand on the door handle when she saw Trent outside, tossing a football with Bobby Flickner under the trees. He wore shorts that revealed a length of muscled, medium-hairy legs. His motion twisted the fabric of his polo shirt tight against his firm abdomen.

Several of Trent's old teammates had gotten in the habit of stopping by. Bobby was the most frequent. She tried hard not to resent his taking up Trent's time. Bobby had been out of work for more than a year, and she'd heard it was rough for him and his wife, getting by on her wages as a cashier at the grocery store. She could understand his needing the outlet.

And, she realized in that moment, watching Trent's easy rhythm and motion as he gathered in the ball, shifted his stance and threw it back, it wasn't even the time she resented the most. It was Trent's reaction.

Oh, he did his duty around Stenner Autos. More than his duty. He had a good mind, and he applied it.

But it was duty. Work.

While there was something of love in the way he gathered in, held, then threw that football. The look of a man doing what he was meant to do.

For the first time in her life she felt a twinge of empathy with Franklin Stenner. If he'd worked half as hard as she had these past several weeks, she could begin to understand his pique with Trent's lack of interest in the dealership. Or had Trent's disregard for the business resulted from his father's disinterest in Trent?

The family version of the eternal chicken-or-egg question.

"Something wrong, Jennifer?"

Jorge O'Farrell came from the men's room drying his hands on a paper towel. Seeing him reminded her she needed to order the list of required tools he'd given her yesterday.

"No, nothing's wrong."

As long as Trent helped make this dealership a success— securing her job and Ashley's financial future—it wasn't any of her concern whether he did it from duty or love. And the Stenner family dynamics certainly weren't any of her concern.

She made sure to smile as she approached the two men.

"Hi, Bobby. Good to see you. How're you doing?"

"Hey, Jennifer. I'm doing great." He smiled back. "Was just telling Trent, here, that I got hired on for the Zeke-Tech construction."

"Oh, Bobby, that's wonderful. When do you start?"

"Next month. Doing some preliminary work on the site, helping them coordinate with local suppliers and such."

Bobby told her more details as she dropped coins in the machine for her soft drink. As far as she knew, Trent never looked anywhere but at the ball that he and Bobby kept exchanging.

"See you later," she said with another smile as she hurried across the flight path of the ball.

But she was in no danger of being hit. Trent had caught the ball and now held it in one hand. He slapped the other hand against its surface.

"Jennifer's right, Bobby. Time for me to get back to work."

"I didn't say—"

"You didn't have to," Trent said, overriding her righteous protest. "You're still right."

"Phone call for you, Trent," Loris called as he was about to walk out the café door.

He knew immediately. So did the bulk of the breakfast eaters who were Drago natives. He didn't even consider trying to get out of it.

He thanked Loris and said hello into the receiver.

"Why did I have to track you down at the café?"

"I'm glad you did," he interrupted. He'd learned as a kid that if you hoped to say anything you couldn't let Franklin

Stenner get a full head of steam up. "I have a question for you. How can I get in touch with Eric?"

"Wha— Why?" his father demanded.

"Found some things of his at the dealership."

"Nothing he'd care about."

"I'd like his phone number and address."

"I don't have it. He calls me."

In Franklin Stenner's voice, Trent heard what a hard admission it had been that Eric was calling the shots.

"And you're no better," his father added quickly, regaining his footing. "I have left messages on your machine, which is the only number you deign to give us. If I didn't have friends in that town, I still wouldn't know we had the dealership back."

"We don't."

"What?" his father bellowed. "I know for a fact that you bought it."

"That's right. I bought it. Not we."

"I know you bought it, that's what I said," Franklin said impatiently. "Now, we have to talk about what to do next."

"No, we don't. I bought it, and I'm deciding what to do next. Bye. If you hear from Eric have him call me. Give my best to Mom."

The only time Trent spared a moment for regretful longing for the gathering he was missing in California was when he was detailed to open hamburger buns and hold them out to receive patties grilled by Jorge.

He looked at the hunks of essentially white bread that were as little like the featherweight, melt-in-your-mouth pastry Linc's mother made as two things made from flour could be, and felt a definite culinary twinge.

To Trent's surprise, Linc hadn't even mocked the menu— much—asserting that it suited the tone they should set with the dealership. Part of the community. A hometown business that would treat customers as friends…so friends should be loyal to the hometown business in return.

Five new cars were strategically placed around the lot—he didn't even want to remember the hours spent discussing where to place them. Followed by more hours of moving them after Jennifer didn't like the scheme she'd picked out in the first place.

Not that he begrudged her that. She'd grabbed on to Linc's suggestion when Trent relayed it like someone wrapping up a game-saving fumble. She'd worked hard to arrange to have the cars here, haggling with the manufacturers' marketing managers until she wore them down.

And then she'd tackled flyers as "teasers" for the reopening, agonizing over each detail of wording, design and color. They looked good, but to his eye so had the other samples she'd produced. And if he didn't hear any more about fonts for the next year that would be soon enough for him. How could a font be friendly and inviting? They were just letters.

So the cars were here and the flyers were here and, lo and behold, most of Drago was here. And Jennifer…Jennifer, wearing a jacketed dress with a skirt that flipped and flirted at her knees, was everywhere.

His gaze followed her as she left one group and moved to another. She did it with such grace and ease he doubted anyone would realize exactly how good she was at working a room—or in this case, a car lot.

One of the high school kids, hired originally to clean and organize the old parts shed but assigned to cleaning the lot to Jennifer's standards and to planting a phalanx of rosebushes out front in preparation for the cookout, hustled up to him.

"Mr. Stenner, Ms. Truesdale says I should take over for you."

"Great." He handed over the package of buns.

"And you should mingle."

Trent groaned. He'd already talked with his fifth-grade teacher, Judge Dixon, a nosy matron named Mildred Magnus and dozens of other people.

The kid, the sandy-haired one with the snub nose and freckles, flashed a sympathetic grin, then pretended he hadn't noticed a thing.

"Did Ms. Truesdale specify who I'm supposed to mingle with?"

"No, sir."

"Good." Trent hitched his hips on the supply table screened from most of the crowd by a Stenner Autos van. "I'll mingle with you."

The kid shot him a look—first startled, then considering. "Then may I ask a question?"

"Go right ahead." He didn't get flooded with questions the way stars did, but he'd fielded his share from kids dreaming of the pros. He had answers all ready, including the one none of them wanted to hear: plan for college, do your course work and get your degree as though it's going to support you for the rest of your life, because it probably will.

"Are you going to need more help here once the shed's cleaned and the parts are inventoried?"

Okay, that question wasn't what he'd expected. "You want a permanent part-time job? After school starts, too?"

"I'd rather work full-time until football practice starts the second week of August, then part-time. When school starts I don't know if I'll be able to work if I make the team."

The last was said in such a low voice Trent almost missed it.

"You're trying out for varsity?" The kid nodded. "What position?"

"Wide receiver. And end on defense."

He seemed too thin for either position, but then Trent was used to pros. "Yeah? You got the hands for receiver?"

"Wouldn't be first-string, but I'm not bad."

"Why wouldn't you be first-string?"

"Because Jonas is the best player on the team. Everybody says he's the best player around here since—"

With color climbing his neck, he stopped abruptly, clearly feeling that having his foot firmly wedged in his mouth left no room for words.

"Since my brother," Trent filled in. "Must be pretty good then. Eric was the best high school player I ever saw."

The boy's gaze flicked at him, and Trent knew the message had been received. Being the best in high school was no guarantee beyond.

"Tell you what. You keep working like you have been and when you find out about your practice and class schedule, we'll work something out."

"You mean it, Mr. Stenner?"

"I mean it." He stifled a sigh as he levered himself up.

"Gee thanks, Mr. Stenner."

Trent lifted a hand in acknowledgment.

He felt Jennifer's gaze pick him up as soon as he emerged into the open.

Their gazes locked. He saw her excitement and pleasure at the cookout's success, sternly damped down. He sent back recognition of her achievement, pleasure at her pleasure.

And then it changed.

The cookout, the dealership, the crowd all faded. She was seeing him as himself, as a man. And she was accepting his looking back at her as a woman.

Then it was gone.

His first instinct was to move toward her, to make her admit what had just happened. To confront what he'd been facing alone.

Second thought prevailed.

Even if he didn't succeed in driving Jennifer's emotions deeper into hiding, there was gossipy Mildred Magnus right there, ready to drink in every nuance. And he suspected there would be enough nuances sparking between him and Jennifer if they got within five yards of each other right now to rival tonight's upcoming fireworks display.

Then he remembered the message the kid had delivered.

Mingle.

He scanned the area. Ahhh. He'd spotted his solution to mingling.

Chapter Seven

"Hey, Coach. Hey, Darcie." As Trent greeted them and smiled at the two other men who formed the group he'd spotted, he shot Jennifer a triumphant grin. She gave the barest hint of rolling her eyes before turning with a charming smile to Mildred.

"Trent, you might remember Zeke," Darcie said. "Anton Zeekowsky."

He extended his hand to the tall man, who once had been skinny but sometime since high school had grown into his height and added a proportionate amount of muscle. "I remember him, but I doubt you remember me, Zeke. I was a runt of a freshman when you were a senior and already full-blown brilliant."

"Sorry," Zeke said with a half smile as he shook Trent's hand. "I'm not the best at remembering people."

"He's getting better," Darcie added, slanting a smile at

him. All the talk about their getting married suddenly made a whole lot of sense.

"And this is Josh Kincannon," Coach said. "He's our principal at the high school. Best one we've ever had."

"And people wonder why I won't let you retire, Coach," Josh said.

He moved like an athlete. He was about Trent's age, a little taller, a little slimmer. Built more like a— "Kincannon! Quarterback for Pepton."

The other man grinned. "You've got a good memory, Trent."

"You're the only team that beat us senior year."

"But you'd beaten us every other year, and that was our homecoming game. And I still remember the blindside sack you laid on me."

"Oh, God. If you're going to do a play-by-play recreation, I'm leaving," Darcie said. "See you at the fireworks. Trent, you're coming with us."

"Fireworks? Us?" Trent asked.

But Darcie had already threaded through the crowd and out of sight.

Beside him, Zeke Zeekowsky laughed. "My best advice is to just relax and follow Darcie's orders. It'll be easier. Even if you end up in handcuffs."

And one of technology's best minds, not to mention one very rich man, lapsed into a reminiscent grin.

"I was telling the boys here a bit ago," Coach said, "that the Bears should do better this season, barring injuries. That new cornerback they traded for—you used to play with him, right, Trent?"

"Yeah. Nobody'll play harder than Ben. He's a good get for the Bears."

"Just a shame you never played for the Bears, near home so folks could come and see you."

Trent bit back the retort that the only "folks" from Drago who would have made the trip to Chicago to see him play would have been Coach.

After more discussion of the Bears' prospects, talk slid to the upcoming high school season.

"Graduated most of the starters," Josh Kincannon said. "So Coach has a lot of teaching to do this year."

"Darcie says there's one hot player," Zeke said, half with pride, half tentatively. "A receiver?"

"Jonas Meltini," Kincannon said. "He's only going to be a sophomore, but he does have good speed. He also has a bad attitude."

"We've got a team with a lot of heart," Coach said. "Lot of young ones. They'll shape up fine. With time." Then he sighed.

Trent was caught by an expression on Josh's face that blended concern and resignation. He saw Zeke also spot it. Then, Zeke looked at Coach. With a reluctance he didn't examine too closely, Trent made himself turn toward his former coach, too.

The man looked tired. Pale under his heat-induced ruddiness. And old.

"Well, I'd best be collecting Mary Jane and getting home," Coach said.

They exchanged goodbyes, then watched him move off slowly.

Josh sighed. "He hates to admit how much the season takes out of him. I wish… Well, no use wishing."

Trent felt discomfort edging in. Not wanting to pinpoint its cause, he changed the subject to the planned fireworks.

He didn't get much detail, since Zeke, looking thrilled at the prospect, said all he knew was he was sticking with Darcie.

"I just want to sit for a minute."

Jennifer sank down on the first horizontal surface inside the showroom, a bench by the door to the service area, pushed the slingback strap down off one heel, then the other, and stepped out of her shoes. Even on the hard linoleum it felt marvelous.

"Ohhh," she moaned, wiggling her toes and propping the back of her head against the wall.

"Tired?" Trent asked.

His voice, like that look he'd sent her across the lot this afternoon, was warm and smoky, filled with communication, connection.

For an instant, another kind of warmth and fire had seeped into her. Just for an instant. Then the clink of the ice cubes in Mildred's glass of iced tea had jerked her back to reality.

It had sounded exactly like ice cracking under her feet.

Thank heavens he had treated her as usual the rest of the day.

"Exhausted."

Exhausted not only from waking at the crack of dawn—and dawn came early in July in northern Illinois—but also from the days and weeks since Trent Stenner left a message on the real estate office's machine.

"Who knew success could be so exhausting, huh?" Leaning against the door frame, Trent rubbed the familiar spot on his shoulder. Trash bags awaited collection, everyone else had left and the place was back to normal inside and out. "You were so worried about nobody coming, there was one thing you overlooked."

She opened her eyes. "What?"

"How it would feel if everybody came."

She chuckled. So many people had taken flyers that she'd had to dispatch Barry to run off a batch of black-and-white copies on the office printer. If a quarter of the people who'd said they'd bring their car in for service actually did, they'd be getting off to a good start. She wouldn't even let herself think of the glorious possibility of half becoming real jobs.

Laboriously, she shrugged off the jacket that topped her halter dress.

"Oh, God, I've been sweltering all day."

"Why didn't you take your jacket off before?"

"I wouldn't have looked professional."

"And I do?"

He bent his head, looking down at his polo shirt, now sporting a smear of ketchup, and cutoff jeans, with beat-up athletic shoes on his feet.

She smiled slightly. He looked like Trent. Powerful and relaxed. "You don't have to be professional-looking."

"How do you figure that?"

"You're the owner. And a Stenner. You're measured by a different standard."

She'd heard about Franklin calling the café. And that Trent had shut him down. Heard about it from a dozen people. But not from Trent.

"Thank God for that if it means I can dress how I want," he said now. "But, if I don't want to attract flies at the fireworks, I'd better go change clothes. Then I'll come pick you and Ashley up."

"Oh, that's not necessary. I can—"

"It is necessary. I expect you to run interference, because Darcie scares me to death."

Jennifer dashed home for a quick shower before Trent arrived, and found Ashley primping in the bathroom.

A knee-jerk wave of insecurity washed over Jennifer. She didn't have time or energy to do more than sluice off the sweat and grime and put on fresh clothes. She sucked in a breath and reminded herself that her appearance wasn't that important, as long as she was presentable.

Jennifer firmly declared that she needed the bathroom, and

Ashley left for the primitive conditions of three carefully angled mirrors in her bedroom with a martyrdom that would have done a saint proud.

From the doorway, she told Ashley that Trent was giving them a ride, then braced herself.

Ashley cut her a sharp look, but said nothing.

Ashley had been distant and preoccupied lately. Jennifer knew it was part of growing up, part of separating from her mother to keep her thoughts and feelings private. And if Ashley had otherwise remained the sunny girl she'd once been, Jennifer wouldn't have been so concerned. But these past few months…

Then again, wishing Ashley was still the sunny child she'd been was the equivalent of wishing her daughter hadn't been hit by the volatile cocktail of adolescent hormones. Which was all part of Ashley's growing up. Or so Jennifer reminded herself fifteen times a day.

Trent, blast him, was early. She'd barely had time to brush her hair and add some lipstick.

"You okay?" Trent asked when he opened the car door for her, having parked down the street from Lilac Commons Park.

As they joined streams of people heading to the park, she called up the smile that had long served her well, that had won her crowns as homecoming, prom and Lilac Festival queen, that so few bothered to look beyond. "Of course. I love fireworks."

Trent frowned. "You should be at home with your feet up and a bottle of aspirin beside you."

She stammered out a protest. God, that smile wasn't supposed to make someone think she needed her feet up and painkillers.

Ashley saved Jennifer from giving herself away more with the first words she'd spoken since Trent's arrival at the apartment. "See you later."

"What?" Jennifer spun around to her daughter, already five yards away. "Wait. Ashley."

Ashley stopped, but remained at a distance. "What?" she demanded impatiently. "I've got to meet Courtney and Sarah by the statue."

"I…" Jennifer's mind raced. She'd assumed Ashley would be with her, as she always had been at Fourth of July celebrations. But it had been a couple years since Drago had fireworks, and Ashley had truly been a child then. Was she overreacting? How old had she been when she'd watched with a group of friends instead of with her family? Just about Ashley's age, she thought. "I thought you'd want to be with all of us."

"Like a little kid? No way. Don't make a big deal of everything, Mom."

Something plucked at Jennifer's nerves. But then again everything Ashley said could pluck at her nerves these days. She suspected that was her daughter's entire purpose in speaking most times.

"Okay. We'll meet you here at the car as soon as the fireworks end."

"Everyone's going to Jessica's to listen to music."

"Ashley. You know the rules about parties. You ask ahead of time and I talk to the parents first."

"This isn't a party, it's—you know—impromptu. You said there could be exceptions for impromptu—"

"It's not impromptu if you knew about it ahead of time. The answer is no. You come to Trent's car when the fireworks end, or you stay with us."

"Fine," she snapped, spinning away and starting to stomp off.

"Ashley."

"Now what?"

"Have a good time."

A flicker crossed her daughter's face, as if the old Ashley resurfaced for an instant. Then it was gone. "Yeah. Bye."

"Jennifer, do you want to—"

"Jennifer! Trent!" Darcie hurried up to them. "We've got a spot saved by the pond. C'mon."

Darcie swept them into the park, congratulating them on the cookout's success and filling them in on the fireworks and who would be part of their group.

"But Mom and the Chief said no thanks when I asked if they wanted to join us."

"The chief?" Trent asked.

"Yeah, my mom's living with the chief of police. I think they want to make out in the dark."

"Darcie," Jennifer protested, laughing. She following Darcie's lead weaving among clots of people on blankets and clusters of chairs.

"Well, I do. You would not believe— Oh, there they are. See Zeke? You know, that's a benefit I never thought about when I said I'd marry him—he's so tall I'm always going to be able to find the guy in a crowd."

Josh Kincannon was there with his three kids when they arrived. Among the greetings, Jennifer heard him say, "Trent, stop by the high school some day next week. Give us a chance to rehash some old games."

Xena Kincannon, Josh's oldest, declared that if they didn't find seats now, there wouldn't be any more left and they'd have to stand. "Again," she added. Josh waved goodbye and headed after his kids.

While Darcie introduced Trent to Zeke's mother, who beamed at her daughter-in-law-to-be and at Trent, Jennifer said hello to Peter Quincy.

Darcie finished the introductions with, "This is Quince— Peter Quincy. He's Zeke's best friend and VP for PR at Zeke-

Tech. Don't you love the way I've learned corporate speak? I sound just like a native."

"One of many vice presidents," the tall, slender man said with a winning smile and a warm handshake.

"And this," Darcie concluded, "is Trent Stenner. He's just bought his family's car dealership."

"Trent Stenner? As in *Trent Stenner?*" Quince interrupted. "As in football."

"Now it's 'as in cars,'" Trent said dryly.

"Oh, yeah," Zeke said. "Coach Brookenheimer said something this afternoon about you playing football."

"Damn right he played football," Quince said. "I saw you against the Redskins a couple years back. If I weren't a Redskins fan, I'd say you played one hell of a game. It never looked like you were going to get to the receiver, but you always did."

"That's why they call me sneaky slow," Trent said.

"I'd say sneaky smart," Quince objected. "A lot of people thought you could have played a couple more seasons."

Trent shook his head. "There's a point when you're getting slower faster than you're getting smarter. I didn't want to be flattened by those Mack trucks they're drafting these days."

Quince nodded slowly. "I can see that. But I'll miss seeing you play. Except against the Redskins."

"Thanks. I suppose I'll miss some things about it, too."

"I'll bet. It's got to be strange with training camp coming up."

"Yeah." Trent seemed struck by that thought. "No training camp."

Zeke spoke up. "But I thought it was your brother, who— ouch." Zeke redirected his puzzlement to Darcie, who looked anywhere but at him.

"It was my brother," Trent said easily. "He was the star here."

"Did it bug you?" Zeke asked.

Jennifer might have wanted to wince at his putting Trent on the spot, but even more she wanted to hear the answer.

"Believe it or not, it didn't. A lot of people don't understand that. He liked being the star. I like the inner workings. The part of the game most people don't see, the part TV cameras don't follow."

Zeke nodded. "I can understand that."

Trent met the other man's gaze, and Jennifer saw a moment of connection between them. "I bet you can," he said.

"You're right that a lot of people don't understand," Zeke said. "They think it's the result we're after, instead of the process."

"If your process didn't bring results that I have to market to people, I wouldn't care," Quince said.

"See what I put up with? Insurrection in the ranks putting hurdles in my way." Zeke turned to Trent. "Bet you've had obstacles, too."

"Mostly what I battled was people wanting to cut me from teams right off because I didn't have one standard selling point. If I stuck around long enough, they'd see what I could do. So my first goal was just to stick. Not to cause trouble, not be a problem, not make any demands."

Jennifer watched Trent as the conversation veered away from football.

He had such determination, such strength. Traits he must have developed from coping with his family from a young age, but then had become the tools he used to move past that upbringing.

"Oh, look," Mrs. Zeekowsky said. "The fireworks began."

Trent tipped his head back along with everyone else to watch the next trail streaking into the sky, then bursting into a shimmering, multicolored ball.

It's got to be strange with training camp coming up.

He resettled in the lawn chair between Zeke and Jennifer.

Why had Quince's words hit like a blow to the gut? Sure, he'd known intellectually—that's what retiring meant. But until now, a couple weeks before he would normally pack for training camp, it hadn't seemed real. He'd mostly been following his off-season routine, even working out with the team at the spring minicamps. But from now on, his life diverged from what he'd known since...

Another explosion blossomed into sparkled confetti.

...Good Lord, since grade school.

Football season had been the structure and rhythm of his years, as certain a part of his calendar as national holidays. And now it was gone.

He dropped his head.

This time he saw the explosion only by reflection in the pond.

Movement among the crowd at the far side of the pond caught his eye. Across a sea of heads looking skyward, he saw a figure amid a group of youngsters that he recognized as Ashley. She tossed her hair and looked up in rapt attention. Not at fireworks. She was looking at a boy. In the flashes of light, he couldn't identify him. Then the group moved, and a clump of broad lilac bushes blocked his view.

Trent looked toward Jennifer. She seemed absorbed by the fireworks.

Another burst, and he saw the fireworks by reflection again. This time in her eyes.

He had never seen fireworks so glorious.

He couldn't look away. Her profile disappeared into darkness between explosions, then reappeared, glowing and sparkling. Not only from reflection, but with its own light.

She sucked in a breath in delight, leaving a gap between her skin and the strap of her sundress, an opening right where her shoulder and her breast met. A gap where his hand could slide under the fabric, fitting perfectly, to feel the soft flesh.

Jennifer turned to him, smiling. "Wasn't that amazing?"

Amazing? Oh, yeah, amazing. Though, he doubted she meant what he meant.

"Trent? Is something wrong?"

Only then did he realize the explosions had stopped. At least the explosions in the sky. How long had he been staring at her?

"Nothing wrong. Just wowed by those fireworks."

Her gaze met his. He extended his hand toward her face. But just short of touching her cheek, he saw the worry surge across her eyes.

Damn.

He redirected his hand, brushing across the skin where the side of her throat turned toward her shoulder. "Mosquito," he muttered.

One of the bloodsuckers might have been there, but he wouldn't have noticed. It was pure excuse. And, as long as he'd invented it, he might as well make the most of it.

Grasping the collar of her feathery sweater, which had slid down her arm, he tugged it back into place, letting his fingers brush her skin again as he did.

"Can't have those mosquitoes eating up a pretty woman," he said.

He'd meant it to sound light. To put her at ease.

It didn't.

First, she went stiff. Then she stood with abrupt, jerky movements.

"They are getting bad," she said, her voice strained, her back to him.

Darcie was suddenly beside him, glaring, letting him know he hadn't fooled her. "That was quite a display."

"The very best display in Drago ever," Mrs. Zeekowsky

said proudly from in front of them. "The fireworks were magnificent."

"They sure were," Darcie agreed, drilling him for another second with her eyes before relenting by looking at her fiancé. "Brenda deserves a bonus, Zeke. She did a fantastic job."

Zeke looked from Darcie to Trent, then back. She gave a slight shake of her head, and the man relaxed. Under other circumstances, Trent might have been amused at the silent communication.

"Don't give Brenda any ideas," Zeke said. "She already thinks she runs the business."

"Nah." Quince grinned. "She just knows she runs the business half of your life."

Everyone laughed, while Zeke protested good-humoredly.

As they folded their chairs, Jennifer looked around. "Has anyone spotted Ashley?"

The question had been general, but Trent was next to her, so he responded. "It's so dark I can barely see you," he lied.

To his surprise, her posture relaxed and she chuckled, sounding like the incident of the mosquito was forgotten. "That's right. Nobody can see anybody at the fireworks."

Pretty damned perfect.

She and Eric had been late for the movie the first time he'd picked her up at her house, because he and her father had talked football for so long. At last, her father walked them to the door, clapped Eric on the shoulder and declared, "You two look pretty damned perfect together."

"Roy! Such language," her mother had said in the background, but Jennifer heard approval in her voice.

Trent and Josh had rehashed just about every play in every game against each other, when Trent leaned back in his chair and grinned at Josh.

"This is a heck of a lot more fun than the previous time I was in this office," he said. "Being lectured by Mr. Grandhier about the dangers of premarital sex. As if we'd gotten anywhere close to that."

It had been hard enough to find privacy to make out, much less do more. He'd never expected to be back in the same situation as an adult.

A vision flashed in Trent's head of experiencing with Jennifer what had gotten him called to the principal's office that long-ago spring day. Holding Jennifer, his mouth on hers, her hands—

Trent blinked away the vision. Vision? More like a hallucination.

Technically, he and Jennifer had been alone the night of the fireworks, since most cars had cleared out while they waited a good half hour for Ashley. But the mood had not been conducive to discussing, much less acting on.

And what would he say? *You don't seem to be worrying every second that I might be Dracula come to suck out your lifeblood anymore, and we work together well, wanna see how we'd be in bed?*

So, they'd talked about the dealership. Of course. She never ran out of things to say about that. Even that had had him edgy, since Jennifer's half of the discussion was in that husky voice of hers.

When Ashley finally arrived, there were looks exchanged between mother and daughter that made him glad they'd decided to save it until he dropped them off. The weird thing was the girl had been downright pleasant to him. Even weirder, it wasn't until then that he'd realized he kind of liked the kid, even when she was being a brat.

Josh laughed. "Got caught at Makeout Lookout, huh?"

"God, it's still called that?" he asked.

"Yup. It's not just kids, either. They say it's where nearly half the babies in Drago are conceived, and more than half the divorces." Josh gave him a considering look. "I hear your brother was there frequently. And I don't mean in high school."

In other words, Eric had cheated on Jennifer, along with everything else. Trent would never have that vision of taking Jennifer to Makeout Lookout again. But the physical aftermath of having the vision in the first place hadn't receded yet.

"What's the matter?" Josh asked.

He must have made an unconscious movement. "A little sore."

"I saw you out running this morning. Feeling your age, huh?"

"You could say that." But it wasn't his leg muscles that felt sore.

"That brings up something I was hoping to discuss with you. I have an idea."

"I heard you need someone to do the books," Anne Hooper said, standing on the far side of Jennifer's desk.

Jennifer knew her a little, as she knew most people in Drago. She knew Anne ran the farm that belonged to her late husband's great uncle. And that they were having even more difficulty than most in the area bringing ends into the same general vicinity, much less making them meet.

"I, uh, well, yes. We do." Trent was right that they couldn't impose on Linc forever. Trent knew investing but not the accounting they needed and her basic-level skills were about to break under the strain. "But we haven't even advertised for the job."

Anne ignored that. "I can do them from home. At night."

"After you've worked all day on the farm?" Jennifer had more than her imagination to tell her how tiring that would be. She could see it in the slump of the woman's shoulders, in the weariness that wasn't so much around her eyes as actually in them. "Won't you sit down?"

Anne did with a quick thanks and a small, tight smile. "Yes, I'll do them after I've worked on the farm. Same time I do our books."

The woman might have been more obvious if she'd been wearing a neon sign proclaiming Sympathy Need Not Apply but just barely.

"The dealership's going to have different issues." Jennifer was sure of that, although she had no idea about farm finances. Not that she'd become an expert at dealership finances. She needed to learn faster. About finances and marketing and management and sales and…everything. "Taxes. Uh, inventory. That sort of thing."

"The basics are the basics. And this can't be worse than figuring out farm taxes. Besides, now I know *how* to find out. That's the toughest part."

Jennifer looked at Anne Hooper, and for all their physical differences, felt as if she were looking into a mirror. A mirror that showed a woman doing her damnedest and afraid it wouldn't be good enough.

"You're right. You're hired."

She could hire someone without consulting Trent. He'd given Barry a permanent job without consulting her, and then extended the offer to Jonas, too, saying it was only fair.

Anne Hooper blinked once, as if shocked, then stood and extended her hand. "Thank you. You won't regret it."

Jennifer met the handshake. "I'm sure I won't. Now, shall we get started? You can use my desk and computer to get acquainted with what we have." She stood and took a wire basket overflowing with papers from the desk. "I'll work on filing, so you can ask any questions as they come up."

* * *

Anne was at the desk and Jennifer was sorting papers behind the open cabinet door when she heard footsteps stop at the doorway from the hall. Then Anne's voice from behind her said, "May I help you?"

"I was told this was Jennifer Truesdale's office."

Jennifer backed up and swung the cabinet door closed. Her ears hadn't deceived her. But she still couldn't believe it.

Chapter Eight

Jennifer watched him skip a rock across the surface of Drago River with the easy movement of an athlete.

She wondered how many people would guess just from that motion that he'd been a high school quarterback.

They'd driven in his car to the river bend just outside of town. From the patch of asphalt off the side of the road known as Makeout Lookout, they'd followed a narrow path through trees and brush to where the river had worn a quarter-moon of sandy earth clear. This was what passed for a beach in Drago. She's always preferred the swimming hole on the other side of town.

"Thanks for coming out here with me, Jenny." The name sounded unfamiliar. He was the only person who still called her Jenny. And she hadn't heard it from him in years.

"You said it was urgent."

He nodded, then skipped another stone across the nearly still water. The droning of insects rose and fell before he spoke.

"She says she'll leave me," her brother finally said.

"Amy said that? Really?"

As astonished as she was, she didn't dismiss his words. Her sister-in-law didn't say things she didn't mean. And she frequently said things other people might not have wanted to hear.

Like on Jennifer's wedding day, when she'd found Jennifer alone during the reception at the country club and had offered her best wishes.

Amy and Mark had been dating less than a year at that point. He was nuts about her, said he wanted to marry her, but Amy was holding back.

"Thank you, Amy. I hope you and Mark might…" She gave her words a questioning lift at the end.

"Maybe." Amy looked around, then added. "Depends on if he can grow up. I love him, but I'm not sure I could be married to him. Your family hasn't done him any favors by making him the center of the universe."

Jennifer had been stunned into silence. Not because Amy was wrong, but because she was right. And because no one ever admitted it. And, maybe, she thought now, because everything Amy had said about Mark also applied to Eric. Unfortunately she hadn't recognized that until several years after she'd said, "I do."

"But you got the worse end of the deal," Amy continued. "I know, I know. Your parents are good people at heart. But, really, Jennifer, it's like they're stuck in the Victorian age with the son the be-all and end-all and you… Well, usually a daughter who's a daddy's girl is also the family princess."

But not you. The words were implicit in Amy's tone and expression.

"Seems like you have to scramble for every bit of attention. Even today," she'd added.

Jennifer's gaze had gone to where most of the guests gathered around three men—her father, her brother and her new husband. Her father was thrilled that she'd married Eric. Thrilled.

Beside her, Amy had sighed. "I suppose it says something about Mark's character that he's not worse than he is, so maybe there's hope."

But after nearly twelve years of marriage and three kids, it now seemed Amy had given up hope.

Still standing by the river, Mark nodded miserably, confirming that Amy had said she'd leave him.

"But why?" Jennifer asked.

"She said to ask you. That's why I'm here. Had to find out where you were from Mom," he added on a note of complaint.

Their parents had moved to a northwest suburb of Chicago six years ago, to be "near the grandchildren," her father had said. Said it right to her face, oblivious that he was overlooking the grandchild he had in Drago. Ah, but Ashley was a mere girl, while Mark and Amy had three growing—and athletic—boys. Her mother had posed no objection to her husband's decision. She'd been happy to have a new house and garden to decorate and design. "And," she'd said with pleasure, "the shopping is so wonderful."

Mark stopped skipping stones and looked back at where Jennifer sat on a picnic table. "Why aren't you living in the house anymore?"

Clueless. Absolutely clueless as ever about other people's lives.

"You do know that Eric and I are divorced, don't you?"

Her sarcasm didn't penetrate. "Yeah, though I don't see why you left the house. And you working at Stenner Autos—that makes no sense."

"It's complicated, but—"

"Oh, God. Divorce, Jenny! I don't want Amy to divorce me. I don't want to lose her and the boys. To be all alone.

Jenny, you gotta tell me what did Amy mean? What are you supposed to tell me?"

"I don't know. I—"

"Think! Think, Jenny. You gotta help me."

A cord that had wrapped tight around Jennifer as long as she could remember, a cord that perhaps she unknowingly had wound even tighter herself, snapped, and with it, the guard on her tongue and her thoughts.

"I don't know what she meant, Mark. And it's not my job to save your marriage. I have more than enough of my own problems to solve. You want to know why Ashley and I aren't living in the house? And, oh, yes, thank you for asking after the welfare of your niece. The niece you haven't seen in nearly three years because you're always too busy. The niece her grandparents barely remember to send a card to because they're taking your kids to Bears games and baseball camps and basketball exhibitions."

She sucked in a breath. She could stop now. Reclaim her calm. Apologize and put things back the way they'd always been. She kept going.

"I'll tell you the reason we're not in the house," she heard herself saying. "Because we're broke. Because Eric left us with way too many debts and way too few assets. Because he's run out on child support. Because I sold the house to pay off what he owed. You want to know why I'm working at the dealership? Because I have this wild-eyed dream of being able to feed and clothe my daughter. And someday sending her to college. That's why."

"God, I had no idea, Jenny. Why haven't Mom and Dad said anything?"

She snorted. "How the hell would they know? And why would they start caring now? Why would anyone start caring now?"

"Jenny! We care. You know—"

"I know that none of you except Amy ever bothered to really look at me. To see my life. Or my daughter's. I've been background—wallpaper—all my life to your great achievements and exploits, Mark. And then I moved on to the same role in Eric's life. Which was probably the only time I've really had Dad's approval. But I will not let my daughter be wallpaper. I will not."

Silence. Her words seemed to spread in that silence like ripples on the water.

"I'm sorry, Jenny. I really am. I had no idea you felt that way. You should have spoken up sooner. I know Mom and Dad made a big deal of what I did, and you were the quiet one, but to feel like this all these years. Wallpaper? I had no idea... Hey! Maybe that's what Amy wanted you to tell me. Maybe she's been feeling that way, too. You think that's it? You think that's what Amy thinks I needed to find out from you so we won't split up?"

Jennifer gaped at the man's colossal ability to make it all about him. Again. Right there in midsentence of actually starting to get a glimpse of how she'd felt all these years, to make the U-turn right back to himself.

And then she laughed. Because crying about it seemed as useless as crying about grass being green.

He stared at her, clearly taken aback. But after a couple minutes, as her laughter eased into gasping breaths and she wiped away tears with her fingers, an expression came over his face that she hadn't seen there before.

Mark Truesdale was abashed.

"I am sorry, Jenny," he said softly.

She met his gaze. Slowly, she smiled.

"Maybe there's hope for you after all, Mark."

* * *

When Trent parked his car beneath the tree between the lot and the car wash, he had every intention of going directly inside.

Then he saw Barry, the kid whose job he'd made permanent after the Fourth of July cookout. Well, one of the two kids. Because it was only fair to make the same offer to Jonas Meltini, the other kid Jennifer had hired. Barry had been grateful; Jonas had been blasé, though he had accepted.

That's when Trent had connected the talented player Coach and Josh Kincannon had talked about with their employee. The one he often had a hard time finding when work needed doing.

Barry appeared to be taking his lunch break from washing cars. Not just running them through the car wash next door, but, judging from the equipment, hand washing any missed spots, along with vacuuming and wiping down the insides. Jonas was nowhere in sight.

But what caught Trent's attention was the football Barry tossed in the air with one hand while he ate a sandwich with the other.

"How 'bout tossing that ball this way?" he asked.

Barry's head snapped around. "Yes, sir, Mr. Stenner."

He scrambled to his feet, dropping the sandwich on a plastic wrapper.

He threw the ball with some juice. Trent had no trouble holding on; as a safety he'd worked on his receiving skills to make the most of any opportunities to intercept.

"You'd better finish that sandwich before the ants have it," he said.

"Oh." Barry sounded deflated. "Yes, sir."

Not moving any closer, Trent turned the ball over in his hands while the kid wolfed down the sandwich. The ball, though worn, felt so familiar, like a talisman of another life.

When the kid's hands were free, Trent tossed it back to him.

"Glad to see you use two hands," he said after the kid caught it.

"Yes, sir. I was only doing the one-handed drill to get the feel. So two-handed would feel easier and if I had to catch one-handed…"

"Not a bad idea. Toss it back."

A grin bloomed that seemed as out of proportion to the kid's face as his feet were to his body.

They tossed the ball back and forth with varied tempos, easy, with a bit of zip, off pace, a passable spiral and Trent's dying-duck specialty to mimic a tipped ball in order to practice snaring those free balls.

They spoke little. A phrase or two of advice or praise from Trent. Heartfelt thanks and unending *sirs* from the kid.

"I gotta quit now," Trent said with regret. "Meeting at the bank."

"No, you don't. I mean, the meeting's off, sir. Ms. Truesdale had to leave. She had Jorge call the bank and reschedule for tomorrow."

Reprieve! And yet also, regret. He pulled in a breath scented from the rosebushes she had planted out front, and it stirred the regret deeper. She wasn't inside. He wasn't just a few strides away from being able to wander into her office to see her.

"Oh, yeah?" Trent gestured for the kid to keep tossing. "Where'd Ms. Truesdale go?"

He shrugged. "Some guy came."

Somebody about taxes? A creditor checking on them? Maybe an automaker rep? One thing for sure, whoever came for whatever reason, it wasn't going to be fun. "Glad I was gone," he muttered.

"Oh, he wasn't here to see you. He was here to see Ms. Truesdale."

"Oh, yeah?" Now why did that please him? Must be a sign he was getting the hang of this retirement business, because he sure liked the idea that this headache wasn't aimed at him. "Maybe he wanted a job."

"I don't think so. She seemed kind of upset when they left."

Trent caught the ball. "They left together." And sent it back.

"Yeah."

The ball returned to him and this time Trent held it for an extra beat. "What did this guy look like?"

"Older guy." That didn't help, since Barry would consider any adult older. "Taller than you. Lightish hair."

Trent held up his hands, halting the game of catch. "I've gotta get to work now. So do you."

"Yes, sir. I will, sir. Right now." The kid practically ran to get started.

Trent swung into Jennifer's office and stopped dead. A woman he'd never seen before sat at Jennifer's desk. An attractive, but tired, woman.

"Who are you?"

"Give me one minute." She hit several keys, her focus intent. Twenty seconds, and she looked up. "Hmm? Oh. You must be Trent Stenner."

"Yes, I am. Who are you?"

"I'm Anne. Anne Hooper." She leaned across the desk and extended a hand that looked as if it had spent more time at hard labor than a keyboard.

"Nice to meet you, Anne. Now, what are you doing here?"

"Oh. Jennifer didn't tell you? I thought she'd called you right after…but clearly she didn't. I'm doing the books. Jennifer hired me this morning. I'm setting up everything so

I can access accounts from home. I've talked to the bank about adding encryption that—"

"That all sounds good, but where's Jennifer?"

"She took off a while ago. She had an unexpected visitor."

"Oh."

"Yeah. Her brother came by."

Trent felt as though he'd been braced to make a tackle, then discovered nothing there to grab except air.

A light was on in Trent's office when Mark drove Jennifer to Stenner Autos to get her car after he treated her and Ashley to dinner.

It wasn't the most comfortable meal she'd ever eaten, through no real fault of her brother's. Ashley had basked and glowed in his presence, reminding Jennifer painfully of herself. And forming a stark contrast to how Ashley reacted to Trent.

They dropped Ashley off at home, but Jennifer still needed her car.

"Uh, Mark, I forgot something in the office. No need to wait for me."

"If you're sure you'll be okay. I'll call you. And thanks, Jennifer."

"Not sure I helped any."

"You helped a lot."

Using her keys, she came in quietly and reached the open office door. Trent frowned at something on his computer screen, his face intense. He should have been intimidating, perhaps even frightening with that expression. For no reason at all, she felt her lips lifting.

"You left the alarm off," she said.

His head jerked up and his gaze locked with hers with the same concentration he'd devoted to the screen.

"No need. I was still here."

"That's not what you told me. You said when I was alone I should have the alarm on."

"Yeah, well…" He hitched his uninjured shoulder. "You should."

Before she could respond to that slight—and totally unapologetic—emphasis on the pronoun, he continued. "You okay?"

"Fine. Why wouldn't I be? Oh—because I missed the appointment. I'm so sorry about that."

"I'll survive."

"Yes, but now we're behind. And it's my fault. I don't know when we'll go over that application before the meeting tomorrow."

"In the morning," he said with a careless shrug.

"I'm scheduled from the minute I get in, and I can't get in earlier, because I'm not dropping Ashley off at her friend's house until nine."

"I'll bring doughnuts to your place in the morning and we'll do it then." She had no time to protest—and really no reason to protest, except doughnuts were not the most healthful of breakfasts—before he continued. "I heard you had a visitor. Your brother, right? Unexpected?"

She sank into the chair beside his desk and expelled a breath.

"Yes, it was my brother. And unexpected isn't the half of it. He's never come to see me. Ever. And now…this…"

She closed her eyes, remembering cathartic truth telling.

"What does he want from you?"

She opened her eyes, nearly as surprised by the edge in Trent's voice as she'd been by her brother's arrival.

"What makes you think he wants something from me?"

"Because you haven't had much contact with your family, and usually when people show up suddenly like that, they want something from you. And frequently it involves money."

She couldn't argue with his logic. Yet she had a sense of something else behind his words. Had he experienced something similar?

You could ask him.

She heard the words as if spoken in her head.

No. She wouldn't ask him. They had gotten along surprisingly well so far, but as business associates. Two people rowing the same boat. No sense in rocking it with personal questions.

"He does want something from me. But it's free—advice."

He leaned back, crossing his hands behind his head, looking from beneath his dark eyelashes. "Yeah? You going to give it to him?"

"Aren't you surprised he wants my advice?"

After her initial pique, she'd been astonished. Her brother, always the darling of their family, coming to *her* and asking for advice.

"No." He left it at that, without giving her any idea of what he meant.

"Well, I was." Although she needed a stronger word— shock, maybe, or better yet, stupefaction—for her brother coming to her for advice and listening to her. Eventually. "His wife's kicked him out. He asked my advice to get her back."

"Maybe he's not as stupid as I thought."

She gaped at him a moment, before a giggle bubbled up from somewhere so deep in her she had forgotten it existed.

"Yes, he is." She giggled again. "He didn't think of it. Amy— his wife—told him to ask me how to make things right."

"Okay. He's still stupid. What does Amy want you to tell him?"

"I told him I didn't know. But he wasn't satisfied with that. He was so desperate... He really does love her."

His upper and lower eyelashes nearly came together as his light-colored eyes pinned her, seeming to see inside her.

Only when she saw that did she realize she'd sounded like a starving urchin with her nose pressed against the bakery window when she'd said, "He really does love her." Pathetic and needy. And she'd vowed never to let herself be that way again. Never to allow herself to need a man's approval so much that she'd fall into that trap.

"Don't you?" Trent said.

Lost, she blinked at him. "Don't I what?"

"Know what Amy wants you to tell him. Seems to me it would be related to your childhoods. You're one of the few people around from his childhood that his wife would know."

Her brain was buzzing. With how he'd zeroed in on it. But also with other thoughts. Thoughts about his childhood. About his relationship with his family.

Why did he never talk about them?

The hell with it, she *would* ask him.

"What about your family, Trent?"

"What about them?" His lack of reaction didn't ring true. He at least should have reacted to the out-of-the-blue question.

"You so rarely talk about them. I can't believe you aren't hearing from your father."

"Hearing from and talking to are two different things."

"Oh." It made her sad. Sadder than she would have expected. "I'm sorry you don't have a good relationship with your family. I know, I know, that sounds weird considering I haven't seen much of mine, either. But…"

A flicker. No more than that. But something crossed his face. Trouble was she had no idea *what* had flickered.

"Oh, I get my fix of family. Just not my family. Linc calls me a family parasite."

"What!" Outrage overrode her suspicion that she was being detoured. "How dare he. How—"

"Whoa, Jen." He laughed. "He was only agreeing with me.

Actually, I suggested the term family vampire and he said it was too harsh, because I don't suck the life out of other people's families. I just don't contribute."

She felt chilled. Chilled to the heart.

She stood. "I'd better go. But... Thank you, Trent."

"No problem, Jennifer. No problem at all. Good night."

"See you in the morning," she said, heading out the door. "And turn on the alarm after I leave."

She heard a chuckle behind her. It's what she'd intended, so the sense of success had to be the reason she felt so warmed by the sound.

The doughnuts smelled mouthwateringly sinful when Jennifer opened the door to Trent the next morning. Her resolve to have only grapefruit slid away unmourned.

"It's such a nice morning, we'll eat on the balcony," she said.

She'd decided to have breakfast outside after considering how she and Ashley bumped and brushed when they sat at the counter to eat. And Trent was a considerably larger presence than Ashley. Jennifer had awakened especially early and finished in the bathroom early so she'd be certain to be ready before Trent arrived, no matter how early he was.

"Sounds great. I've been wanting to see this balcony. Where is it?"

"The far end of the apartment, which isn't very convenient for the kitchen." She shrugged, guiding him down the hall. "They took space from the second floor of each of the stores, so the apartment's long and skinny, with the hallway winding around."

"I smell guacamole," Trent said as they neared a turn in the hallway.

"Guacamole? I don't have any guac—"

At that moment, Ashley emerged from the bathroom.

Jennifer took in the situation in less than a heartbeat, which put her way ahead of the other two. But then she had an advantage—she was female, and she wasn't in shock.

At least not as much shock as her daughter.

Trent gawked. But give him credit, he did clamp his mouth shut almost immediately. Ashley, on the other hand, could have used this jaw-dropped, eyes-starting, hands-to-heart pose to audition for any horror movie ever made—and she'd get the part.

Green goop covered her face except for a strip of orangish red down her nose and bare circles around her eyes, explained by green disks held in hands slathered in white. Her hair hung in slimy hunks on a shawl-wrapped towel over her old chenille bathrobe faded to the color of dust.

Clearly, Ashley had used the extra bathroom time made available by Jennifer's early rising to try out remedies culled from the most recent stack of beauty magazines from the library.

"Ahhhggg!" Ashley's squawk was strangled, probably because the green goop appeared dry enough to keep her face from moving.

It didn't stop the rest of her from moving, however. Jennifer grabbed Trent's arm and pulled him against the wall to keep from being run over as Ashley made for her bedroom.

The door slammed behind Ashley, and Trent jumped.

"What on earth…?"

"Beauty regimen," Jennifer said, pushing open the sliding-glass door to the balcony.

There went her hopes that Ashley and Trent might be edging away from the tension that had seemed to exist between them from their first meeting, and toward a true niece-uncle relationship. Ashley would redirect her embarrassment to anger, and she'd divide it between the witnesses to her embarrassment, Jennifer and Trent.

Jennifer sat wearily, then poured Trent's coffee.

"She smelled like…like a salad." Trent still sounded shocked.

He sat opposite her, his knee brushing the side of her leg as he settled in. The contact sent a shiver of shock through her, like static electricity from rubbing a carpet during the winter.

"Avocado facial mask, tomato and lemon to bleach freckles, mayonnaise to condition hair and cucumbers to treat eyes." And now Jennifer understood Ashley's willingness to do the grocery shopping lately.

"My God." He peered at her across the small table. "Did you ever…?"

Well, if that wasn't just like a man. Forcing her into a corner. What did he want her to say? That she'd used every potion and concoction that magazines, her allowance and ingenuity had allowed in pursuit of beauty?

"At that age? Sure."

His hand hovered over the largest chocolate doughnut in the bakery box he'd opened. "Why?"

He was mean. No two ways around it. He'd take candy from a baby, a bone from a puppy, and the last shred of feminine ego from a woman.

"Because I foolishly cared what guys thought of me then. Now, shall we get started?"

He didn't respond. She had the feeling his thoughts were continuing on a track unconnected to her words.

"At first, I mostly saw how much Ashley looks like you. But she's got Eric in her, too."

Jennifer stiffened. "I know you have issues with your brother." He lifted one eyebrow as if to say, *And you don't?* She ignored that. "But I will not have you playing out any sibling rivalry on my daughter."

"Whoa, retract those claws, Mama."

In silence, she continued to glare at him.

"I wasn't saying she's a bad kid, Jennifer." He raised his hands in pantomimed surrender. "I swear not to take out any sibling rivalry on your daughter."

"Don't look at Ashley and think of Eric," she warned him. "She's not Eric. No mother could ask for a better daughter."

"Okay," he said with enough skepticism to let her know he didn't believe it, but not enough for her to make an issue of it.

Still, she had two satisfactions.

First, he looked positively pained as she handed over the bank papers. Second, she snagged the biggest chocolate doughnut before he could.

The sky boiled with clouds. Not a drop of rain had fallen, but wind shook the trees, bending them before its will and shaking loose clusters of green leaves and small branches.

Jennifer stood in the second service bay's open doorway, head lifted, arms at her side. She didn't look frightened. But she didn't move.

The rain wouldn't hold off much longer. They were lucky this front hadn't moved through earlier and prevented their balcony breakfast.

"Hey, you awake?"

"Watching the storm come." She didn't take her eyes off the sky.

"I can see that. Are you planning on moving when the storm arrives?"

"Probably."

He stifled a chuckle. She sounded awfully dreamy for a woman talking about getting drenched when they had a meeting at the bank soon.

Wind came tearing in with a prolonged rush that shook the trees so they bent and swayed and shimmied like souls possessed. The blast, still hot, still dry, pushed against them, flagging their clothes behind them, swirling the scents of old oil, metal and men from the area behind them.

"It's like standing in front of a huge blow-dryer," he said.

Her only reply was an eyes-closed "Mmm."

He'd forgotten about midsummer storms in the Midwest. How big they felt. How raw. How awesome. In California they'd been an inconvenience delivered from a realm disconnected from him.

But here, now, he remembered how he'd felt a part of them as a kid. As if he were another element, along with the wind, the lightning, the thunder, the rain. As if he, too, roared and blustered.

"I used to love storms as a kid," she said quietly. "I wanted to stand out in it and drink it all in."

Surprised, and something more he didn't examine, he said, "Me, too."

"You didn't have much choice, did you?"

"Huh? You're going to have to explain that one, Jennifer."

"Didn't you have to walk places in the rain as a kid?"

"Doesn't every kid?"

"You more than most."

"Just come out with it. What are you getting at?"

"I saw you running home from practice. In the rain."

"What? When?"

"Your freshman year. Your father had come to pick Eric up because of the rain, and he was giving me a ride, too. I saw you head across the field, going toward your house. I could have pointed you out to your father, so you'd get a ride, too. But I didn't. I didn't say a word."

"Don't worry. I wouldn't have thanked you for sentencing me to ten minutes in the car with my father," he said easily. "Besides, me dripping all over his car? No thank you. Believe me, I much preferred the run in the rain. You did the right thing."

"Not for the right reasons."

"Afraid of my outcast cooties, huh?" he asked cheerfully.

Her mouth twisted. "More like I was afraid that being around you might reveal my own case of them. At some level I'd recognized you were the equivalent in your family to me in my family. Not consciously. I wasn't that deliberate about it. But I'd developed skills, including never calling attention to my status. Pointing you out to your father might have made him or Eric see me as I really was. Unworthy. Or worthy only by association with Eric."

For the first time, she shifted her gaze from the sky, aiming it full at him. The sight was even more stunning than at the fireworks. The entire sky seemed to be reflected in her eyes. Roiling clouds of trouble, flashes of sharp lightning, rumbles of pained thunder and even glimpses of clear blue.

"I'm sorry, Trent. I'm sorry I let you run home in the rain without making any effort. I'm sorry I shunned you."

He shook his head, but not enough to dislodge the connection between their gazes.

"You have nothing to apologize for, Jennifer. Nothing."

In that long look he felt something fundamental shifting. Like the earth he stood on. A subtle earthquake, if such a thing were possible. As if the earth's crust had developed a fine trembling that communicated itself to his feet, into his legs, pausing to rattle his knees, before continuing on to his chest, where it lodged.

"It was never that big a deal to me, Jennifer. I suppose I'm a loner. And I never have cared about most people's opinions. It never got to me."

"You're lucky— No," she corrected herself. "Not lucky. You're strong. It's a shame you had to be so strong. But it's a good thing you were."

He shrugged. "I figured out a long time ago that some parents get their mind set on a certain sort of kid. If the DNA dice come up with a different kind, they don't know how to react, how to understand that kid or connect."

"That's awful."

He acted as if he hadn't heard her. Sometimes sympathy from a particular person could open a wound so long healed that the scar seemed to have always been there. Sometimes those wounds were better left scarred over.

"I've seen what happens when the parents try to make a kid over, and I know I was real lucky to be left on my own."

He looked into her wide eyes, still clouded with the storm of concern.

"I *was* lucky, Jen. I'm still lucky. It took some hard knocks, but I learned important lessons being on my own—on my own in a lot of ways even before I left home. I've got a good life. And no regrets."

In that moment, he knew that's what he wanted for her. A good life and no regrets. And that was damned crazy.

Him, wanting things for Jennifer Truesdale. Especially those kind of soul-deep things. Wanting to make sure she and his niece had the necessities? That made sense. But this?

A single large drop struck him on the cheek and slid down. Five more hit hard and fast, like a flourish on a drum.

She gave a small gasp that morphed into a laugh.

It was the laugh that did it.

He took her hand, long and slim, and sprinted with her across the pavement toward the showroom door, all the while knowing he should be letting her go and running the opposite direction.

After two long weeks, the heat broke. This night was one of those midsummer coolings-off where everything smelled like crisp, line-dried sheets.

As they walked to their cars, the last two to leave the dealership as usual, Jennifer told Trent about a program through the dealers' association that would let them have contact with other dealers of about the same size.

"Not dealers from our area, because they're competitors, and who wants to give away their secrets? But from other areas. Think about it, people facing the same issues we do, exchanging ideas, telling each other what works and what doesn't."

"Uh-huh."

She stopped. After another stride, he stopped, too, and looked back.

"What's wrong?"

"That's what I want to know. What's wrong?"

"Nothing's wrong. What makes you think—"

"You don't want to be doing this, Trent. I know you don't."

"Talking about the dealers' association? It's not my favorite—"

"This—you don't want to be doing this." Her wide-flung arm took in all of Stenner Autos. "Any of this."

"I…" He'd started to lie, she could see it. Then he shook his head, muttered a curse, and looked her in the eyes. "I never had any interest in the dealership growing up. I thought it was because it was so important to my father. Turns out, I just don't have much interest in selling cars."

"I see."

"No, you don't. You think I'm going to turn tail and run. I don't do that, Jennifer. C'mon. Let's sit."

She didn't resist as he took her arm and led her to his car. With her in the passenger seat, he went around and got in the driver's side.

"Want to go somewhere?"

She shook her head. She wanted to get this out. "It's not even opened yet and you hate the dealership."

"Hate's strong. I—" he rubbed his neck and along his shoulder "—I don't get excited about the details. I don't come in with ideas like you do. When I'm away from here I don't think about it."

"You work so hard... But it's driving you nuts, isn't it?"

He made a sound between a snort and a laugh. "Yeah, it is."

"Why haven't you told me how you feel?" Although she had seen how he felt, she realized now. When she would let herself.

"What could you do? I'm not going anywhere, Jennifer. I don't want you to worry about your job or Ashley's fund. I'll stick with it. And I'll keep working hard to make it a success. Hell, if it gets to be big enough we can hire a general manager, like I planned—or make you general manager—then I can do something I like. So that's good incentive."

She didn't return his grin. *Something he liked...* "What would you do if you could do anything?"

"Coach," he said immediately.

"Then why aren't you coaching? Couldn't you get a job with your old team after you retired?"

His mouth quirked. "I'm not sure I'd really accepted that I'd retired until you put me to work here. Besides, I'd rather stick with the real kids."

"Why am I not surprised?" she said dryly.

"What?" He grinned wryly at her. "You see me fitting in with kids?"

"Absolutely. I've seen you out throwing that football every opportunity you get with Barry. Or Bobby or anyone else who comes by."

"Barry's afraid of the mean, big boss lady, so don't tell her."

"Right. She can be vicious."

"Well, she is driven, and unfortunately she drives other people half as much as she drives herself, so everyone else is exhausted."

"Very funny."

"Very true. But back to Barry. He's a good kid. He's trying to get on the team and I'm helping him out a little."

She made a decision in that moment. She didn't think it through or examine it. She just knew it was right. She couldn't see him miserable.

"You should help him all the time. You should coach."

Trent's eyes narrowed. "This damned town. I don't know how the gossip got back to you, but they forgot one thing, I turned him down."

"Turned who down, Trent?"

He stared at her in the minimal light here under the trees. "You didn't know? I thought you must have heard. Damn."

"Well, now you have to tell me," she said calmly.

He swore again, more vociferously. Then heaved a sigh.

"Josh asked if I'd consider assisting Coach Brookenheimer with the team. He's getting older, and it takes a lot out of him. He doesn't have any assistants who can take on the responsibilities. Or who can ride the kids' butts. A few think pretty damn well of themselves and Coach doesn't have the energy to knock their heads together like they need. Josh thought I... But I told him no. Told him my first responsibility is here."

Her mind was going a hundred miles an hour. So fast that only one word came out. But it was an emphatic command.

"Coach."

"What? But—"

"Coach, Trent. It's what you want to do. You can help those boys, and Coach Brookenheimer. You'll be good at it." And he'd be happy.

"But—"

"We can handle it here without you. *I* can handle it. You said yourself, I could be general manager eventually. Why not now? Because I do like it. And I'm good at it," she said with pride.

"You're damned good at it. Seeing how good at it you are has helped me see I'm not cut out for it. But how could it work?"

"Just the way it has been working," she said with a wicked grin. "When there's a problem I set out the options, we discuss which one's best, and I implement it. You'd still have to work—might need to be here every day, but you can't coach until after classes end anyway, so—"

"Well, there's planning and preparation and—"

"Don't push your luck, Stenner."

"Okay, okay. So, I'd be here daily to go over things, pick up the slack. But you'd be in charge day-to-day."

"Right. And you'd be here for the big things. If you're not here for the Grand Reopening weekend, I will personally slash every football in town."

He laughed, still sounding stunned. "I swear. I'll be here for the entire weekend. Practice doesn't start until the following week."

"Okay. Say, we try this a month. Or two. Then we reassess."

"You're serious?"

He looked at her with such light in his eyes that she couldn't help but smile. "I'm absolutely serious."

"Hot damn!"

He took her face between his hands and kissed her.

It wasn't much in the way of a kiss.

It reminded her of films of soldiers and sailors celebrating the end of war by grabbing the closest available female and planting one on them. More a celebration of the moment than anything to do with the individuals.

He lifted his mouth, still holding her face. He was so close that his grin was almost out of focus.

Then it was gone. She looked up, right into those dangerous eyes. Hot and intent.

So hot that they seared the air she drew in with a quick breath.

His gaze dropped to her mouth, and the heat she'd drawn in as oxygen became a lit fuse racing through her body.

"Jen."

And then he kissed her again.

Chapter Nine

Trent would drown in this trouble, and be happy to go to the bottom.

Drowning in Jen. The scent and sensations of her. The touch and taste of her.

Her mouth welcomed his tongue. Her hair enveloped his fingers in sliding silk. Her hands brushed and stroked his neck, his jaw, his head.

The heat rose as if kindling, gasoline and wind all hit it at once. A blast of heat so fast and hot it burned right through something in him that had held hard and solid as long as he could remember.

Her skin—revealed to his touch in greedy swaths as he opened her blouse, then her bra—started cool, but in not even a second burned with the same heat. A heat that could only be consumed by the fire that had given birth to it.

She'd opened his shirt, trailed the burn down his chest

with her hands and her lips, lower to where his stomach muscles contracted and jumped. Then she came up, back to his mouth. Kissing, and kissing. Each a blaze in itself.

He stroked her breasts, deserted her mouth only to explore her nipples.

Abruptly, Jennifer slid down his body. He felt the graze of her breasts against his chest like charges that set off larger explosions throughout his body and instantly primed the main fuse.

Those reactions were so strong that it took a couple extra beats to realize several things.

She wasn't headed where his libido had hoped she was heading. Instead, she was curling into him while trying to refasten her bra.

Also, a bobbing light grew brighter and larger as it approached.

As much as he'd been lauded for quick thinking on the football field, it still took him a second to put it all together.

If he'd been turned on like this on the football field, he would have been crushed to smithereens. Then again, he didn't remember being quite this turned on *off* the football field, either.

"What's going on here?" came Darcie's in-charge cop voice.

Trent grabbed the sides of his open shirt and held them to shield Jennifer as best he could from light pouring in through her open window.

"Uh, Darcie—Officer Barrett. It's okay. It's me, Trent."

"Trent? What are you—?" Darcie swallowed the last word.

Clearly she knew what he was doing. The question was whether she realized who he was doing it with.

"This is not a good spot for this, Trent." Her voice was strained.

"Sorry, I wasn't thinking."

"I don't suppose you were." And now he could tell the strain came from efforts not to laugh. "I'd tell you to get a room, but I happen to know you have one over in Pepton. That wouldn't do, though, huh?"

"Not really. And this was rather spur of the moment."

He thought he heard a groan from Jennifer, who still had her head down, so that hot, faintly damp puffs of her breath played across his chest. That was not helping to get his brain back in charge of this production.

"I can't encourage this sort of thing in public under any circumstances, but I do hear there's a spot overlooking that S-bend in the river where people aren't likely to get disturbed."

"Uh, thanks, Darcie."

"You're welcome." That came out a little garbled because she was working so hard at not laughing. "But you cannot do this here. Another officer might have thought you were burglars or something. And if they called for backup…"

He got the picture. Lights, sirens, a whole lot of excitement. Not good.

"I understand, Darcie. Thank you."

"No problem." She backed up a few steps and clicked off the light. "I'll be back in, say, a half hour. I expect everything to be peaceful by then."

"It will be. Thanks again."

She said good night and he heard her retreating steps, then a car door open and close.

Only when the car was gone did Jennifer straighten away from him. She kept her head down, still fumbling with the clasp of her bra.

"Want me to do that?"

"No!"

Her horror at the idea of him putting on a piece of clothing she hadn't complained about him taking off—not to mention his extremely pleasurable exploration of the flesh that piece of clothing had covered—struck him as illogical. But he knew enough about women not to mention that.

"Okay. You want some light?"

"No! No light." She sucked in a breath that hitched in the middle. She started buttoning her blouse, apparently having given up on the bra. "I just want to get out of here. And forget this ever—"

"No you don't."

He clamped his hand around her wrist, halting her from buttoning the shirt to her throat. "You're not going to run off and pretend—"

"I'm not pretending. This was a mistake, Trent. A crazy, stupid mistake. I can't believe I…we…I just can't believe it."

"Tell me why it was a mistake."

"Why?" In three letters, her voice skidded up the register about an octave. If the word had been any longer, she would have had dogs responding by the end of it. "Because we work together. Because you're younger than I am. Because we have nothing in common except this dealership. Because we're just being thrown together by circumstances, not because we're a…a real couple. Because you're Trent *Stenner*—my ex's *brother!* Because the town would go nuts. Because your parents would go nuts. Because the last thing I want to teach Ashley by example is to forget everything else I've taught her the first time some guy kisses her."

And then she delivered the knockout punch.

"Because I don't trust you."

Tell me why it was a mistake.

Was he nuts? He hadn't really said that, had he? He must have still been lost in the hot haze of passion, because he sure hadn't been thinking. But now, sitting in the motel room alone, sleepless hours later, he knew she was right. Absolutely right. It had been a mistake.

For all the reasons she'd listed. And for about another dozen she hadn't gotten to.

He paced to the window. Even without any lamps on, the glow of the muted TV and the night-light in the bathroom reflected the empty room back at him rather than letting him see into the dark outside.

Because we're just being thrown together by circumstances, not because we're a...a real couple.

Liz had said something similar when she broke it off last summer. That circumstances had made them convenient for each other, that they weren't a real couple, that she wasn't even sure they liked each other.

She also had said that she was sure they didn't want the same things.

She wanted a family. And he didn't.

He yanked the cord that closed the drapes, masking the window.

Too bad it didn't shut up the voices.

Linc's voice, followed by his own.

Plenty enough people who don't find what they want in the family they were born into build a good family themselves.

Not me. It's the last thing I want.

And yet there he'd been, kissing Jennifer, wanting a whole lot more.

Jennifer Truesdale. A woman who put her daughter ahead of everything else. A woman who would tie him up in family in ways he couldn't even begin to sort out.

Because the last thing I want to teach Ashley by example is to forget everything else I've taught her the first time some guy kisses her.

Damn right it was a mistake.

Because now he had her taste on his lips. He had the feel of her skin. He had the scent of her hair.

What he didn't have was her.

Because I don't trust you.

Jennifer accepted Darcie's invitation to have a glass of wine and view her house renovations.

Ashley was at the movies with her friends, and after last night's sleeplessness and her difficulty concentrating at the dealership today—even after she'd prevented Trent's efforts to open the subject—the last thing Jennifer wanted was to be alone.

Darcie hadn't said a word about last night, so she must not have known who was with Trent. Jennifer relaxed as they toured the house.

In late spring, Zeke had bought the Barrett family home secretly in order to surprise Darcie and her mother, thinking Martha Barrett had moved out because of money problems. He'd gotten a surprise right back when he discovered she'd moved out so she could move in with the chief of police.

Once Darcie accepted his marriage proposal, they'd decided to renovate the house for themselves. In the meantime, the two of them were living in Darcie's old apartment over the garage whenever Zeke's duties as founder and CEO of Zeke-Tech didn't pull him back to northern Virginia.

First, Darcie gave her a tour, spinning vivid pictures of what the house would look like when it was finished.

Then they sat on the couch in the apartment with a tray on the cushion between them holding wine, their glasses and munchies.

"So, tell me about the wedding plans," Jennifer urged.

If Darcie kept talking, maybe Jennifer would stop thinking about Trent. About what a mistake she had made. What a horrible mistake.

At some level, she'd known she was attracted to him. But she'd succeeded in keeping it under her conscious radar. Now…now, the dragon was out of its cave. The dragon that had spent the night flaming her with memories of his mouth on hers, of the sensation of his short, prickly, yet soft hair against her palm…oh, lord, against her breast. And then his mouth on—

"We're still negotiating the place," Darcie said. "But it's definitely the first weekend in October, because we refuse to wait any longer. Mom and Mrs. Z are in a dither, saying there's not enough time. But all I have to do is suggest that Zeke and I take over the arrangements and they back off. I think they have visions of us in Vegas, married by an Elvis impersonator."

Jennifer laughed. This was what she needed. A good dose of Darcie to take her mind off her troubles. To forget her mistakes.

"So, how's Trent?"

Jennifer started in heated guilt, then masked it with a detailed listing of all the things she'd done and what needed doing at the dealership.

"I didn't ask about Stenner Autos, I asked about Trent Stenner."

She met her friend's curious gaze with her best effort at blandness. "What about him?"

"Is he as hot as he looks?"

Oh, God. Jennifer had awakened so many times during the night in hot, aching want that she'd given up and taken a cold shower around four, then sat on the balcony waiting for dawn. "I don't know what you—"

"Oh, yes, you do, Jennifer. I've seen you two together. I thought at the fireworks…and now I know I'm right."

"No, you're not right." She made the words as stern as she could. Was there also a thread of sadness there?

"Don't tell me you're letting the age thing stop you."

Because you're younger than I am. The memory pricked Jennifer.

"Or the specter of Eric," Darcie continued.

Because you're Trent Stenner—my ex's brother! Because your parents would go nuts.

"You've got to admit that would be horribly awkward—talk about in-law problems!" Jennifer defended herself, producing a laugh. Then she hurriedly added, "If this were anything other than your imagination, I mean."

Darcie sailed on. "Lots of people have in-law problems. You can't let it stop you because it might get complicated. Really complicated," she amended. "If you and Trent get together—"

"Darcie."

"Wait a minute, don't say anything. Let me figure this out. You and Trent getting together would make him both Ashley's stepfather and uncle."

"Not going to happen, Darcie," Jennifer said.

"So when she has kids they could be... Got it! They could be their own mother's cousins."

"Oh, God. That would be worthy of being on *Oprah.*"

"Or *Jerry Springer.*"

Jennifer felt the blood draining from her face, at the same time she caught the contagiously wicked glint in Darcie's eyes. "Don't you laugh, Darcie Barrett, don't you dare."

But she did.

Worse, far worse, she lured Jennifer into joining.

When they were both exhausted, Jennifer flopped back against the cushion, one hand on her aching ribs.

Darcie pushed an item across the tray. "This is for you."

"What is it?"

"The key to the house's back door. You'll need a flashlight, because you can't count on electricity downstairs. But we've kept the electricity to the guest room I showed you, and the bathroom next to it, so Quince can use them when he's in town. He's a great guest. Even changes the sheets before he leaves so it's ready for other guests."

"What?"

"Quince—remember him? The one I wanted to fix you up with? But, oh, no, you had to go for the family plan."

"Not who, Darcie. What's this for?" She pointed at the glinting object. "And why—why would you—?"

"Oh, c'mon, Jennifer. It doesn't take a world-class detective to solve this one. I do have eyes. And I know your clothes. Even if I hadn't caught you guys making out in the dealership's lot—"

Jennifer's effort to protest came out as a choking sound.

"I do know a little something about chemistry, thanks to Zeke."

Darcie's face got that glow she'd had the past few months, and her voice softened, so Jennifer didn't have the heart to interrupt her.

"Add to all that, that I know you," Darcie said. "For starters, I know you would never take Trent back to your apartment with Ashley there. And you wouldn't go to his motel room, because word would be all over Drago before you closed the door. But if you're discreet, like bring one car, put it in the garage and close the door, then there's no reason anybody has to know. Lights are on variable timers to go off and on all over the house. Who's to say that's not the explanation if there are lights at weird hours."

She knew Darcie had kept talking to give her time to recover.

"I know you mean well, Darcie. But, really this isn't necessary. I saw to that."

"Oh, yeah? How'd you do that?"

"I told him all the reasons it never should have happened."

"Reasons besides being on *Jerry Springer?* No." She held

out a hand as if Jennifer had been about to reply. "There's no reason you should tell me anything. Me or anybody else. I know about feeling you have no clue what's going on. But it'll settle down. At some point everything will just be real obvious. At least that's how it worked for me."

"You didn't have a nearly teenage daughter," Jennifer said dryly.

Darcie gave her a considering look that for some reason reminded Jennifer of Trent. "What's that got to do with it?"

"That's the thing about being a mother. You're supposed to be sure of things."

"Nah," Darcie said. "You're supposed to be human and do your best. Besides, I said you didn't owe me or anybody else any explanation. That includes Ashley."

"Well, it's all moot anyway." She gave a shaky laugh. "I told Trent I don't trust him."

"Ouch."

Less than two weeks before the Grand Reopening, Jennifer halted at the threshold of Trent's office when she saw he was on the phone and started to back out. But he waved her in.

By the second day after that encounter in the parking lot, they were close enough to their usual way of dealing with each other that she'd felt confident no one else could sense the underlying tension, though she did.

His gaze followed her as she took the chair across the desk, while he listened intently to whatever was being said on the phone.

He sighed a concession. "Okay… Yes, I mean it.… You know me better than that, Tracy. I'll be there…I've got all the info." He snorted, amusement and annoyance in the sound. "Fine, fax it again just in case.… Yeah, it'll be good to see you, too, Tracy." His voice gentled on those words.

She shouldn't have come in. She should have ignored his gesture. She didn't need to hear his private conversation. She didn't need to know about his life outside of Drago—outside of this building for that matter. He could have a harem of hundreds for all she cared.

No, she definitely shouldn't have come in. Because she had a lot of work to do. She couldn't afford to just sit here.

But could she walk out? Wouldn't that look like…well, something?

She would look through the papers she'd brought in, act as if she'd forgotten something, give him that one-finger-raised be-back-in-a-minute gesture, then slip out. By the time he finished his call she could have gotten all sorts of things done.

Jennifer opened the folder with the list of parts sales from the first weeks of their Web site and started flipping through them. Before she could proceed with her act, however, he was wrapping up the call.

"Right, I'll see you then. Bye, Tracy."

His hand still on the receiver, he gave Jennifer a rueful smile and said, "How'd you like to go to Chicago with me Saturday night?"

Visions of harems didn't exactly burst into oblivion, but they did grow hazy. But that might have been from feeling suddenly light-headed. "What?"

"It's this benefit thing downtown. The wife of a former teammate who's with the Bears now got involved, and she heard I was in the area, so she's twisted my arm to go. It'll be a really nice event—Tracy never does anything halfway. I can guarantee it'll be worth the trip."

"I don't think that's a good idea."

His gaze on her sharpened and the skin over the bones of his face seemed to tighten. But his voice remained easy when he said, "I won't cause you any trouble, Jennifer. You made yourself clear. I wouldn't mistake this for a date, so you needn't worry about that."

"I'm not—" She started to lie before he cut her off.

"It is, however, a great business opportunity. If you knew Tracy, you'd know that the top movers and shakers in the Chicago metropolitan area and beyond are bound to be there—and I do mean bound. She'd tie 'em up and drag 'em if she had to. So think of the contacts you could make. These kinds of contacts can be golden."

To succeed in business, she could not let personal feelings of discomfort prevent her from making the most of opportunities.

Oh, she didn't have any delusions that Stenner Auto could compete with major Chicago area dealers. But they could aspire to nibble market share from outfits in the suburbs always stretching hungry fingers to the west. Why couldn't consumers take a pleasant drive to the country to look for a car? The right contacts might help.

"Golden," she agreed. "What time do we leave?"

"What on earth am I going to wear?"

"The dress you wore at the Lilac Ball," Darcie said.

"It's a dozen years old."

"This is a new group of people—they won't have seen it before."

One of the things Jennifer most liked about Darcie was her hardheaded sensitivity. She didn't ask why Jennifer didn't buy something new, she simply plunged into the problem at hand, recognizing the realities.

"They would have seen the original it was patterned after fifteen years ago when it was in style. This is Chicago," Jennifer said. She sounded remarkably like Ashley in the moment, and she didn't even care. "And these are society types. They'll probably be wearing Versace, Valentino and Dior."

"Sounds like a law firm." Darcie chuckled.

Jennifer gave her a harried glare. "I need to look good—great—for this event. Because it's such a good business opportunity," she rushed to add when Darcie's eyes lit up.

"You can wear my dress—the one I wore to the Lilac Ball. You said it was a classic style, and Zeke sure liked it. Though there's a button or two you'll have to sew back on."

Jennifer forgave her friend's reminiscently lascivious grin. Darcie deserved that good—and apparently hot—memory, especially considering the way she'd suffered when Zeke left the day after the ball. It had taken the dope several long weeks to come to his senses and come back to Darcie.

"It is a classic style and it looks fabulous on you. But in case you haven't noticed, we have different shapes."

"Sure, rub it in," Darcie grumbled.

"You've got to be kidding. You *are* kidding, right?"

"I don't know what you're talking about."

"I sure hope you lie better than that when you have to interrogate dangerous criminals. I am talking about my disbelief that you could still be stuck on that thing from high school of thinking you don't have a good figure. You have a fabulous figure." She eyed her friend's curves. "But that means that, in addition to being several inches shorter than you, *I* don't have enough to fill the top of that dress the way it needs to be filled."

Darcie wouldn't accept that. She made Jennifer try on the dress.

Standing in front of the mirror with the fabulous dress of varied shades of red hanging loosely from her shoulders, Jennifer sighed. This dress matched Darcie's figure the way Darcie matched Zeke.

She sighed again. Would the pieces of *her* life ever fit?

"So, it's a little long," Darcie said. "We can hem it."

"Length isn't the major problem."

"So, we'll take it in."

"We? We both flunked that section of Home Ec. And even if we could…" Jennifer reached behind her and pulled the fabric tight.

"Geez, you look like one of those anorexic Hollywood starlets. Like a Popsicle stick wrapped in pretty fabric."

Jennifer gave a pained chuckle. "Just what I always wanted to hear."

"But you don't usually look like that. You're gorgeous. When you wear that clingy, swingy purple dress, the place has to go under a flood watch for all the men drooling."

This chuckle was more genuine. "Nice image, Darcie."

"Well, it's true. I don't suppose you could wear that purple dress. No, no, you're right. Not for this. Let me think. I'll come up with something."

Which is how Jennifer came to be standing in Josh Kincannon's basement Thursday night trying on dresses.

She'd said absolutely not when Darcie explained that she'd asked Josh if they could try on clothes his designer wife had left behind when she left him and their three children several years ago. But Darcie was driving.

"How could you even ask him, Darcie?" she demanded. "You know how devastated he was when she left, even if he did jump right into Super Dad mode. And how could I think of wearing his wife's dresses?"

"Why not? He's over her now. And the clothes are sitting in the basement. He said he'd tried to ship them to her, but she was out of the country or something and they came back. Xena won't let him get rid of them." Alexis Kincannon, now nine years old, had been nicknamed Xena practically in babyhood for her warriorlike and commanding personality. "He said he'd love to see the things get some use."

"And what's Xena going to say?"

"Are you kidding?" Darcie pulled to the curb in front of the Kincannons' comfortable brick house. "I'm not stupid. I asked her first."

So, Jennifer tried on dress after dress that Melissa Kincannon had designed and made, then left behind, along with her family. The dressing room consisted of ducking behind the trio of tall wardrobe-style moving boxes that held the dresses. Instead of a three-way mirror, she checked her image in two precariously stacked mirrors that left the region of her upper thighs a mystery unless she shifted to just the right angle that then blocked a view of her waist. Her panel of judges, seated in two rows on the stairway, was distinguished and varied.

Darcie, of course. Xena, who added expert commentary. Darcie's mother, whose arrival had surprised Jennifer. And Ashley, who had come with Martha Barrett, and whose arrival had stunned Jennifer.

Darcie had waggled her eyebrows at her to communicate that she'd explain later, and Jennifer had had to be satisfied with that.

Ashley had assumed a veneer of boredom that kept cracking into heated debates with Xena.

"If she's not going to choose the blue one—" Jennifer heard Ashley say from the far side of the moving boxes, referring to a dress she would never in a million years wear in public, since it had taken décolletage to a new low. Xena had said something about her mother being inspired by the movie *Gypsy,* and Darcie had muttered that a stripper wearing that dress would have nothing left to lose. "Then this last red one should be it."

"Blondes can't wear red," Xena declared.

"Says who?" Ashley sounded closer in age to Xena than to the thirty-year-old sophisticate who inhabited her daughter's body all too frequently.

"Everybody knows reds wash out blondes," Xena declared

in eerie imitation of Melissa Kincannon. "Maybe that dark red one from the beginning. The one that's the color with the other name. You know," she insisted, impatient, "like your ring, you said, Mrs. Barrett."

"Garnet," Darcie's mother supplied.

"Eeeuw," Ashley said. "That was an old lady's dress."

"That was from Mom's *African Queen* period. But she didn't want to make it in white. She said it had more depth in that other color."

"Garnet," Mrs. Barrett repeated.

"Are you ready?" Darcie called.

Jennifer stifled a grin. Darcie had about had her fill of fashion.

"Just a second." She zipped herself up, and emerged.

The discourse cut off instantly. The four females stared at her.

"Well?" she asked.

They just kept staring. She went to the stacked mirrors, moving forward and back, trying to see if the narrow-skirted black dress looked as good as it felt. She twisted, trying for a view of the distinctive cutout back.

"That's it," Darcie said, slapping her thighs. "That's the one."

"That's from Mom's *Breakfast at Tiffany's* period." In the mirror, Jennifer saw Xena's pride, as well as a wistfulness quickly hidden.

"I have the perfect necklace for you to wear," Mrs. Barrett said.

"I have an evening bag that'll be great," Darcie said.

"Thank you, thank you both. But what do you think about wearing black in late July?"

"Black is always appropriate for a formal event," Mrs. Barrett said.

"If I looked like that in that dress, I'd wear it as my wedding dress," Darcie said.

"Darcie!" Her mother gasped. "Not black."

"I said *if*."

Jennifer turned to her daughter. "What do you think, Ashley?"

She narrowed her eyes. "You'll have to wear your hair up."

"Good idea, Ash." Darcie nodded.

"But what do you think of the dress, Ashley?" Jennifer persisted, not knowing why she did, fully aware that this could backfire into a snippy comment in a heartbeat. "Is this the one I should wear?"

Ashley looked up. For that instant, she was once more the loving, sweet girl she'd been until this past winter. "You look beautiful."

Then the instant was gone.

"I can't believe you got Ashley to come," Jennifer admitted to Darcie in the car on the way home.

"You kidding? A chance to go through another female's clothes? Did you see the way she coveted that 'slit to the belly button' blue number?"

"Please, don't remind me. But really, Darcie, I was astonished to see her. When I told her I was going to this benefit with Trent—"

"She had a hissy fit."

"She wasn't happy. She's going through a rough time. Plus, she didn't exactly take to Trent, and then there was the guacamole incident. Even when I explained that Saturday is strictly business—"

Darcie cut her a look that Jennifer ignored.

"—she accepted it grudgingly only when she realized it was the same night as Courtney's sleepover."

"I suspect she thinks being rude to Trent somehow upholds her loyalty to her father. Though it's both parents she's worried about."

"Me? There's no reason for her to worry about me."

"Right. No way a kid could ever worry that if her mother falls in love with a guy that the kid might lose her, too. But that's not the most interesting thing. You must be nuts—"

"Definitely nuts," Jennifer said with an attempt at a laugh. "About the guy."

"What?" A surge of panic hit her stomach.

"Yup," Darcie continued as if she hadn't spoken. "Nuts for Trent Stenner. Otherwise you would have jettisoned him the way you've jettisoned other guys at the first sign of disapproval from Ashley. And she always objects if she senses you could really like a guy. "

Feeling as if the car had become a torture chamber, Jennifer forced herself to reason with her best friend. "Darcie, you're talking nonsense. I told you, this is not a date. Trent made that very clear. It's business."

"And that night in his car?"

Heat surged through Jennifer along with memories. When would that stop? "I told you, that was a mistake. One we've put behind us."

"My point still holds, because it has nothing to do with the lies you and Trent might be telling yourselves. For you to go out with Trent—"

"I'm not going out with him. It's not a—"

"—when Ashley disapproves, there's something there for sure."

"Darcie, I'm telling you this isn't a date. I promise you."

Chapter Ten

Bad move, Stenner.

It wasn't the first time Trent had that thought since Tuesday, when he'd invited Jennifer to come to the benefit. The thought had hit almost as soon as the words left his mouth. But he couldn't undo the invitation. Not after his oh-so-clever extolling of the contacts she could make.

Why had he asked Jennifer to be his companion—not his date, just as he'd assured her—to this benefit in the first place?

He had no problem going out alone. He'd even become fairly adept at sidestepping Tracy's attempts to fix him up when he arrived at an event solo.

He couldn't claim to have invited Jennifer because he thought she'd enjoy it, either. Some women, he supposed, would get a kick out of hobnobbing with the city's elite. But that wasn't Jennifer's style.

Heck, she'd looked downright pained when she'd agreed.

She'd tried to hide it with a smile, but that had made her discomfort even more obvious.

So, maybe he should be asking that question, too— Why had she agreed to come?

If he'd had any brain cells left to work on the problem, he should have been able to solve it. But all his brain cells were devoted to reminding himself that this was not a date.

So it didn't matter what Jennifer looked like standing across the hotel ballroom with chandeliers sparkling stars in her hair.

He'd nearly been burned to ash when she opened her apartment door. Seeing the back of the dress when he put the wrap around her shoulders had finished the burn. With her hair up, the dress's low back highlighted the exposed, perfect line of her neck. The drive from Drago to Chicago had tormented him with the desire to lean over and kiss that length.

And the burn was just as hot each time he saw her now.

Not a date. *Not* a date.

Jennifer shook hands with the silver-haired man, smiled and moved away. The books she'd read said closing a conversation was as important a skill as opening one.

She huffed out a breath, and decided she deserved a break.

She'd done darned well, if she said so herself.

Trent had been the perfect companion. He'd stayed by her side at the beginning, introducing her to Tracy and her husband Ben, Trent's former teammate. Tracy, in turn, had introduced them to two other couples. Trent had circulated her through the room for another half hour.

At dinner, he'd made conversation easily with their tablemates, naturally drawing her in, too.

After dinner, he'd asked if she wanted to strike out on her own. When she'd said yes, a flicker of something crossed his eyes before he'd smiled and said, "Go get 'em, killer."

Twice, just as she'd finished a conversation and drifted away, he'd been between conversations, too, and their paths had crossed long enough to check in with each other, to take a few sips from the drink she'd been carting around, and for him to make her smile.

All in all, it had been a perfect evening.

Except for that moment when she'd opened the evening bag Darcie had loaned her to freshen her lipstick and found a key she recognized as the one to the Barrett house glinting up at her from the satin-lined bottom.

Darcie Barrett did not give up.

Jennifer looked around now, not spotting Trent. But she did see her hostess approaching with a determined smile.

"It's a marvelous party," Jennifer said, meeting her partway.

"Thank you. Having everyone willing to come and help out is what makes it." She tilted her head, eyeing Jennifer. "You're remarkably pretty."

Jennifer felt herself stiffen. "Thank you."

Tracy laughed a little. "No need to thank me, it wasn't really a compliment. I've been smiling and handing out compliments so much tonight I think my face will crack if I don't take a break to just be plain honest and nosy. That's why I headed for you when I saw you alone. So, definitely don't thank me. I intend to ignore every one of those signals you're emitting that you want me to butt out, and to satisfy my curiosity."

Jennifer froze. She'd had plenty of people corner her and try to pry into her personal life, but that was in Drago, where she knew the person doing the prying so well that she knew exactly which evasionary tactic would work. She didn't know this woman at all. Except that she was Trent's friend. Why hadn't the books covered this sort of situation?

"The reason I remarked about your being so pretty is it surprised me," Tracy went on. "Trent doesn't usually date remarkably pretty women. Striking, cute, interesting, attractive, yes, but not pretty. So there must be a lot more to you than being pretty."

Solid ground came up under Jennifer's flailing feet and she almost heaved a sigh of relief. "Oh, we're not dating."

"No?"

"No," she replied firmly to Tracy's blatant doubt. "We're business associates. In his family's car dealership."

For a long moment Tracy stared at her. Then her brown eyes widened so much that Jennifer thought her eyelashes were going to meet her hairline. Her mouth formed a circle before it produced a delayed, "Oh…"

"Trent thought this would be a good opportunity for me to meet people who would be good business contacts."

Tracy waved off business with the flip of one elegant hand. "Omigod! Why didn't I put that together? I must have been even more crazed about this benefit than I knew. You're the ex-sister-in-law. The one married to that goon of a brother—Evil Eric."

She immediately gripped Jennifer's forearm. "Sorry—sorry. I shouldn't have called your ex a goon. It's just that we all think they've treated Trent so… Well, we love Trent. He's family."

For absolutely no reason, Jennifer's eyes stung, sharp with salt, but soft with another ingredient she couldn't identify. Trent did have family. A family that loved him and protected him, the way a family should.

"Oh, God. I really am sorry. I didn't mean to make you cry."

"No, no, it's okay." Jennifer found herself smiling at the same time she blinked would-be tears into submission. "You're Linc's sister. I don't know why *I* didn't put *that* together."

"I am. And he says you've got a good head on your shoulders. Not much experience, but lots of potential—and you have no idea what a compliment that is from my brother."

"He's been so wonderful to us. In those first few weeks I must have called or e-mailed him a dozen times a day."

"He loves it. And he thinks the world of Trent. Why, he even had you—"

"There you are." Trent stepped in between them, sliding one arm around Tracy's waist and shifting her to his other side.

Tracy peered around him, grinning at Jennifer. "You get the feeling he doesn't want us to compare notes?"

"Not at all, not at all," Trent said. "It's just that we have a long drive back, so we should get started, and I'm sure your other guests would like to have the pleasure of your scintillating company."

"It's been a pleasure meeting you, Tracy," Jennifer said. "Thank you for letting me come to this wonderful event."

"I'm so glad you could come."

Trent hugged his longtime friend. "I'll talk to you soon, Trace."

"You bet you will. And—" she grinned at Jennifer "—I'll call *you*, too."

Jennifer leaned her head back and watched out the passenger window, relaxed to a near-dozing state. Nerves over how she would conduct herself at a benefit in downtown Chicago were behind her. Done. Now, carried by the security of Trent's capable driving, she could simply be.

Swooping elevated cloverleaf entrances and exits, like some gigantic carnival ride, divided travelers according to their destinations. Interstate signs for Wisconsin, Michigan, Indiana and Illinois jostled for position.

All the places. All the possibilities. All the roads she hadn't taken.

Should she have left Drago, come here to try to find work? Would that have been better for Ashley?

No answers came from the buildings flashing past. Impressionistic layer cakes of gray and tan, utilitarian concrete boxes, odd curves and arches all stating the human need to express individuality. The boxes wider spaced and the trees more numerous. Although no trees could arch over these six lanes of traffic the way trees did over the streets of Drago.

Now, well outside the city, suburbs spread wide blankets of houses. But the Interstate outlasted them, diving into the farm-dotted space.

The moon glinted on the surfaces of road, cornfields, barns and trees. An occasional clapboard farmhouse appeared in the brighter glow of security lights; harsh lighting for houses that, more often than not, showed hard usage, like proud old ladies trying to disguise wear on aging silk dresses. She understood the pride and the determination.

Trent steered smoothly onto the exit to Drago, then down the highway.

Her heart thudded hard in her chest as they slipped through the night. This was her land. This was where she belonged. She had made the right choice in staying in Drago. The right choice for herself and for Ashley.

Everything would be okay. They'd work out their mother-daughter differences. The dealership would thrive. They'd have financial security. Maybe get a house.

"Are you awake?" Trent asked quietly.

She rolled her head toward him and smiled. "Yes. It's been a wonderful drive."

She saw only the profile of his smile. "We aim to serve."

"It's been a wonderful night, too. Thank you for asking me."

He rolled to a stop at the light on Main Street—its red had a knack for catching solo cars in the dead of night.

He faced her. "Thank you for coming with."

She knew what he was going to do. She didn't move. Not as he leaned toward her. Not as his mouth touched hers.

It was a brief kiss. Neither hard nor soft. Neither passionate nor "just friends." Nothing connected except their lips.

And then he straightened, and eased the car forward.

"Trent—"

"Just let it be, Jen. Believe it or not, you can trust me, including about this. So, just let it be."

So she let it be. Even though it felt as if a solitary key in the bottom of her purse might burn a hole right through it.

Jennifer sat on her balcony in the early-morning light, sipping water and listening to her town stir, called first by birdsong, then the less subtle exhortation of church bells.

She felt as if she were standing on the edge of something. The way she used to feel at the swimming hole as a kid. Standing on the dive-rock, poised to slice through the air, then into the cool water, shadowed by surrounding trees. Down into its dark mysteries. Finally, pulling the water to start the ascent, kicking toward the growing light, kicking hard, that last time as she broke the surface, head back, face to the sky.

Somewhere in the distance, a screen door clanked closed, and a woman's voice called for Gary to hurry or they'd be late. A child's voice responded with "Okay, Mom," sounding totally unhurried.

Jennifer sipped from her glass, her gaze falling on the evening purse she'd brought out with her. Only because she hadn't emptied it last night, so it still held her cell phone.

Along with other things.

She recrossed her legs and tugged the edge of her robe into place.

She wasn't going to dive into anything. Not anything as

familiar as the old swimming hole and definitely not anything as unfamiliar as…well, unfamiliar.

Oh, but it *was* nice when he'd smiled at her. And the way his eyes looked in that second before he'd kissed her…and in the seconds after.

He'd insisted on walking her to the door and waiting while she checked that all was right inside. She'd wondered if he would kiss her then.

He hadn't. He'd taken both her hands in his, looking down at them, then simply said good-night and smiled at her again.

Her cell phone rang. The ordinary sound jolting through Jennifer like an alarm.

It was Jill, Courtney's mother. Calling two hours before the scheduled time to pick up Ashley.

"What's wro—?"

Before she could finish the universal maternal concern, Jill said, "Ashley's fine. I wanted to talk to you before you pick her up, though."

"I'll be there in fifteen minutes."

"Let's meet at the café? My husband will stay with the girls. They're all sound asleep now."

Jennifer was there waiting when Jill slid into the seat opposite her in the back booth with the wan smile of an adult who'd hosted a sleepover.

"Coffee," she said with deep gratitude when she saw that a steaming cup awaited her. "I've already had two cups and I still feel half-dead."

Jennifer barely curbed her impatience while the woman took a sip.

"I'm sorry to be mysterious about this, Jennifer, but I wanted to talk to you out of Ashley's hearing. She slipped out of the house last night—well, really this morning. About two."

"Slipped out," Jennifer repeated.

"To meet a boy. Nothing happened." The other woman ran the words together as if they were one. She reached across and put her hand over Jennifer's. "Nothing happened," she repeated. "As far as Ron and I could tell, nobody was ever even there. I heard the girls sounding more and more excited, but trying to be more quiet than usual—you know what I mean?"

Jennifer nodded numbly.

"It was the quiet that really alerted me—all the shushing each other. I went to the family room, and they were all glued to the windows, trying to see out. A quick head count, and I grabbed Ron out of bed and we went outside. She was out by the street. She said she was waiting for a boy named Jonas. Do you know him?"

Oh, God. Not just a boy, but a nearly sixteen-year-old boy. "He works part-time at the dealership."

Jill made a face. "I should have remembered that. Well, as I said, we never saw him, and Ron looked around pretty thoroughly. Ashley just blurted out his name when Ron demanded—in that 'I am the father' bass that always gets to Courtney—to know what she was doing outside.

"As for the girls, I gave them all a stern talking-to, locked the outside door and kept the key."

"I'm so sorry, Jill. I'm so terribly sorry."

Jill shook her head. "Ashley went out, but they all participated. Looking back, I knew they were egging someone on to something, I just didn't know what. So I hold them all responsible—and I told them that."

Jennifer didn't doubt the other woman's sincerity. But that didn't change that Ashley had been the only one to leave the house and go to meet a boy—a much older boy.

* * *

"We were just going to talk." Ashley drew her leg up on the couch after Jennifer ordered her to sit. "They made a big drama of it. It was no big deal."

A *ping* of acid-sharp panic plucked against Jennifer's ribs at Ashley's defiance.

"It *is* a big deal," she said. "To start, you left without permission."

"They never said—"

"Ashley Elizabeth Stenner. It doesn't matter what they said or didn't. *You* know you are not to do that. Do not tell me you didn't."

Her daughter's mulish expression didn't change, but she held her tongue.

"You know you would never have received permission, so you sneaked out. In the middle of the night. I can't begin to tell you how disappointed I am in you. When did Jonas arrange this meeting with you?"

For the first time, Ashley's expression softened, looking vulnerable.

"I, uh, told him about the sleepover. And he said that was, you know, cool. He was interested, really interested. And I said I could get outside if I wanted to, if he wanted to talk or something."

The ton of worry that had clamped down on Jennifer's heart lightened by a bare ounce. Maybe…maybe this wasn't what she'd feared. Maybe…

"And what did Jonas say?"

"He laughed. Not at me," Ashley added, instantly defensive. "Laughed like it was cool. So I knew he wanted me to get out. So we could talk."

"Ashley—"

"You don't understand!"

Ashley's face crumpled, making her look so much like she had as a baby that Jennifer's breath caught in her throat. Her daughter. Her baby.

At some level Ashley recognized that this boy, this object of her first crush, wasn't really interested in her. And it hurt. It hurt her so much that she wouldn't—maybe she couldn't—see it. But Jennifer was certain her daughter had no grasp of another aspect of this crush. A crush on an unattainable football player who couldn't be bothered with her—just like her father.

"He talks to me," Ashley wailed. "To *me!* He's going to be the star of the high school football team, but he likes to talk to *me*."

"Ashley," Jennifer said gently, "Jonas is in high school. He's—"

"You're horrible! You go off with *him,* you're always off with *him*. He's more important to you now. But you won't let me have anybody!"

It took Jennifer a second to untangle the pronouns. "This has nothing to do with Trent. Or me. It's—"

"I hate him! He's more important to you than I am, more important than anybody."

"That's not true!"

"God, you just don't want me to be popular!" Ashley exclaimed in another of her abrupt turns. "You think you're the only one who can be popular in this family. But I can be. I will be. Just you wait. I will be. Because Jonas likes me. He doesn't think I'm some stupid kid, and he's the star! The team's best player! Everyone says so. I won't let you stand in my way. I won't!" Her wail desolved into sobs and she stormed off.

He doesn't think I'm some stupid kid, and he's the star! The team's best player! Everyone says so.

And if only she could stand within the glow of his star, everyone would think Ashley Stenner was okay.

The slam of her daughter's bedroom door reverberated through Jennifer's bones with the truth she had feared for months.

Ashley Stenner was becoming Jennifer Truesdale.

Ashley was on the same path to making the same mistakes that she had. Her own teen years might serve as a cautionary tale…if Ashley were old enough and wise enough to recognize that. But if she were, then they wouldn't be in this situation.

What mattered now was making sure that her daughter saw her making good decisions, being a good businesswoman, making her own way. Ashley needed to look up to her so she would follow Jennifer's current path, not her past one.

Jennifer went to her room, took the key to the Barrett house from the evening bag and put it in the change section of her wallet. She would return it to Darcie the next time she saw her.

Jennifer stepped into Trent's office almost as soon as he arrived Monday morning. He knew that wasn't a good sign.

"Trent—"

"I thought we could go to a movie next weekend."

"Trent—"

"I know it means an expedition to get to a theater. But I've got a craving to be overcharged for popcorn, have a hard time hearing the dialogue over the audience and step in goo that makes my shoes stick to the floor. Can't go this weekend because of the Reopening. But next weekend is the last one before practice starts, so that works. You pick the movie— though a big screen is wasted without a car crash, explosion or battle."

She sucked in a breath, and he knew the answer wasn't simply *no*. It was *never*.

"Trent, I'm sorry if you misunderstood—" she shook her head at herself "—if I misled you Saturday. After telling you it was not a date, I sent mixed signals, and I apologize for that. It was wrong."

He'd expected backtracking. It's why he'd hit her so fast with the idea of another date—and Saturday had been a date, damn it—so he would have time to work on her, get her over the hurdle of going on what they both would acknowledge as a date. But this, this was something else.

"What happened?"

Her head snapped up. So much swirled around in the drowning blue of her eyes that he felt it like a punch.

"Nothing happened."

"Has anybody ever told you you're a rotten liar, Jen?"

She turned away.

"I'm sorry, Trent. Truly. You have every right to be angry after Saturday. But it would be an untenable situation to have any relationship other than business colleagues under the circumstances. The circumstances here at the dealership, I mean. Because we're coworkers. Business associates. And that's all we can be."

She'd overdone it. All that emphasis on the dealership and business. It was a misdirection play. And he wasn't falling for it.

"Ashley," he said.

She spun around to him. "What? No. I told you—"

"I know what you told me. And I know the bits and pieces I heard at the café."

"Oh, God." She pressed her fingertips to her temples. "I should have known. In this town, I should have known."

"Something about sneaking out. She was at a sleepover, right?"

Her sigh seemed to come from the core of the planet. "Yes.

But… Oh, God. I might as well tell you, before you come to even worse conclusions."

He'd had people confide in him before, but didn't remember any who had been less happy about it. At the end of her tale, with her working so hard to not cry that it would have been easier on both of them if she'd just gone ahead and let the tears fall, he waited to be sure—sure she wouldn't say anything more and sure she wasn't going to give them both a break and go ahead and cry.

Then he spoke. "I'll fire him today."

Her head jerked up. He was glad to see the tears receding under the effect of her surprise. "No, I told you, I really don't think it's his fault."

Trent couldn't pin down the itch in him that wanted not only to fire the cocky kid, but to pop him one. He reined it in with reluctance as he recognized Jennifer wasn't going to let him scratch that itch.

"Then what do you want me to do?"

More surprise washed across her eyes. "Nothing. This has nothing to do with you. I told you only because you'd already heard pieces of it and… And…." She shook her head. "I seem to always tell you more than I intend."

He stared unfocused through the window into the show-room. "If you really think this is just a case of a girl's first crush, what's worrying you so much?"

Her response took so long in coming that he started to think she wasn't going to answer.

"You said that sometimes when parents get a child who's different from the kind they expected or wanted, that they can have trouble understanding or connecting with that child."

"Yeah." He remembered that conversation. Standing in the open service bay door while the storm brewed. *That's awful,* she'd said. He should have known she was thinking about her daughter.

"I worry that I put my expectations between me and Ashley. That—"

"That you're human?"

She frowned.

"You worry that you're human," he explained. "Because every human being puts expectations on everybody else."

After a pause, she gave a single nod. "Okay. But with Ashley—"

"She's a kid. Worse, she's the not-yet-beautiful daughter of a beautiful mother."

Heat shimmered between them for a second, burning the oxygen in his lungs, singeing in the blood pooling fast in his groin.

He looked away. Had to. Self-preservation kicked in at the last second. And finally, a lick of sense reported for duty.

He cleared his throat. His toes curled in his shoes as if they were holding on to a cliff edge. She looked slightly dazed. Unfocused. He knew what it would take to snap her out of this trance. One word.

"Ashley—" *yup, that did it* "—is dealing with all that. Give the kid a break. More important, give yourself a break. Wanting the best for her isn't the same as not accepting her for who she is. You're a great mother, Jen."

She tried to smile. His imagination thought it had faint tendrils of steam still attached to it.

He continued. "I understand if you're worried what people will think of you as a mother, but you can't really believe—"

"No." The word was fierce. "I'm not worried what kind of mother people think I am. I'm worried what kind of mother I *am*."

Chapter Eleven

In four and a half hours, at 10:00 a.m., the doors of Stenner Autos would officially reopen for business. Jennifer thought she might be sick.

She hadn't been able to sleep. She left Ashley a note and came to check her list one more time.

She'd forgotten something. She was sure she'd forgotten something. But every item on her list was checked off. So what…?

Trent strode into her office.

That was it. The alarm system. She'd failed to turn the alarm system back on after she came in.

Without a word, he took the legal pad with her checklist out of her hand and replaced it with a cup of coffee.

"Decaf with lots of milk," he said. "The last thing you need is caffeine or acid. Now, relax. It's going to be fine."

She meant to ask him what he was doing here, making it

sound as if she weren't glad to see him. What came out was, "How do you know it's going to be okay?"

"I know because we have one of the smartest women I know running Stenner Autos."

She stared at him blankly.

He leaned forward from his seat on the corner of her desk. "That's you, Jen. I'm talking about you."

"Oh. Thank you."

"Hey, that was a compliment."

"I know. I said thank-you. I've been thinking about the display of used cars. If we—"

"No. Not until you tell me why you flinched."

"I didn't flinch."

"The hell you didn't. I say you're smart and you look like I'd just slapped you with a raw fish."

She opened her mouth to deny it again. Instead, laughter came out.

She put her hands over her mouth, as appalled as she would have been if she'd belched, but the laughter kept coming. Until it brought tears.

Finally, with mingled sighs and minisobs, she got her breathing under control.

"Okay," he said, "that was good for you. You certainly needed it."

"You're right, I did. Thank you." She meant it this time.

"You're welcome. But if you think that's going to get you out of telling me why you flinched when I said you're one of the smartest women I know, you're wrong."

"It's nothing, really. I just…" He locked gazes with her, implacable. She cleared her throat. "It's something my mother used to say to me."

"And that was?" he prompted.

. "'There's no such thing as too pretty. But you can be too smart for your own darned good.'"

"You're kidding. What century did she come from?"

She chuckled, but it felt dry and tight. "It took me a while to realize that it was how she negotiated the world. Most people, I think, blend a lot of ways in order to negotiate the world. But some specialize. Some use smarts, some use anger, some use manipulation, some use niceness. My mother mostly used her prettiness. And she trained me the same way."

"That's not true. You work too damned hard to think you're getting by on your looks."

"Damn right I work hard. That's part of her training. You have no idea how much hard work went into meeting her standards. There was no question of *getting by* on looks, not with my mother. I've often thought that if she had applied all the energy she put into appearances to business, she'd be CEO of General Motors by now, and they'd be doing a lot better."

She saw a certain look in his eyes and she shook her head. "It wasn't that bad. Nothing like with your family. I know my parents love me in their way. And I've realized the prettiness is just how my mother interacted—connected—with my father. It worked for them, and she thought it would work for me, so that's what she taught me."

"'No one truly knows what goes on inside a marriage. Sometimes not even the two people who are married.' My mother said that to me recently."

She smiled slightly. "Who knew Mother Stenner could be so wise?"

He muttered something, then added, "But for you to be taught that you shouldn't use your brain—that's damned near criminal."

"Why do you think that's worse than how your parents— your father—treated you?"

That silenced him. Because as much as they talked around

the edges of his nonrelationship with his father, he never got to the heart of it.

"It wasn't like I was emotionally abused or neglected," she said. "My parents did the best they could. It's just…"

"That you want better for Ashley."

"Yes." He knew. He understood. Eric never had. How strange, his own daughter and he had never understood about wanting more for her. Wanting *better*, as Trent said.

"I've learned—a lot—from the mistakes I've made. I want Ashley to learn those lessons without having to go through the mistakes."

"Sometimes lessons don't take hold if you don't learn them through knocks on the head."

"Sometimes knocks on the head put you so low you never get up."

His quick nod acknowledged she might have a point…and she might not.

Then he smiled, slow and wide. The smile that changed his face from darkly interesting to heart-hammering fascinating.

"What?" she demanded, trying to stop herself from smiling back.

"You get a look now and then that kept reminding me of something. I just figured out what—Ashley when she was learning to walk. A look of absolute determination, followed by absolute satisfaction that she wasn't holding on to anyone or anything, but was standing on her own two feet."

Jennifer Truesdale was more than happy to get off her feet by the end of this business day, some two weeks into the new life of Stenner Autos.

She took her shoes off and set them on the desk next to her purse. The place had closed hours ago and she was alone, so there was no reason to keep the darned things on.

There was no reason to go home immediately, either, since Ashley was at Mark and Amy's house. Mark had been calling "just to talk," which was starting to seem normal. He and Amy had surprised her by coming to the dealership the day after the reopening. "Not back together yet, but better," Mark told her. They'd also brought her parents, who had seemed pleased for her, if a little vague on the details of what she was doing.

That's when the idea of Ashley visiting them before school started had been hatched.

Things were going well. With her family. With the dealership. With her running the operation. With Trent coaching. Even with Ashley, who'd served out her two-week grounding with no more eruptions.

Yes, things were going well. Not absolutely smoothly, but nothing she hadn't been able to handle. Although there was an odd blip on the statement from the bank. She'd have to look at that more closely.

They'd sold their first car the first day they were open for business—a reliable used model to Yolanda Wellton, Warren's mother.

By the next weekend, when Trent's friends Ben and Tracy came out to see Trent—and for Ben to sign autographs that drew Bears fans to the showroom—they'd sold six cars.

Trent had insisted she join him and Ben and Tracy for dinner afterward. And they'd had a lovely evening. Though there'd been an awkward few moments when Tracy cornered her in the ladies' room and refused to believe there was nothing romantic going on with Trent.

He hadn't repeated his invitation to the movies. So that was good. Very good.

"You didn't turn the security system on again."

"Oh! You scared me, Trent."

It was a lie. Her heart had started hammering when she'd

seen him leaning against the doorjamb of her office, but it wasn't from fear.

"Good. Hope you're scared into turning the alarm on from now on."

"What are you doing here?"

"Saw your light on my way back from the high school. You shouldn't be working so late."

"Look who's talking, Mr. Coach Stenner, just leaving the high school. Besides, there's a withdrawal on the bank statement I want to look at. I could show you—"

"Oh, God. Please don't make me look at bank statements now. That session last week was bad enough. C'mon." He jerked his head toward the front door. "It's time for you to be in—to go home."

A pulse of heat gripped her, her heartbeat skittered. All because he'd started to say *in bed*.

"You're right." She levered herself up, hooking her shoes with two fingers and her purse strap with the other hand. "I'm not even going to take paperwork home tonight."

"Living wild," he said from the doorway.

She smiled as she came around the desk.

Just before she passed him in the doorway, he flipped the light switch. She stopped and turned toward him.

With the dark office on one side and the lighted hall on the other it was like the day he'd arrived, facing each other in the showroom, light on half of his face, dark hiding the rest of it.

But now she knew him. She didn't need the light to see all of him. To know all of him. To know the good man he was.

She leaned up and kissed him.

As simple a kiss as he had given her in the car the night of the benefit.

But after her lips left his, she didn't step back. She held still, and felt his even greater stillness. With his head bent, she felt the rhythm of his breath on her cheek, a whisper of it on the side of her throat, as he must feel the rhythm of hers on his skin.

She dropped the shoes, freeing her hand to curve around the back of his neck, to feel the soft-harsh prickle of his hair against her palm. She didn't need to draw him to her. He bent to meet her mouth. Kissing the side of it. Then letting her capture his bottom lip between hers.

Kissing. And kissing again. New angles, different pressures.

She dropped her purse, and used both hands to explore the shape of his skull, to hold him.

He gripped her shoulders, pulled her tight against his hard chest.

Without warning, his hold changed. He grasped her shoulders and put her away from him, against one side of the door frame, while he remained at the far side.

"We can't do this, Jen."

"Why?"

His mouth twitched, even while lines drew it tight. "Aren't you the one who had all the reasons—we work together and I'm younger and you want nothing to do with the Stenners. And you don't trust me."

"Trent. I shouldn't have—"

"You're right. You had no cause to trust me. But I'll give you reason now. I won't promise anything but to tell you the truth. I want you, Jen. I want to make love to you every way we can think of. So don't do this if that's not what you want, too."

Each breath burned her lungs. Each pulse of blood seared her veins.

She reached down for her purse, opened the change keeper and found what she was looking for without fumbling.

She gripped the solitary key in her fist.

"It's what I want, too."

* * *

Trent didn't ask why they'd come to Darcie and Zeke's under-construction house instead of going to his motel or her apartment.

He wouldn't have taken her to that motel regardless. Even if it wouldn't have led to gossip, it wasn't what he wanted for her. And her apartment…even with Ashley away, he wasn't surprised Jennifer didn't take him there. It would be too much of a declaration, letting him too deeply into her life.

He mentally stepped around that thought, watching her.

She switched on a small light on the dresser, setting her purse and the key there.

Echoing her moves without coming close enough to crowd her, he went to the nightstand, turning that lamp on low, dropping his car keys there, then adding the condom packets he pulled from his wallet.

Her gaze seemed to stick on the glint of those foil packets.

If she wasn't sure… It might kill him, but they would not do this if she wasn't sure.

He didn't move, waiting.

With her gaze still on the packets, she stepped out of one shoe, then the other.

He started to breathe again. He balanced on one foot to remove shoe and sock, then freed his other foot. His shirt followed in a hurry.

But with his hands on the snap of his jeans, he slowed.

Jen still wasn't looking at him. He'd have traded his best season in the NFL to know what she thought—better yet, what she felt—at that moment. She unhooked the waist of her skirt, unzipped the back and let it drop, leaving her in a blouse that teased the tops of her thighs and whatever she wore underneath.

Trent couldn't imagine anything hotter than Jen stripping for him. But this wasn't a tease that flirted with heat and humor.

Head down, she started unbuttoning her blouse.

He watched her, looking for doubt, for regret, for the flicker that would say she had changed her mind, that her mind had overruled her heart.

What he saw was that she was shy. Not uncertain, exactly, but nervous.

Her eyes came to his as he closed in on her, her fingers slowing with their work, then stopping.

He came in close, but not quite touching. Her hands dropped to her sides.

His gaze following his own movement, he put his right palm on her chest, flat against the center of her breastbone, the tips of his fingers reaching to her throat. Making no attempt to even brush the rise of her breasts at either side of his hand. Not stroking, not moving at all.

Just his palm, solid and still, against her flesh-covered bone.

Then he looked into her eyes, already locked on his. Those marvelous eyes that could hold a life, a heart, a soul, all in shades of blue.

Under his palm he felt her heartbeat, jittery at first, settle to a solid rhythm that quickened. But this quickening wasn't a sprint, it was a slow, steady climb that picked up his own heart rate, connecting them, pulsing them in sync.

Harder, then faster, then harder still.

Her chest was rising and falling in quick, harsh breaths, his hand riding with it. From some distance, he realized his own chest was doing the same.

Her lips parted. A sound came from them. Not a word, just a sound. Then, "Trent."

For a dozen more torturous beats of their hearts he waited, still connected, still in sync. Reluctant to lose this, yet knowing so much more could come.

A groan wrenched from his throat and he swept her up, an arm under her knees, her arms locked around his neck.

He followed her down to the bed, the need driving now. And hers as demanding as his.

They were united in this, too—a bare restraint, layered over the hunger, which both made the hunger stronger and the feeding of it sweeter.

He refused to tear her blouse, unbuttoning the last few buttons with concentrated caution. She unzipped his jeans with precision. He unhooked her bra and pulled it away from her in measured movements. She slid down the bed to draw his jeans and briefs free, each inch a deliberate decision. He repaid the favor—and the torment—with her panties. She positioned the condom with exquisite care. So exquisite that he had to stop her twice, his hands over hers, while he regained restraint.

Finally, naked, he rose over her, her hands at his ribs.

"Jen?" he asked. Because what he wanted for her was no regrets.

"Yes," she said.

She skimmed her hands across his ribs, then down, his muscles dancing in teeth-clenching reaction. She guided him to her entrance, opening to him.

Hunger roared hard against the veneer of restraint. He stroked into her, felt her arch under him, against him.

"Jen, are you—?"

"Okay. I'm okay. Don't—" she raised her hips against him "—stop."

He didn't. He couldn't. Not with her body and her voice surrounding him.

Need and hunger shredded restraint in a stroke.

There was only Jen. Soft. Strong. Yielding. Powerful. Holding. Meeting. Straining.

All that she was swirled around him, in him. Circling him,

twisting him as he tried to stay with it, to hold on to control even with restraint washed away.

He felt the power growing.

The eddy rose, with him, then higher and higher. Over his head, sucking him in, so he spun with it. Faster and harder. Until his lungs burst with the hoarse, harsh cry of it. And he drowned.

In Jen. For Jen.

They lay on their sides, facing each other. His bottom arm stretched across the mattress between them, his hand curved around the back of her neck. Her bottom arm crossed over his as she rested the back of her fingers against his jaw.

In her eyes, he saw possibilities. Possibilities he had never imagined for himself.

Possibilities he feared he could never fulfill for her.

"Jen—"

"Shh. Not now, Trent. Not yet."

Her voice, just her voice, had him hard again.

Maybe it was the memory of how that voice had sounded calling his name as she climaxed.

She took his top arm from where it had rested at her waist, and positioned it so his palm was once more flat against her breastbone, then she put her own palm against his breastbone.

Their heartbeats stuttered, raced, then settled. As they lay there, looking into each other's eyes, they felt the heartbeats come together. Then slowly begin to rise, each beat harder and faster than the one before.

Jennifer woke without doubt. Without confusion. Without fuzziness.

Clear and sharp and sure. She knew where she was and why and with whom.

Trent.

That's the way she'd awakened each time they had made
love in these three nights before Ashley's return.

During the day, they worked as usual: her, all day at the dealership; him, splitting between coaching and the dealership.

At night they came back to this bed in the guest room of
Darcie's house.

He brought her a new rose each night. She didn't know
whose garden he was raiding, but they were lovely.

Sitting on the bed, they ate peach pie and cinnamon ice
cream from Loris's Café. He talked about coaching, about the
individual players and about the team. She talked about the
dealership, its progress, the concerns. Stenner Autos remained
in the red, but it wasn't bleeding Trent's money as badly after
only a few weeks of being open. She was proud of that.

Once, she brought up the sales of the old parts, how the
effort was picking up steam, having already paid for the cost
of the Web site. She'd said Franklin had done them a favor by
accumulating those parts, and he might enjoy hearing that he
was contributing to the dealership's revival.

But Trent teased her about bringing the bottom line into
the bedroom, and closed the conversation with a kiss.

She would have liked to have talked to him more about his
feelings about his family. About his childhood. About what
was happening between them. But any time she considered
opening one of those doors, she had a vision of Trent opening
doors that she'd kept closed.

So they didn't talk of important things. They made love.
Long and slow, fast and hard. Always good.

And each time she woke to certainty, and to Trent.

Solid and real, he lay on his stomach beside her now. No,
half entwined with her. His arm angled across her torso, his
face turned on the pillow so each of his breaths breezed her
shoulder. And she was half entwined with him. Lying not

quite on her side, with the hand closest to him curled under his side and her opposite leg flung over his.

She listened to his breathing—felt his breathing—and tried to make sense of her own emotions. How could this be? How could she feel so certain?

"What are you thinking?" His voice was as deep as the black of his lashes, as rough as the stubble on his chin.

"I'm—I'm thinking that bodies are weird."

He chuckled. "There goes my ego."

"No, I meant mine."

"Weird is not the word that comes to mind." He kissed her shoulder. Then skimmed his mouth down to her nipple, circling it with his tongue, drawing on it until she moaned.

She held his head to bring his mouth to hers, kissing him, long and slow.

But when the kiss ended, she came back to the topic. "But I'm serious. Bodies truly are weird."

"Uh-huh." He nibbled at her shoulder.

"I was never more comfortable in my skin than when I was pregnant with Ashley. And at the same time it was as if it wasn't my body at all. As if an alien had taken it over and I was just along for the ride. That's sort of how I feel when we make love."

She expected him to tease that she was likening him to an alien taking over her body. Instead, he propped his head on his hand and watched her, his eyes solemn.

"You feel the most comfortable in your skin when we're making love?"

"Yes...well, no." She had said that, hadn't she? "I mean, because it's not exactly a comfortable sort of thing. But the most like I belong, like—" Like she was doing something higher, belonged to something bigger than herself. The way she'd felt when she was carrying Ashley. So she forgot herself. Lived beyond her body, beyond herself. But she couldn't tell him that. It sounded too…too big. "Like I did when I was pregnant."

She shifted one shoulder, acknowledging her verbal ineptitude.

"Would you like to be pregnant again? Have more kids?"

"You know, I never thought I would ever want to for a long time. But I think it's connecting with Mark, and even some with my parents that has me feeling different. My family isn't perfect, but there's good in them. I think there must be good in every family."

He said nothing.

"No family's all bad," she added.

Even if he argued with her, it would mean talking about it. It would open the subject.

"So, now you're thinking you'd like to have more babies."

"I doubt I'll be in a place in life where it would be right to have another baby, to give a child stability and the kind of home…" She couldn't finish the banalities. "Yes, I'd like to have more babies. But I accepted a long time ago that I won't."

The next two weeks were an exercise in juggling.

She had a daughter and the dealership pulling her away from him. He had the football team and the dealership pulling him away from her. And they both had desire drawing them together.

But there was no time and even less privacy. She couldn't leave Ashley alone at night and they couldn't use Darcie's guest room during the day with the renovators there.

Alone in her windowless office with the door closed, Trent had groaned, but said, "Okay. But I get to hold your hand at dinner."

"Trent, I don't think that's a good idea."

"Hey, even the high school kids can hold hands in public."

"I meant dinner. It's just that everyone would read so much into it. You know what Drago's like."

"So? Let everyone read. Who cares?" He looked at her. "Uh-huh. You care. You don't want anyone to know."

"It's not the way you make it sound. But there's the situation here at the dealership—"

"Yeah, I bet there's never been a relationship between people who work together."

"I have Ashley to consider."

"Ah."

"What does that mean?"

"It means I understand that you don't want to leave her alone at night. And I understand you wanting to keep our making love private. But at some point, you're going to have to break it to her that I'm in your life, so dinner doesn't seem unreasonable."

"There's been so much going on this summer, so much has changed, I just… Not yet."

He'd left then. She'd known he wasn't happy. But she couldn't just breeze into Ashley's room one night and say, *Oh, by the way, I'm involved with Trent, who happens to be both your uncle and the man you seem to like least in the world.*

She couldn't.

He hadn't said anything more about it. And they'd even found one night last week when they'd worked so late that everyone else had left…. And then her windowless box of an office had become a haven, with the door locked and some creative use of her desk chair.

She had welcomed his kiss, his arms, his body, feeling him slide inside her with a rightness that sang along her skin and deep in her soul.

They would work this out.

It needed time. That was all. Some time.

Chapter Twelve

"Hi, Jonas."

Trent barely recognized that happy chirp as Ashley's voice.

He held his position bent double in the backseat of the black sedan Jonas had supposedly finished cleaning. Trent had been pressed into service checking used cars because Jennifer was up to her neck in dealing with the new cars that would be coming in. He'd found cigarette butts under the driver's seat and had collected sixty-four cents from the floor under the passenger seat when he heard Ashley's voice.

He raised his head and, with the car door open, he could see her, Jonas and Barry over by the car wash.

She was smiling as if she'd just won the lottery, with her jackpot Jonas's face. Trent happened to know that Jennifer had told her to stay away from the boy.

If Jonas's bored mumble was a greeting, it wasn't much of one.

"I thought I'd come see what you're doing," she said brightly.

"I'm working. What does it look like? Go away."

"Oh. I just…" Even from this distance, Trent saw color surging into her face. She leveled her chin the way he'd seen her mother do, and walked away.

Trent came up behind the boys before either knew he was there.

"Jonas," he barked from just behind the kid's shoulder.

He pitched forward, knocking his head against the car's side panel and swearing.

When he saw who it was, he scrambled up—a task made more difficult because Trent's position crowded him against the car—and muttered an apology for cursing.

"Barry, take a break," Trent ordered, not taking his gaze off Jonas.

Jonas looked anywhere but at Trent. When his gaze fell on the sedan, he said. "I didn't get all the way finished with that one yet. Barry must have moved it by mistake. I know my initials are on the form, but—"

"What do you think you're doing with my niece, Jonas?" Trent could barely believe the words came out of his own mouth. Where the hell had this surge of protectiveness come from?

"Huh? Your niece? Oh. Ashley? Nothing. I mean, I asked some stuff about you and she talked about her father and now she just keeps bugging me." The kid came to a full stop. His mouth opened so wide Trent thought he could see his tonsils. "You don't mean— You can't. My God, she's a *kid!*"

Jonas's reaction was unfeigned. A knot eased from Trent's gut.

"Yeah," he said, his voice so low Jonas had to go still and intent to hear it. "She is a kid. And you stay the hell away from her."

"I will. I— Yes, sir. Yes, sir."

He was talking to Trent's back.

God, he better be careful or he'd be acting as though Ashley were his kid. He'd be well and truly caught, not just in a family, but in the last family on earth he should be in.

"Be careful of this step."

Trent had her hand gripped in his, and shone the flashlight over the step he was on and she was about to climb.

The deconstruction of Darcie's house was in full swing. "This is crazy," she muttered as Trent tugged her along the hallway.

"A little chaos is a small price to pay," Trent said, sweeping aside protective plastic and opening the door to the bedroom that formed an oasis.

An oasis within the construction and an oasis in their lives.

"I know why I'm in this," Jennifer said, unbuttoning his shirt. "You're kind. You're down-to-earth. You're capable. You're comfortable with who you are and where you are. You're just so *sane*. You're—"

"You are going to get to sexy eventually, aren't you?" he demanded, holding up the sock he'd just shed.

She laughed. "And you're sexy. Incredibly, incredibly sexy." She kissed his chest, then straightened. "And then there's me. I'm a mess. With a daughter who makes me more of a mess every day. Why would you want to get involved with us? How does it benefit you?"

"You mean besides the obvious?" Having disposed of her blouse, he made a lightning strike to kiss, then suck, then soothe with another kiss the delicate skin where her shoulder met her throat.

She sighed with pleasure. "Yes," she said. "Besides that."

"Then the answer is the same to both questions—why I'd want to get involved with you and how it benefits me. It's you."

"I said besides that."

"Sex isn't all you are, Jennifer. Being around you—well, let's say I'm a whole lot happier guy than I used to be. I have a life. Look at the way you got me to start coaching. You not only encouraged me to go for what would make me happier, you made it possible."

"Maybe I just wanted to run the dealership alone."

He laughed. "Maybe? I *know* you wanted to. But that doesn't mean you didn't have my best interests at heart. Actually you did twice—because you knew I'd be happier not running the dealership and you knew the dealership would be better off without me getting in your hair every five minutes." He slid his fingers into her hair, pulling free the pins that had held it back. "Though getting in your hair does have its benefits.

"I'll tell you something, Jennifer Truesdale. From the time I was a kid I've done my damnedest to study hard and anticipate what was coming my way so I could handle it. That's how I am. I study, I look ahead, I anticipate."

"I know. But—"

"But not with you. Because with you I feel things. With you I enjoy now. And with you… Ah, Jen, don't you know? I never could have anticipated you."

At some point after Jennifer collapsed on Trent's chest, she'd shifted, so when she opened her eyes after dozing, she was on her side, one of her legs over his.

"This will be the last time we can be together for a while," she murmured.

She'd agreed Ashley could attend the summer's final sleepover only after extracting pledges of perfect behavior from her. It was a small gathering—Ashley, Courtney and Sarah at Sarah's house for her birthday and a farewell to summer. At noon the next day, the last Friday of summer, the girls would go to school for a two-hour session of getting class schedules, locker assignments and books.

Come Monday, the school year began for real.

Back at the beginning of summer, when this was planned. Sarah's mother had talked with Jennifer and Jill, as the other mothers, and they'd all decided that, in addition to falling on Sarah's actual birthday, it was a better plan to give the girls more time between the sleepover and the start of school than a weekend date would.

But first, she and Trent had the whole night to be together.

They'd been so eager to make use of this opportunity that she hadn't taken the time to explain when they'd arrived.

Trent rolled his head on the pillow to look at her.

"Yeah, I heard Quince is going to be in town more often in the fall. I need to get my own place."

"You probably do, but that wouldn't change that we wouldn't be able to do—" she gestured from him to her "—this."

"You can't leave Ashley alone," he said.

"No, I can't." She levered herself on one elbow. "What?"

"I didn't say a word."

"You didn't have to. What?"

"You let her manipulate you. You let her—"

"Stop. This is because you think you see Eric in her. I don't—"

He raised one hand, the one not wrapped around her. "Fine. I won't say another word about your perfect daughter. I'll butt out."

"Oh, I know she's not perfect. And you want to know something else?"

He looked as if he wanted to say no, but wasn't that stupid. "What?"

"I see a lot of someone else in her, too. I see a lot of the Stenner genes that landed in her uncle in her. Stubborn. Proud. Closing out hurt, determined to never let anybody get back inside if she's been stung once. Refusing to talk about it. What have you got to say to that?"

She thought she'd reached him. She thought she might have gotten through to him. Might have cracked the protective covering he kept around his feelings about family.

"What I've got to say is if this is our last time for a while, we should make good use of it."

Trent heard the phone ringing inside his room as he put his key into the motel door. It wasn't yet seven o'clock. He'd only dropped Jennifer off at her car a short time before.

Could something have happened?

He slammed the door behind him, and in two long strides had the phone. "Yes?"

"Trent? Finally."

It was Linc.

Worry fell away, only to be replaced by surprise. "What are you doing calling at this hour? It's not even five your time."

"Don't I know it. I've been calling since last night. Your cell phone's off, too."

Eventually, both he and Jennifer had slept. Neither had awakened until the light breaking through the window jerked him into alertness later than they'd planned. They'd scrambled up—catching one kiss over the bed as they'd changed the sheets, and another in the car before he backed out of the garage. Because they couldn't—or Jennifer wouldn't—kiss goodbye out in the open where anyone might see them. Where anyone might know they were together.

But he wasn't telling Linc any of that. At least not now.

"What's up, Linc?"

"A buddy of mine called me last night. Strictly on the Q.T. He saw my name connected to yours, and figured I'd be interested. Do you trust all those people you've got working for you at that dealership?"

"What's this about, Linc?"

"First, tell me who's running the accounts?"

"Anne Hooper does the books—she's the one you said was top-notch after I sent you the first month's worth."

"Just you and Jennifer can write checks off the accounts? Not this Anne Hooper?"

"Right."

Linc hissed a breath out through his teeth. "There's no easy way of saying this, Trent. Somebody's set up a side account. Separate from the ones you sent me papers on. Money's going into this account from the dealership, and then it's going out."

"Where?" Trent asked, his chest suddenly tight.

"It's not clear where—not yet. I'm working on that. But if it's just you and Jennifer who can—"

"Don't say it, Linc. Don't say something I won't be able to forgive you for."

Silence hummed over the phone line.

Linc expelled a breath of exhaustion. "Okay, I won't say anything unless I know for sure. But if I do, Trent, I'm going to say it whether you want to hear it or not. Because if I didn't, I'd never forgive myself—not as a professional, not as your friend."

"It won't be an issue," Trent said.

"I hope not. I sure as hell hope not. Will you dig around there? See what you can find out?"

"Yeah." It might have come a beat slow—would a man who was sure be reluctant to put it to the test?—but it came. "Yeah, I will."

So, after he took a shower and dressed, he returned to Drago, opened the dealership and went directly to Jennifer's office.

He hesitated a moment, then tried the door. It was unlocked. He went in.

* * *

Jennifer had her key in the apartment door lock when she heard a sound from inside.

She knew all the advice said to leave, to run down the stairs and call the police. But a stronger instinct shoved that good advice aside.

She swung open the door and heard her daughter's sobs.

Racing through the apartment, she found Ashley curled on her bed, clutching a pillow to her middle the way she used to as a child.

"Ashley! Are you hurt?"

Her mind cataloged the facts. No blood, no sign of injury, disheveled hair, tearstains down her face, wearing the clothes she'd taken with her to the sleepover for this morning, her cries sounding more of fear and anger than of pain.

She gripped her daughter's shoulders. "Ashley Elizabeth. Tell me right now—are you hurt?"

"Noooo," she wailed.

"Are you sick?"

This response was less distinct, but Jennifer recognized it as negative.

Okay, not the worst. She could deal with this then. She could.

"Ashley, tell me what's happened. Why are you here?" She was supposed to have stayed at Sarah's until they all biked to the school. "How did you get home? What's wrong?"

"Everything's wrong!"

"Ashley. You have to tell me what's happened."

Her daughter jolted upright, wrenching out of her hold. "Everyone knows. *Everyone.* They said they had to tell me because they're my best friends and everybody's been talking about it for weeks and they all say you're in love with that man."

I am.

The recognition came so fast, so hard, that Jennifer gasped at it.

Oh, God. She loved Trent.

He was the one. The one Darcie had told her was all she needed. *And then it makes no difference if it's never lasted before.*

The one who didn't believe in family. The one who didn't get along with her daughter. The one who would complicate her life beyond belief.

The one who made her so happy.

"I said they were crazy. You'd never do that. But they said you're going to marry him. That you chose him!" her daughter wailed. "You let him come between us!"

Jennifer made it past the smiling good-mornings of the dealership staff, none of whom seemed to be concerned that she had come in at nearly noon instead of being here before anyone else.

She wasn't sure she'd done the right thing sending Ashley out to keep her date with her friends. But she'd seemed calmer after they'd talked. Even though Jennifer had refused to make any promises.

She saw motion in Trent's office, and felt as if a vise inside her—one that had been twisting tighter and tighter since she'd put her key in the apartment door lock five hours ago—had just clamped down to the max.

With the football team's final roster being posted this morning, then practice this afternoon, he wasn't supposed to have been here until this evening. She'd thought she would have more time.

She went directly to her office, putting her purse on the desk. Some level of her mind took in that someone had moved the pad with today's list on it. And the stack of papers ready for her to look through had been shifted, as if by someone's elbow when they sat by the computer.

But that minor mystery would wait.

First, she had to break her own heart.

She went to Trent's office, knocked on the open door and walked in, knowing she had to do it now. Do it fast. And do it here, where they would be constrained by potential witnesses through the window to the showroom.

"Trent, we have to talk."

Belatedly, she realized he'd been pacing. What on earth...?

He'd spun around at her voice, his eyes alight and his mouth smiling at seeing her. "I was thinking exactly the same thing."

He came toward her.

Before he could touch her, before he could make her forget what she needed to say, she rushed out the first words that came to her. "There are all these things between us, and we've never dealt with them, and they just sit there getting bigger and bigger."

He'd stopped at the words *between us*. "Like what?"

"Like why you really came here this summer. I know why you wanted to get away, I can understand that, but why did you come back? I thought it might have been for your father, to try to finally win his approval."

His face twisted.

She reached toward him, then dropped her hand.

"No, no, I know that isn't the truth now. And I'm glad, because I don't think that man will ever...but Trent, why? And why did you stay?"

"I stayed because you and Ashley needed help."

She sucked in a breath. "You stayed out of charity? Duty?"

"At the beginning, yeah. I started asking questions and—"

She didn't think so many emotions could be packed into one heart at the same time. God, she didn't want to be a charity case, especially not his charity case. And yet, how could she pretend she hadn't needed financial help? How could she ignore that if she hadn't been the one receiving his aid she would have thought what a kind and generous man he was?

"I knew Eric left you with nothing but debts."

"And is that what this—" she gestured from him to herself and back "—is about? Stepping in for Eric?"

"God, no, Jen. You've got to—"

"But why don't you ever ask about Eric? It's there—my past with him—right there between us. It would be natural for you to want to know about my ex-husband, and my God, he's your brother! But you never ask. It's like he doesn't exist."

"I asked at the start. You made it clear you didn't want to discuss it."

"You were a stranger. You don't think now—? Well, I'm telling you now whether you want to hear it or not. I left him because he'd started to tear down Ashley the way he'd been tearing me down. Not with fists, not with big, dramatic scenes, but with a word here, a word there. Making her think she was only as good as she looked. That nothing inside her head mattered."

He reached toward her. She backed away, but his fingertips brushed her arm, and the warmth and the ache were so strong she knew she'd never finish if he really touched her.

"Trent, we can't be together anymore. Ever."

Silence roared like a dam bursting in her head.

No, like ice cracking all around her, splintering into fragments that pitched her deep into the frigid waters, just as she'd always feared.

Just when she thought it might take her under for good, the phone rang, a slash of sound scraping her nerves.

Trent didn't move, didn't take his eyes from her.

It rang again.

And a third time.

She stepped toward the desk.

He moved between her and the phone. His shoulders were tight, his face hewn close to its strong bones, the thin scar on his nose standing out white against his skin. "Let it ring."

"It could be Ashley. She was upset this morning."

His expression shifted. She could almost hear the *Oh, was she?* going through his mind.

Without breaking their look, he swung around closer to the desk.

"We haven't finished this talk." He reached over and punched the speaker button. "Yes."

"Trent? It's Linc."

"Linc—"

She wasn't sure what had been in that solitary word. Warning? Weariness? Impatience? And his friend was too intent on what he had to say to hear anything in Trent's voice.

"Have you questioned Jennifer about if she had anything to do with that fishy account yet?"

She sucked in a breath that burned through her lungs into her heart and down to her gut with the flame of betrayal. *Questioned. Her.*

The man she'd fallen in love with. The man who'd believe in her more than she'd believed in herself.

"Linc. That's not—"

Trent was looking at her, trying to connect with her gaze. She turned her back.

"Well, don't," Linc said. "I mean, *do* talk to her, but I wanted to get to you before you did. My friend did more digging, and it turns out Jennifer's the one who was making the inquiries that got them started looking at this. I was as wrong about this as I was about investigating her at the start."

Silence.

"Trent? Did you hear me? I thought you'd be glad."

"Yeah." Trent sounded weary, depleted. "I gotta go, Linc."

"You want me to keep checking into this account?"

"Sure. Thanks."

The phone cut off before Linc finished his goodbye.

"You investigated me," Jennifer said. Her voice sounded almost normal. She was a better actress than she'd known.

"No, I didn't. Linc did. But, yes, I listened when he told me what he found out. It was mostly about the divorce, and how you and Ashley were struggling. I also talked with Judge Dixon."

Still with her back to him, she nodded once, the movement rigidly precise. "I can understand that. You had to be careful about the person you were going into business with."

"Jen."

"When this other thing came up, of course you had to look at everyone. It's not Anne Hooper, you know."

"I already figured that out. She doesn't have the authority."

She faced him then. "And, of course, you thought it was me, so you didn't need to consider Anne."

"I never thought it was you."

"You looked in my office. That's why you came in early."

"Yes. I came in early. And yes, I went in your office."

"You could have asked me, Trent."

"Could I? I went in your office, and I sat there, but I didn't look in your desk or on your computer or at your papers. I know you didn't do it. But tell me, when could I have asked you? When you were making sure nobody ever saw us in public? When you were hiding our relationship from your daughter?"

"That's not fair."

"Yeah? Well, then on a strictly professional level, why didn't you tell me about the inquiries you were making about this account? Why didn't you even talk to me about that?"

"Because you didn't want to hear about the dealership.

Because you wanted to wash your hands of it, push it away from you, just the way you do with family. Because you think hiding away from it will make it all better, just the way you think hiding away from family will make that all go away."

"So I'm going to be cut out of your life because I don't want to buddy up with Franklin Stenner? Or is it Eric you want me to bond with?"

"They're not your only family. Ashley's your family, too. But you've had nothing to do with her. Ever since you came to town—"

"She wants nothing to do with me."

"She's a child and she's been hurt."

"Even if she wanted to get to know me, you wouldn't let it happen. Any time I talk to the kid, you come running to get between us."

"Do you think I want her to hear how much you hate your family?"

He raised his hands. "You're right. You're right. I'm no good at family. Never have been, never will be. You're doing the right thing. Dump me now, before this gets any harder."

"I—"

"What the hell is going on here?"

Jennifer spun around, gaping at Franklin and Ella Stenner standing in the doorway.

Before she could react, Trent moved in front of her, practically shouldering her aside, knocking her hip against the desk.

"What the hell are *you* doing here?" Trent demanded of his father.

"What else could I do when I heard what a fool you were making of yourself? And a hell of a trip it's been, with the damned incompetent airline leaving us circling forever before finally getting us on the ground. And the rip-off car rentals can't even get a simple reservation straight. As if it weren't bad enough to hear the things I've been hearing about what's going on here—giving away my parts collection to fools on the Internet, some idiot idea about a fund going to that money-grasping woman, along with a charity job that—"

"That fund is for Ashley," Jennifer said. She didn't give one damn if this man considered her money-grasping, but she would not let the other lies stand. "And my job is not charity."

Franklin stared as if she had two heads. She couldn't blame him for being surprised. She'd never stood up to him in all the years he'd known her. Hell, she hadn't stood up for herself much at all for most of her life.

He dismissed her with a one-word opinion.

Trent stepped forward menacingly, further masking her from his father. "Apologize."

The phone rang. No one even looked toward it.

"Wha—? I will not. What is the matter with you?"

"You heard me. Apologize to Jennifer. Now."

"Oh, my God. She's got her hooks into you!" He laughed, a nasty sound.

The phone rang again. Ella Stenner edged around her husband.

He didn't even look at her. "I was a fool to think you were man enough to deal with this dealership. Like you could do better than your brother. He had mountains to overcome." He glared at Jennifer. "But he escaped, and now you're fool enough to walk right in and—"

"I love Jennifer."

That silenced the entire room so completely that it almost seemed to Jennifer that they were caught in freeze-frame. Never to be released. They would be caught like this forever.

Then the phone rang again.

Ella lifted the receiver and said a soft, polite, "Hello?"

It seemed to unfreeze Franklin. He advanced on his son.

"You idiot. You fool. You think you want her because Eric had her? I always knew you were jealous of him. Never could keep up. You aren't worth—"

"Don't!" Jennifer cried, drowning out Franklin's words. "Trent is the smartest, hardest working—"

But she couldn't stop the man. He shouted over her, thrusting his face at Trent. "To think I thought having you run Stenner Autos—"

"I'm not running it." Trent was still icy-cold. "Jennifer is. She's the general manager. And she's doing a damned good job of it. Better than any Stenner ever has."

Red-faced, veins on his forehead bulging, Franklin Stenner could not get a word out.

Ella's voice came over the garbled sounds. "Jennifer."

She turned to her ex-mother-in-law, who stood behind the desk, her face white.

She held the phone receiver toward Jennifer. "It's someone from the police. They say Ashley's been in an accident."

Chapter Thirteen

The nurse firmly escorted Jennifer out of the curtain-enclosed cubicle where her daughter lay, bloodied and hurt.

"We'll make her more comfortable," the nurse said, "then move her to where you'll have some privacy. Give us a few minutes. We'll come get you."

Jennifer was vaguely aware of Trent beside her, hand under her elbow, holding her up, as he had from the moment the phone call came.

She'd taken the phone, heard Darcie say, "She's going to be okay. You hear me, Jennifer? She's hurt, but she's going to be okay. She's at the hospital."

She'd hung up and started to walk out, when Trent grabbed her arm.

"You're not driving."

"I'm fine. I'm going—"

"You are not driving." He'd held on to her arm, while he

shouted to someone to get Jennifer's purse, then he'd guided her to his car. He had the motor running when someone ran up with the purse.

At the hospital, he'd simply refused to leave her, no matter what she or the nurses said. He stood beside her, silent, as he was now.

The doctor who'd been treating Ashley came out of the enclosure. "Doctor," Jennifer said, her throat tight. "Please tell me. Is Ashley—"

He kept walking, so she kept pace with him, aware of Trent on her other side.

"She's going to be fine," the doctor said. "The concussion's mild. No internal bleeding. She'll need stitches in her leg. I'll do that shortly."

"But…you're sure? All that blood… She looks so…"

"She split her scalp. That bleeds a lot, but it'll heal okay and her hair will hide any scarring. She'll be good and sore for a while."

"I see. Yes, thank you, doctor."

He peeled off to a side corridor. She stopped, and Trent's hand immediately came under her elbow.

Darcie, in uniform, appeared at the end of the corridor, coming toward them. "How is she?"

"She'll be okay." Jennifer's voice wobbled for the first time.

"Mild concussion, cuts, bruises," Trent said. "They've stitched her scalp, but have to clean her leg more before they stitch up a cut there."

Darcie expelled a relieved breath. "Okay. There's a boatload of people waiting to hear how she is. Do you want to—?"

Jennifer shook her head. "They're moving her. I'm waiting here until I can go back. Darcie, how did this happen? She said something about a car? Did someone hit her with a car?"

"No. She was in a car when it crashed."

"Whose car? She and Courtney and Sarah were supposed to ride their bikes to school."

"From what I can tell, they did. They were locking them up in the lot between the middle school and the high school. Then she saw Jonas Meltini about to get in a car nearby, and her friends said Ashley just got in the passenger seat, even though Jonas was shouting at her about it being *all her fault*." Darcie slanted a look at Trent. "Turns out Jonas was upset about not being named a starter on the football team. The car wasn't his. It was Coach Brookenheimer's. Apparently kids around when the team list was posted heard Jonas shouting he was going to *show him, show them all*."

"Jonas was wrong about Ashley being any part of his not being the starter," Trent said from behind Jennifer. "He earned that all on his own—but I did tell him to stay away from Ashley."

Jennifer twisted around to look at him. His eyes were so intense she thought she could dive into them and never return.

But Darcie cleared her throat.

"Jonas isn't saying, but I suspect he was heading for the dealership, possibly with a demolition derby in mind. But he blew a stop sign, and a garbage truck hit the passenger side."

Jennifer closed her eyes, fighting off nausea.

"The truck wasn't going very fast or it could have been a whole lot worse. The driver radioed it in, and I was there before the ambulance. She was scared, but she knew me, her color looked good, and she didn't lose consciousness, so I was pretty sure…"

She grasped her friend's arm. "Thank you, Darcie. I'm glad you were the one there. Is Jonas okay? Anyone else hurt?"

"Jonas has a cut on the head and bruises. I've parked him in the waiting room for now. Nobody else is hurt. The garbage truck barely had a dent. I've got to go talk to the driver now."

"Okay. Thank you, Darcie. Thank you so much."

After Darcie left neither she nor Trent said anything for a period of time that she felt no watch could measure. She found herself leaning into him, her shoulder against his chest. Still able to stand alone, but seeking the comfort of contact.

"Jen, I need you to know that I meant what I said before." His voice came low and steady and warm, the faint vibration of his words communicating to her through his chest wall to her shoulder and into her bloodstream. "I love you."

"Trent, you were angry at your father. You had every right to be. And to strike out at him—"

He turned her toward him, holding on to her shoulders.

"Jen, loving you has nothing to do with striking out, or with my father or Eric or anyone else. What's between us is between us. I know you're feeling good about your family, with your brother and your parents coming around some. But it's different with my family. You should know that better than anybody. As a kid, I kept my distance as self-preservation. But for a long time now it's been a conscious choice. If it weren't for Mom...

"Remember what you said when I asked if you knew what a great mother you are?" He seemed to know she couldn't answer, because he went on. "You said what was most important was whether Ashley knew it. But that's not true, Jen. No more than it's my father or Eric or me or the whole damned world who says if you're okay. It's you." He pressed two fingertips just under her collarbone. "Here, Jennifer. This is where you need approval from. The only place you need it from.

"No, don't pull away." His arms encircled her shoulders, drawing her into his warmth. "Let me say the rest. I need to say this now. That's why, whatever you want, I'll back you. Even if it's my walking away. But it's got to be what *you* want, Jen. Not what you think Ashley wants. And if you're willing to give us a chance, I'll do my damnedest to make us a family. To help you teach Ashley the lessons it took both of us all those hard knocks in the head to learn.

"The idea of being a father scares me to death. And I know…" His voice broke, and Jennifer thought that if he hadn't had his arms around her she might have sunk to the floor. "I know it won't happen in some blinding miracle. It'll take time and hard work—I've got time and I'm good at hard work. The only miracle I need is you."

"Ms. Truesdale?" The nurse came down the hall toward them. "Would you like to come in and see Ashley now?"

"Yes." She cleared her throat. "Yes, please."

Trent held her a second longer, then released her.

"I'll let the folks in the waiting room know."

"Thank you, Trent." Her eyes filled with tears, though he wouldn't be able to see them because she had taken a step away. She reached back, and found his arm, curling her fingers around it. "Thank you for everything."

Then she followed the nurse down the hallway to her daughter.

Jennifer stopped just inside the door, and tried to gather her strength so she could lend some to Ashley, just as Trent had done for her.

She wasn't sure that seeing Ashley looking so small and pale in the hospital bed wasn't worse than that first sight in the emergency cubicle. Despite the blood and frightening view of her clothes cut off her, there'd been the clarity of paring life to its essential fact—her daughter was alive.

Now, the complications of living came rushing in.

"Don't let him come in here, Mommy," her daughter said in a small, weak voice.

It broke Jennifer's trance and she went to the bedside.

"What, darling? Who?" She smoothed Ashley's hair back from her forehead.

Her daughter clasped her hand.

"I don't want him here. He's not Daddy. If we can't have Daddy, I want it to be just us. Like it used to be. Just us."

The girl's voice trailed off, and her eyelids drifted closed.

Jennifer smoothed her hair and refused to cry.

Her daughter was alive. How could she ask for anything more?

Trent immediately spotted Jonas, with a white gauze bandage on his forehead, in the crowded waiting room. Barry was there, too, along with three more boys from the football team, a couple of girls he recognized as Ashley's friends and a woman who appeared to be one's mother. Also Josh Kincannon. And Anne Hooper and Jorge O'Farrell from the dealership.

And his parents.

"Well?" his father demanded. "How is she?"

Trent addressed the worry in his mother's eyes. "She'll be okay."

Exhalations of relief came from every corner.

Before anyone else could pull in the oxygen to say anything, Trent looked at Josh and tipped his head toward the hallway. "You got a minute?"

Josh responded immediately, as if he'd been wanting the same thing, and they were out of sight around the corner before Trent heard the first reaction—his father's voice demanding to know what the hell he thought he was about disappearing like that.

Part of Trent might have wished his discussion with Josh took longer, but they were in agreement on every point, so they returned to the waiting room before his father's bluster had expended itself.

"It's about time! I have questions for you, Trent. I want—"

"Not now." He turned his back on his parents. "Jonas, Mr. Kincannon and I want a word with you in the hallway."

"What the hell's this about?" Franklin demanded from behind him.

Trent kept his eyes on Jonas.

"Talk to me here," the kid said.

"Jonas," Josh said, "this will be better handled in private."

"Talk to me here," he repeated.

Trent had had enough. "You're suspended from school for two weeks. And you're off the team indefinitely."

"Wha—?"

Jonas half rose from his chair, but the wail came from behind Trent.

"He's the best player on that sorry excuse for a team this season. What the hell is your problem, Trent?"

"You can't," Jonas said, apparently bolstered by Franklin's outrage. "You can't win without me."

"Then we'll lose."

"You can't—"

"He can, and I back him all the way," Josh said evenly. He nodded to Darcie who'd just returned to the waiting room. "Officer Barrett, we hope the police will work with the court system to see Jonas is appropriately punished."

"Jail? You can't send me to jail," he whined.

"You'll also need to make reparations for the property damage you've done. You can work off the cost of repairs to Coach's car at the dealership."

Jonas brightened until Trent added, "As Barry's assistant for no pay."

Barry looked nearly as appalled as Jonas for a moment. Then a gleam stole across his eyes, and he stood straighter.

"Th-this is—is—" Jonas stuttered.

"Just the beginning," Darcie said, taking his arm in a firm grip.

Jonas's cool was nowhere to be seen as Darcie led him off. He looked shocked. If the kid truly absorbed that there were consequences for his actions, there might be hope for him after all.

"C'mon, all of you," Josh said. Barry and the other team members stood. "It's time you're all getting home."

As they filed out the door, followed by the younger girls and the mother, Josh looked at Trent. "Call if there's anything anybody can do. If I can't help, I can find somebody who can. And if there's any more news—"

"I'll call. Thanks, Josh."

They shook hands. Jorge and Anne followed with the same offer, then they, too, left, leaving only the Stenners—parents and son—in the waiting room.

Slowly, Trent turned to face them. His mother's hands worked at the shreds of a tissue. Her eyes held a sheen of tears, and a message she seemed to be trying to communicate to him without words.

Probably the same old message. Don't anger your father. Don't rock the boat. Go along with him. Keep the peace.

At all costs.

His father sat bolt upright, the fact that his period of silence had resulted from rage rather than restraint apparent in the popping muscles of his jaw and the rusty color of his cheeks.

"That was quite a performance," Franklin said between gritted teeth. "I've always known you were a fool. Good God—the best player! How is Drago going to have a decent team again when you go throwing away your only decent player. And for what?"

"For nearly getting a girl killed. For crashing someone else's car and putting his own life at risk. For being too damned stupid to know how damned lucky he is. How damned lucky we are. Ashley —" He swallowed hard. "Your granddaughter. Your only grandchild, lying in there, hurt."

"He's just a boy—"

Trent swore, sharp and emphatic. "Don't excuse him. Don't even try to excuse him. Who are you going to blame, huh? Who are you going to blame? Ashley?"

"Of course not. She's a child, as well. You're blaming children when it's clear it's that woman's fault. After this there can't be any doubt that that woman's not a fit mother. She can't control her daughter. We can sue for custody and—"

"Good God. I didn't think even you could twist logic that much." The sound that came from Trent's throat wasn't a laugh. It hurt too damn much for that. "I mean, I know that in your rule book, a talented football player can't possibly be at fault— that was the core tenet of our family life. So there had to be another cause for Jonas's misbehavior. Your favorite scapegoat was always the girl. But this time the girl's your granddaughter. Uh-oh. That would make Ashley bad, and you can't have that, so what are you going to do? Of course—fall back on your old standard. Jennifer Truesdale is the root of all evil."

"That woman ruined Eric's life."

"Bullshit. Eric ruined Eric's life. With a strong assist from you."

His mother stood abruptly.

Franklin's head snapped around. "Where the hell do you think you're going?"

"To see Ashley."

"We need to talk," Jennifer said firmly.

Ashley hadn't slept long. Jennifer had given her ice chips, and with the nurse's help Ashley had used the bedpan— sounding nearly like herself when she declared it "gross."

So, once her daughter was settled again, the covers smoothed and her face relaxed, Jennifer felt it was time.

"I can't help how I feel. I just don't like him." Ashley sniffled.

"I know Dad isn't really coming back. And another guy would be okay. It's not like I've ever objected to any other guy."

That wasn't true. Ashley had heartily disliked Zeke for the short time when a few misguided people—basically Ashley and Darcie—had thought he was interested in Jennifer instead of desperately in love with Darcie.

"We can discuss Trent later. What I want to talk to you about first is what happened today. And the consequences of your actions," she said firmly. "Darcie's going to be here later to ask questions about what happened, and she's going to be here as a police officer. You will tell her everything she wants to know. With full details and absolute honesty."

"But—"

"No buts. And a little later, you and I are going to have a discussion about what you did today—the decisions you made—and the consequences that will follow those decisions."

Jennifer thought she heard a faint noise from behind her, like the door opening. But no one came in, and she didn't take her gaze from her daughter.

Ashley's eyes filled with tears and her lip quivered. "If it means it's just you and me like it used to be, I don't care what the consequences are. I don't want him around anymore."

"Ashley, Trent cares about you. It would be a major change in our lives, and it would be different. But he's a good man. Such a…" How did she tell her daughter that he was a man unlike her father, that Trent was a man she could trust? "Such a good man. Give it time."

"Time won't change that he just gets in the way. I've missed you so much, Mom," she sobbed.

Jennifer's head screamed at her that Ashley had been acting out before Trent came into their lives. That her daughter had pulled away from her, not the other way around.

But her heart and her arms and her throat and her eyes all

ached with the pain her daughter was experiencing. So that she felt a pain that wasn't merely reflected, but was amplified, a pain far more acute than she would have felt on her own behalf.

Wasn't that what motherhood was about? Feeling your child's pain, and doing whatever was necessary to stop it?

"Oh, Ashley…" She hitched her hip onto the bed and gently held her daughter's head to her breast. "Honey, if you feel so—"

The door opened wide suddenly. Ashley sat up, out of Jennifer's hold.

"Grams! What are you doing here?"

Ella Stenner advanced into the room. A smile on her lips, worry in her eyes as she surveyed her granddaughter.

Jennifer got off the bed and went to the window.

She would never interfere with Ashley's connection with her paternal grandparents, but she would never understand it, either.

"What matters is how you are, sweet girl."

Ashley groaned and her voice sounded tear-clogged. "It was so awful, Grams."

"I'm sure it was. Especially when you expected to be having such a good time."

Jennifer heard the words in Ella's usual placid tones, ran them back through her head, and still came to the same conclusion. She was criticizing Ashley.

Ashley must have felt the same shock, because all she got out was, "Uh, I…"

"I'm so glad you have not been permanently hurt, my dear. And I hope to visit with you more later. But right now, I would like to speak with your mother." Jennifer turned from the window. Ella held Ashley's hand but she was looking at her. "If you don't mind?" she added.

"Ashley might—"

"She can ring for the nurse if she needs anything, can't

you, dear? Yes, see. The buzzer is right there. It is important, Jennifer."

Jennifer wasn't sure if it was the novelty of Ella being forceful and determined or a craven desire to avoid committing to Ashley that she would cut Trent from their lives, but she found herself following Trent's mother into the unoccupied room designated as a chapel and taking the chair beside her.

"Did you know that Trent came here to Drago because of me? He thought it would please me if he could form a better relationship with his father. Ever since my heart attack this winter, he has been divided between being the man he is, and trying to forge some truce with Franklin. All because he believes that is what I want."

Now it made sense. He'd come to please his mother, not his father.

Trent's mother continued, "My greatest joy in life is also my greatest sorrow. And both are Trent. Because he is a good man, and because he had to become a good man on his own."

Each of Ella's words pierced Jennifer like a thorn. A thorn carrying a peculiar poison that made her body unable to move while her mind raced.

"I have many regrets in my life, Jennifer. That is one. Or, rather, it is part of perhaps the largest one that I carry. The regret of years of watching in silence as my elder son followed the path of his father."

She studied Jennifer, then gave a small nod, as if satisfied.

"Do not misunderstand. I love Eric, because you do love your children, even if they are jerks. I suppose, at some level I even still love Franklin, though he also is a jerk."

Jennifer felt her mouth gape. She fought sluggish muscles to close it.

"But that is my problem now, not yours any longer." Ella patted her hand in seeming approval. "What I want to say now is that Trent is not at all like his father or brother. And although I had little to do with making him the man he is, I want more than anything for him to be happy."

She looked directly at Jennifer, and Jennifer could do nothing but look back. It was as if the older woman willed her words into Jennifer's mind as much as she spoke them.

"But I know that a mother's wishes can't simply make a child happy. And I know I have no right to talk to you of your relationship with Trent. But I feel I do have the right to say something else. Something very important. Don't make the mistakes that I made as a mother, Jennifer. I let Eric manipulate me—play me, I think you young people say—and it hurt us all. It is hard to know whether it hurt him more or Trent, but only Trent had the strength to overcome it. I've had a great many years to think about what I did, and why I did it. I am ashamed to say that I think the primary reason was that I wanted my husband to like me."

She gave a pained smile. "A sad admission. But after my heart attack I finally began to take stock of my choices in life. I did not do all that I could have to help Eric become a good man because I needed my husband's approval. Approval I never gained anyway."

A quake seemed to rumble through Jennifer from the core of her being. A quake that echoed with voices. Ella's, Darcie's, even Jennifer's own. But the voice that came through most clearly was Trent's.

You said what was most important was whether Ashley knew it. But that's not true, Jen. Here, Jennifer. This is where you need approval from. The only place you need it from.

Maybe it wasn't poison that the pricks of Ella's words carried into Jennifer's system. Maybe it was medicine. Just the right medicine.

"Don't let Ashley play you the way I let Eric play me. It will only harm her, and that will break your heart in the end. Living your life, welcoming Trent's love, are the best examples you can give Ashley," she said. "Now I'm going to leave you here to think about what I've said."

She rose, hesitated a moment, then stroked Jennifer's hair once.

His mother's departure from the waiting room had left silence.

His father's silence had seethed with words unspoken—or in Franklin's case, unshouted.

Trent's silence had stemmed from having nothing to say to the man. And much to think about.

Giving control of what happened between them to Jennifer was the hardest thing he'd ever done. He was the man who looked ahead, who planned, who anticipated. Now he couldn't do any of those things. Because everything was in Jennifer's hands.

He had no idea what shape his life would take, what future his heart had. All out of his hands, and into hers.

Yes, the hardest thing he'd ever done, and the easiest decision to make.

Because it's what she needed. She needed to know that she was in charge. Of herself. Of their future.

If she chose to be with him, she needed to know she hadn't acted in response to what someone else expected of her. Hell, if she wanted a life with him, she would have to ignore his parent's vociferous disapproval, along with her daughter's and probably a fair amount of talk in town.

He swore to himself. How could he ask that of her? How could he make her overcome all that by herself, along with the past and the undeniably sticky issue of convoluted family ties? What an idiot—

"Where have you been?" His father's demand broke the silence.

Trent saw his mother had returned.

"I went to Ashley's room, then went with Jennifer to the chapel—" his father snorted in disgust, but his mother continued smoothly "—and then to the cafeteria."

"Great, just great. We'll don't just stand there, give me my coffee."

"It's tea."

"Tea? You know I don't like tea."

"Yes, I do know that. This is for me."

"What?" Franklin blinked, as if he had just noticed his wife's calm. "What's gotten into you?"

"I had a very interesting discussion with Jennifer."

"What could that woman have to say that could possibly be interesting. She ruined Eric's life. She's not a fit mother. She's—"

In the instant before the next word, several things happened.

Trent opened his mouth to let the hot words steaming through his brain out. But he spotted Jennifer just outside the doorway, where his parents couldn't see her. He thought her lips curved ever so slightly up, even though she had to be able to hear Franklin's indictment.

His mother clunked down the cup and stood.

Franklin's next word remained unspoken as he gawked at his wife.

"Shove it, Franklin," Ella Stenner snapped.

Trent's gaze whipped around to his mother.

"What did you say?" Franklin demanded.

"I said shove it. What would you know about being a fit parent? You gave Eric too much and Trent too little. You haven't been much in the way of a husband, either. I don't know why I was so worried about losing you."

She looked at Trent, then toward the doorway, where Jennifer had entered. For some reason Jen didn't look as poleaxed as Trent felt.

"You both should hear this. Your father has been siphoning money from the dealership to send to Eric."

"Ella!"

"It's an account he set up with a crony at the bank before he retired. I don't know if it's illegal, but I do know it was done without your knowledge and it's underhanded. Get your accountant to look into it." She turned to her husband. "I've told the children what they need to know. I think the rest of this should be between us, Franklin."

As if she'd been waiting for that cue, Jennifer walked to Trent, took his hand, and started leading him out.

"Jen—?"

She kept going. He could have held her back. Easily. But that was one thing he never wanted to do to Jen, hold her back.

As he followed, Trent heard his father demand, but not with his usual bluster, "What do you think you're doing?"

And his mother's reply, "Sit down, Franklin. It's my turn to talk. I figure you owe me about forty years."

Wordlessly, Jennifer led Trent down the hallway. Acutely aware of how much could be communicated through the touch of hand to hand. The sureness of his grip. The power of his hand, gentled now, but there if she needed it. The way he kept up with her, but had no need to take the lead.

And then, as she turned the corner into the short corridor where Ashley's room was, his slight tensing, and the questioning.

But when she started to push the door open, he didn't hesitate to use his arm to push it wider for her, making it easier.

Ashley was lying propped up in the narrow bed.

"Where'd you go? I've been all alone. They gave me all these shots and—" Then she saw Trent. "What's he doing here? I don't want him here."

"Ashley, as your mother, I will do my absolute best to keep you safe and to give you all that you need. Your wants, however, are another issue."

"But, Mom…" The protest became a wail as her eyes filled with tears.

Jennifer stroked her hair with her free hand, but she didn't release Trent's hand and her voice was firm.

"How can I teach you to value a good man if I turn one away? How can I teach you that you have the right to be loved as you are if I refuse that kind of love? How can I teach you to value yourself if I don't value myself enough to love?"

Jennifer saw anger at being thwarted in her daughter's eyes, but she also saw confusion, and she took that as a good sign.

She'd spent a good part of her own life being certain of things that turned out to be wrong. In the past few months, confusion had been a step toward enlightenment. At the same time, though, she felt the certainty and joy of Trent's firm grip on her hand, of his solid presence at her side.

"Mom—"

Ashley's renewed wail was cut off when the door opened and the doctor and nurse walked in.

"Ready for those stitches? If you'll wait outside, Ms. Truesdale."

"Stitches?" Ashley's voice wavered. "Mom?"

Jennifer knew her daughter needed to learn some tough lessons in life, lessons that wouldn't be easy for her, especially not since her mother had let her believe that too much of the universe revolved around her. Not only had Ashley been following in her mother's mistaken footsteps, she'd also been in danger of becoming like her father.

But being alone now was not one of the lessons she needed to learn.

"I'm staying, Doctor. And so is Trent."

The doctor clearly intended to give her an argument.

Then the young man looked at Trent, and the argument went right out of him. And she didn't mind. Because she knew she would have won if she'd had to. So having Trent spare her the effort was fine with her.

"You'll have to go to the other side of the bed," the nurse told Trent.

He squeezed Jennifer's hand once before releasing it to follow the nurse's gesture to the far side of Ashley's bed.

Ashley slanted him a look of enmity that evaporated when her gaze fell on the medical cart the nurse had pushed forward. Ashley went white.

"I think, we'll just…" the nurse muttered, as she used a frame to rig a bridge over Ashley's hips. She hooked a sheet across it as a screen, then lowered the bed so Ashley couldn't see what the doctor was doing.

Jennifer turned so she couldn't see, either, focusing on Ashley's face, while she grasped her hand.

Trent reached across Ashley and offered his hand to Jennifer. She immediately put hers in it. His hold was so warm and so right. The ice under her feet hadn't cracked, it had melted under the summer sun, slipping her into sunlit waters.

Trent extended his right hand to Ashley. She turned her head away and grabbed onto the sheet.

"All set?" the doctor asked. "This shouldn't hurt a bit."

Ashley gave a small whimper, then twisted her head to glare at Trent.

"You've had surgery and stuff. Is that true? It won't hurt?"

"No, it's not true. It'll hurt. But not more than you can bear, Ashley."

Her lips parted, as if she would say more. But then came a faint clink of medical tools from the vicinity of where the doctor leaned over her leg.

Ashley's hand released the sheet she'd clutched and inched across the bed to slide into Trent's.

He wisely said nothing. None of them did.

Maybe they didn't need to, now that they were linked, hand to hand. Like a real family.

Epilogue

Trent found Ashley sitting on the old bench behind the service area. Some of the techs used it for breaks, even now that the weather was downright chilly. She sat with her knees drawn up under her jacket and her heels resting on the seat.

He'd just heard a customer who used to know Eric asking Ashley about her father. Well-intentioned questions about how he was doing and where he was living now and when did she expect to see him—but wrenching ones for a child who hadn't heard from her father in years.

Trent handed Ashley a can of root beer and popped the top on his cola, sitting at the far end of the bench.

She gave her usual mumbled thanks.

They sipped in silence.

He debated a couple smooth introductions, then decided to cut to the chase. "You have every right to be ticked that your father isn't around. Some people just don't have an ability to think about anyone but themselves."

She tossed her hair. "Some people are different. Special."

"Like who?"

"Famous people. You know. Movie stars. Singers. Athletes. Models. People like that. The really good ones. The best ones."

He eyed her. *My dad was the best quarterback this town ever saw.*

He'd thought she'd had an awful lot invested in that declaration when she'd made it that first night by the soft drink machine. More invested than just being proud of a father.

Did she think that if her father had been a great player that it excused him from being a good person? Was that how she held on to loving him? Excusing his not coming to see her, dropping out of her life, not helping support her, by telling herself he was a great athlete and therefore the rules for mere mortals didn't apply?

God knows, it was how Eric had always operated.

But Ashley…Ashley deserved better than dealing with males who thought like that.

"Nobody gets a free pass on being a good human being. And anybody who passes out free passes for somebody famous or infamous is just as bad as the person who takes that free pass."

Her eyes welled up too fast for her, because even though she turned away, he saw the tears glinting. She shot off the bench.

"Ashley."

She stopped, though she kept her back to him.

"I'm not going anywhere. I love your mother and you're starting to grow on me."

She looked over her shoulder at that. The look held questions and doubt, rather than anger. And she didn't look away. A major breakthrough.

"So, that's my promise to you," he said. "I'll be here as long as I live, and I won't lie to you."

He thought he saw a memory of his not lying to her in the hospital flicker across the eyes that were becoming more like Jen's every day.

"That doesn't mean I have to like you."

He held up his hands. "Heaven forbid."

And damned if her mouth didn't twitch as if she might smile.

She clamped down on it and ran off, but he could almost swear he heard her actually say, "Thanks for the drink."

He took another sip and waited. In another half a minute, Jen came around the corner.

"Eavesdropping?" he asked as she took a seat on the bench beside him, settling naturally into the curve of the arm he put around her just as naturally.

They'd eaten dinner together at the café the night after Ashley's accident, so it was public knowledge that they were together. After football season they would look for a house. He'd promised he would plant as many rosebushes as she wanted. He'd even given her catalogues full of them to start choosing.

"How would I know what a wise man you are if I didn't?"

He kissed her hair. "Faith? Trust?"

"Yeah, right."

They could joke about it now, because they had it.

Because they had everything.

"How much longer before you think I can ask your daughter for your hand in marriage?"

She tipped her head back to look at him without raising it. "Are you serious?"

"Serious." He kissed her, letting her know how serious. "Because we got to get started soon on having babies together, babies who are born into a family where their mother and their father love each other and love them."

* * * * *

Set in darkness beyond the ordinary world.
Passionate tales of life and death.
With characters' lives ruled by laws the everyday world
can't begin to imagine.

Introducing NOCTURNE, a spine-tingling new line from
Silhouette Books.

The thrills and chills begin with UNFORGIVEN
by Lindsay McKenna

Plucked from the depths of hell, former military sharpshooter
Reno Manchahi was hired by the government to kill a thief,
but he had a mission of his own. Descended from a family of
shape-shifters, Reno vowed to get the revenge he'd thirsted
for all these years. But his mission went awry when his target
turned out to be a powerful seductress, Magdalena Calen
Hernandez, who risked everything to battle a potent evil.
Suddenly, Reno had to transform himself into a true hero and
fight the enemy that threatened them all. He had to become a
Warrior for the Light….

Turn the page for a sneak preview of
UNFORGIVEN
by Lindsay McKenna.
On sale September 26, wherever books are sold.

Chapter 1

One shot...one kill.

The sixteen-pound sledgehammer came down with such fierce power that the granite boulder shattered instantly. A spray of glittering mica exploded into the air and sparkled momentarily around the man who wielded the tool as if it were a weapon. Sweat ran in rivulets down Reno Manchahi's drawn, intense face. Naked from the waist up, the hot July sun beating down on his back, he hefted the sledgehammer skyward once more. Muscles in his thick forearms leaped and biceps bulged. Even his breath was focused on the boulder. In his mind's eye, he pictured Army General Robert Hampton's fleshy, arrogant fifty-year-old features on the rock's surface. Air exploded from between his lips as he brought the avenging hammer down. The boulder pulverized beneath his funneled hatred.

One shot…one kill…

Nostrils flaring, he inhaled the dank, humid heat and drew it deep into his massive lungs. Revenge allowed Reno to endure his imprisonment at a U.S. Navy brig near San Diego, California. Drops of sweat were flung in all directions as the crack of his sledgehammer claimed a third stone victim. Mouth taut, Reno moved to the next boulder.

The other prisoners in the stone yard gave him a wide berth. They always did. They instinctively felt his simmering hatred, the palpable revenge in his cinnamon-colored eyes, was more than skin-deep.

And they whispered he was different.

Reno enjoyed being a loner for good reason. He came from a medicine family of shape-shifters. But even this secret power had not protected him—or his family. His wife, Ilona, and his three-year-old daughter, Sarah, were dead. Murdered by Army General Hampton in their former home on USMC base in Camp Pendleton, California. Bitterness thrummed through Reno as he savagely pushed the toe of his scarred leather boot against several smaller pieces of gray granite that were in his way.

The sun beat down upon Manchahi's naked shoulders, grown dark red over time, shouting his half-Apache heritage. With his straight black hair grazing his thick shoulders, copper skin and broad face with high cheekbones, everyone knew he was Indian. When he'd first arrived at the brig, some of the prisoners taunted him and called him Geronimo. Something strange happened to Reno during his fight with the name-calling prisoners. Leaning down after he'd won the scuffle, he'd snarled into each of their bloodied faces that if they were going to call him anything, they would call him *gan,* which was the Apache word for *devil.*

His attackers had been shocked by the wounds on their faces, the deep claw marks. Reno recalled doubling his fist as they'd attacked him en masse. In that split second, he'd gone into an altered state of consciousness. In times of danger, he transformed into a jaguar. A deep, growling sound had emitted from his throat as he defended himself in the three-against-one fracas. It all happened so fast that he thought he had imagined it. He'd seen his hands morph into a forearm and paw, claws extended. The slashes left on the three men's faces after the fight told him he'd begun to shape-shift. A fist made bruises and swelling; not four perfect, deep claw marks. Stunned and anxious, he hid the knowledge of what else he was from these prisoners. Reno's only defense was to make all the prisoners so damned scared of him and remain a loner.

Alone. Yeah, he was alone, all right. The steel hammer swept downward with hellish ferocity. As the granite groaned in protest, Reno shut his eyes for just a moment. Sweat dripped off his nose and square chin.

Straightening, he wiped his furrowed, wet brow and looked into the pale blue sky. What got his attention was the startling cry of a red-tailed hawk as it flew over the brig yard. Squinting, he watched the bird. Reno could make out the rust-colored tail on the hawk. As a kid growing up on the Apache reservation in Arizona, Reno knew that all animals that appeared before him were messengers.

Brother, what message do you bring me? Reno knew one had to ask in order to receive. Allowing the sledgehammer to drop to his side, he concentrated on the hawk who wheeled in tightening circles above him.

Freedom! the hawk cried in return.

Reno shook his head, his black hair moving against his

broad, thickset shoulders. *Freedom? No way, Brother. No way.* Figuring that he was making up the hawk's shrill message, Reno turned away. Back to his rocks. Back to picturing Hampton's smug face.

Freedom!

* * * * *

Look for UNFORGIVEN by Lindsay McKenna,
the spine-tingling launch title from Silhouette Nocturne™.
Available September 26, wherever books are sold.